LAST MAN RUNNING

CHRIS BOUCHER

B B C

Other BBC DOCTOR WHO books featuring
the Eighth Doctor include:

Published by BBC Worldwide Ltd,
Woodlands, 80 Wood Lane
London W12 0TT

First published 1998
Reprinted 1999

Copyright © Chris Boucher 1998
The moral right of the author has been asserted

Original series broadcast on the BBC
Format © BBC 1963
Doctor Who and TARDIS are trademarks of the BBC

ISBN 0 563 405945
Imaging by Black Sheep, copyright © BBC 1998

Printed and bound in Great Britain by Mackays of Chatham
Cover printed by Belmont Press Ltd, Northampton

For Lynda

Chapter One

Leela was not impressed. This travelling hut might be cleverly made and strong but no structure was completely impenetrable, and that buzzing noise sounded like a parasitic worm to her. She pulled the long-bladed hunting knife she carried on her tunic belt and poked at the point on the console she judged the buzzing to be coming from.

'Don't do that!' the Doctor snapped, not looking up from the holographic star chart he was projecting over the TARDIS's sampling image locator. The match was inexact but it was still too close to be random, which meant either the chart or the locator was malfunctioning, or possibly both. Just identifying the fault was going to be a long and boring process of elimination and there was no guarantee even then that he could repair it himself. The prospect was annoying him intensely. And so, of course, was Leela.

'There is a Bloodswimmer in there.' She continued working with the knife. 'You clearly do not know how dangerous they can be. You do not leave one to swarm. Get it now, or it will get you later.'

'What you can hear,' the Doctor said with all the exaggerated patience of someone barely controlling their rage, 'is not biological. It's a mechanical circuit. Well it's a biomechanical circuit actually but I don't imagine the difference will matter to you.'

Leela was not having much success with her efforts to dig a hole in the top of the transdimensional-drive housing so she turned her attention to one of the flimsier-looking side panels. 'If it is what you say it is then tell me what it does,' she demanded.

'It reacts badly to primitive abuse, especially by abusive

primitives,' the Doctor said with a certain unkind relish.

'If it is what you say it is you do not *know* what it does, do you?' she challenged. Soon after she had first entered the travelling hut, Leela had come to the conclusion that the Doctor had very little idea of how it worked and nothing she had seen had done anything to change her mind. 'And if it is what you say it is, why is it moving? I tell you it is a Bloodswimmer and it knows I am here now and it is trying to get away from me.'

'It has a point.' The Doctor stopped trying to guess what was causing the system identification anomaly and set the TARDIS to locating the nearest viable landing site.

'It has *many* points,' Leela said. 'More than have been counted. It has three needle-sharp points on every one of its heads. Each head has a point to paralyse and a point to dissolve.' There was a pause.

'And the third?' the Doctor asked finally, his curiosity getting the better of him as it always did.

'It is a spare of course.'

'Of course,' he muttered. 'Stupid of me.'

'That is what the Elders said anyway. Nobody ever survived an attack long enough to tell us for certain.'

There was a sudden ripple in the floor, a lurch which was not quite movement, an action oddly without reaction. The TARDIS had identified its ground and started the time-looping systems. The approach and retreat of the materialisation-shock diffusers caused the familiar grating howl as the TARDIS crossed and recrossed the timelines.

The Doctor had once told someone that this roar of not quite noise was music to him, that he thought of it as the overture to adventure. He had been showing off a bit at the time and the phrase appealed to him a lot, but it was not strictly accurate then and it was certainly not appropriate any more. In the short time she had been travelling with him, Leela had already managed to complicate even the most routine matters of existence. He looked at her now. Absurdly young and determined to be fearless, she was half crouched in a fighting stance with the knife held slightly in front of her. Long dark hair fell back from a handsome face deliberately set to be expressionless but still dominated by bright brown eyes. She was reacting to the situation like the warrior she had been brought up to be. Any threat was to be fought. The response to danger was immediate and unthinking aggression. But then before he could point this out to her she relaxed abruptly and sheathed the knife and smiled.

'The TARDIS is stopping. It startled me.'

'No need to apologise,' he said grudgingly. 'It's frightened people from societies far in advance of your own.'

She frowned. 'I was not apologising. And I was not afraid.'

Leela's problem – at least as far as the Doctor was concerned – was that her quick and inquiring mind was coupled with an uncertain temper and a youthful, edgy pride. While an intelligent young primitive was potentially a delightful companion with whom to share the wonders the TARDIS could offer, an opinionated savage who could not recognise her own shortcomings was less appealing. 'What about the Bloodswimmer?' he asked. 'You seem to have forgotten the Bloodswimmer.'

Leela recognised the undertone of petulance. For a powerful shaman the Doctor could be quite childish sometimes. 'You can smell acid?' she prompted.

'No.'

Wheezily the TARDIS flexed and moaned through its last checks and balances and gradually fell silent.

'Neither can I. So I was wrong. I am sorry if I frightened you.'

The Doctor ignored the jibe. 'My theory would be that the third needle is probably to disconnect the segments when it swarms,' he said. 'That would explain why no first-hand evidence survived.'

Leela was almost impressed.

* * *

'Didn't you hear it? Quiet. Listen. *Listen*!' Sozerdor held up his hand and for the second time in as many minutes the patrol stopped in its tracks and listened. 'An eerie, wheezing, moaning sort of noise?' He looked around at the other six, who in their different ways were showing signs of increasing tension.

Kley, the ranking officer and Chief Investigator, glared at him. Sozerdor was the oldest and most experienced member of the team and was supposed to be a steadying influence on the rest of them. He was not supposed to behave like some gibbering hysteric every time something rustled in the undergrowth. Second planet second class. She should have insisted on an all-firster team. Even the best of the toodies were useless.

'One of you must have heard it,' Sozerdor insisted, 'or is it just me?'

'Wheezing and moaning?' Pertanor was grinning. 'It's just you, you useless toody. You should have taken that base job. You're getting too old and fat for the field.' Everyone breathed a little easier without really knowing why. Pertanor seemed to have that effect.

'You can mock me, son,' Sozerdor said, and in truth it was only Pertanor who could have got away with the insult, 'but you'll be an old fat toody yourself one day.'

'And we'll still be stumbling around this *unexpected* jungle when he is if we stop every time some rodent breaks wind.' Monly's comment was also made smiling but it was pointedly directed at Kley and made the others uncomfortable. The criticism that the word 'unexpected' clearly implied was a matter for her and the pushy young second in command. Monly was ten years Kley's junior and a star of the rapid-promotion programme so he would probably outrank her within a year unless he did something seriously indiscreet. But in the meantime he seemed to be missing no opportunity to undermine her, apparently hoping she would make a mistake serious enough to justify his taking over command. Under normal circumstances this too would have been of concern only to the Chief Investigator and the Assistant Chief Investigator, a question of the ambition that drove them both. The trouble was that these were not normal circumstances – in fact this team had been selected precisely because these were not normal circumstances. On this mission any mistake could be very expensive. It could cost them their quarry and all the bonuses that came with success. More to the point, it might even get one or two of them injured.

'If that's what passes for a rat fart on this planet I should hate to stand behind one of their horses,' Rinandor said.

'You heard it too!' Sozerdor was triumphant, then immediately annoyed. 'Why didn't you say something, woman?'

Rinandor pushed tightly bound black ringlets away from her eyes. Her round pale face remained impassive as she said, 'I heard something. It was a long way off.' She shrugged slightly. 'It could have been wind.'

Pertanor smiled but no one else seemed to get the joke.

'All right, we've wasted enough time,' Kley said. 'There's some way to go before we reach that drop zone, so let's get on with it, shall we?' She moved off quickly to preclude further discussion, firing up the short-range thermal imager as she went. The others automatically fell into step behind her.

Although it was energy-hungry, enhanced imaging was the obvious system for picking an immediate line of march through the dense tropical scrub. When this was combined with data from the low-orbit microbeacons the ship had seeded on its way down to the surface, finding the route from anywhere here to anywhere there on the planet was mindlessly easy. The real-time navigation computers on the grounded ship did everything except choose the objective and the method of attack. Kley made those strategic decisions and despite Monly's continuous bitching she was satisfied that the careful approach – like using the limited but difficult-to-detect microbeacons and landing a long way out and walking in – was sensible.

If she had needed reassurance that she had it more or less right, then Fermindor's professionally routine agreement would have been enough. He was the best Investigator she had ever worked with: the exceptional toody who proved the rule. When he called yet another halt and made his way up the line to her she was irritated but more inclined to listen than before, especially when he leaned close and lowered his voice so that only she could hear.

'I think we've got a problem with the landing site, Chief,' he said.

'Like what?'

'Like maybe it's too far away. Like maybe we should be carrying more equipment.'

Now Kley was more than just irritated; she was furious. 'This is not the time for a debate about tactics,' she whispered fiercely. 'Have you lost your mind, man!'

'No,' Fermindor murmured, 'I've lost the ship.'

'What do you mean? What are you talking about?' Kley asked, knowing they were stupid questions but unable to think of anything immediate to say.

'Check your homer, Chief,' he said. 'The ship's gone. It isn't there any more.'

The Doctor liked to believe that his attitude to dress was one of lofty indifference; he was altogether too busy thinking serious thoughts to be concerned with what he was wearing. When Leela pointed out that the long coat was cumbersome if you needed to run, the long scarf would get in the way if you needed to fight, and the hat was ridiculous on top of all that curly hair he maintained a calm dignity and pointed out that rational beings should seldom run and never fight, and that hats were *supposed* to be ridiculous. And anyway, someone who insisted on wearing a short tunic of nondescript animal skins, crude calf-length moccasins and a belt with enough Stone Age weaponry stuffed in it to fight a small tribal war was hardly in a position to criticise. But then, he occasionally had to remind himself that fighting small tribal wars was exactly what Leela had grown up to do and that he himself had some responsibility for the circumstances on her world that gave rise to them.

Leela had noticed before that the Doctor had a rather selective memory, and wondered if this was because it was impossible to hold on to memories when you were constantly travelling backwards and forwards to them as he did. She hoped the same thing would not happen to her now she too was passing time in the travelling TARDIS hut. Of course all shamans were mad, which made it difficult to decide when they were telling the truth or even if they knew what truth was. She was fairly sure that the Doctor was different there. He understood the truth and he knew how to find it. He was probably still mad, though.

'I want you to stay here,' he said wrapping the scarf round his neck several times and clamping the hat on his head. 'In the TARDIS.'

'Why? Where are you going?' Leela looked at the doors, which were so large in here and so small out there. She knew there was a trick to that which involved not believing what your eyes were seeing, and eventually she would work it out. In the meantime, what she could see on the scanner screen was limited and as always the Doctor was ready simply to trust the TARDIS to tell him that it was safe outside. He appeared to think that the doors would not open unless it was. She peered hard at the picture of where the travelling hut had stopped. The ground looked flat, there were trees which looked like standard forest vegetation, and there was nothing obvious lurking in the immediate vicinity. All was silent stillness, not even a breeze moved in the trees.

'I'm going for a walk,' the Doctor said.

'What for?'

'I need to stretch my legs. Walking helps me think.'

Leela turned back to watching the screen for signs of movement. 'The larger predators will wait to see what we are and how we move. It would be wise for us to do the same.'

The Doctor began to show renewed signs of exaggerated patience. 'There are no large predators,' he said as if addressing a troublesome child. 'The conditions are unsuitable for their development.'

'How do you know that?' Leela was not to be cowed by his tone. 'You do not even know where we are. Why will you not admit that you cannot control this – this –' She gestured round the console room.

'Travelling hut?' the Doctor offered.

'TARDIS.' Leela managed to sound appropriately dismissive of the slur on her understanding of the travelling hut.

'Which means?' The Doctor said, adjusting the door control sequence.

She struggled to remember what the acronym stood for, finally managing, 'Time And Relative Dimension In Space.'

'Which means?' He was rather shamefaced about that one. It was not a fair question. There were one or two Time Lords around who had trouble giving concise and coherent summaries of the theory.

'It means, I think,' Leela snapped, 'that we are lost.'

Without warning the Doctor strode towards the doors, which opened as he approached. 'I shan't be long,' he said, walking through.

Leela moved to follow him. 'I will come with you,' she said, but he had already gone. The doors closed behind him and did not open again when she reached them. She pushed at them. She took out her knife and tried to insert the point in the crack where the two halves met.

'The doors won't open,' the Doctor's voice said from the screen.

'It's for your own good.'

Leela turned to look at the scanner. He seemed to be looking directly at her, though she knew he was not. 'Any sounds you hear in the TARDIS are normal, so try not to attack anything while I'm gone,' the picture said. 'You are perfectly safe. Nothing can get to you in there.'

'And what happens when you do not come back?' she shouted at the Doctor, but in the picture he had turned away and was strolling off through the trees. 'I am not going to die in here,' she said more quietly to herself, 'like an animal in a trap because you think nothing can get to you out there.' She stood perfectly still for a moment and took a couple of deep breaths. She must reason this out carefully, as the Doctor did. As the Doctor did on most other occasions. A door was a door: a way of blocking up an entrance hole in a wall. There were only so many things you could do to make a door open and close and none of them was magic. Something is done and something happens as a result. What did the Doctor call it? Cause and effect? So what did the Doctor do to cause the door to open? Leela crossed to the control console, parts of which were still glowing and flickering in a sleepy sort of way, and stood where the Doctor had been standing. She examined the available knobs and switches and buttons and levers. She decided on a process of elimination. Tentatively she reached for one of the levers.

'This is so stupid,' Rinandor complained. 'The homers are obviously crap. Malfunctioning pieces of reconditioned crap.' She slapped the wrist unit against the thick stem of a tropical vine and checked the result. 'Crap!' she repeated.

Pertanor used his side-arm and burned down some more foliage to make the path they were following clear and obvious. They were going to have to walk back the same way to link up with the rest of the party again and their guns' depleted power packs could be recharged when they got to the grounded ship. 'What a nightmare if they're not,' he said, and then, as though he was bothered that this might upset her, added with a slightly forced grin: 'If she has to call in a rescue mission guess who'll be carrying water and digging latrines while we wait for them to pick us up.'

It was little more than a token gesture because they both knew that if there really had been some catastrophic failure in the ship's automatics the survival training they had been given on joining the Out-system Investigation Group would be barely adequate. Camping routines would be the least of their worries.

'You shouldn't keep volunteering,' Rinandor said, checking her own weapon to confirm that she had used up most of the charge.

'That's what my grandad always said. If you must join the chasers, he said, you need to remember three things. Keep your bowels open, keep your mouth shut and never volunteer. And don't hide in the washroom when it's your turn to buy the drinks.'

'That's four things.'

Pertanor nodded gravely. 'Grandad never made it beyond Investigator grade. Why was that, do you suppose?'

But Rinandor was feeling exploited and her dark mood was not to be lightened so easily. 'Being a toody wouldn't have helped,' she remarked. 'Second planet second class, firster class or no class.'

Pertanor frowned. 'I don't know,' he said, serious for a moment. 'Maybe it's time we stopped making that excuse to ourselves. Maybe if we stop believing it then it'll stop being true.'

'Well you've certainly convinced me,' Rinandor said. 'Why couldn't I see that? How could I have been so wrong for so long?'

Pertanor giggled. 'When I'm in charge you'll change your mind. Or else I'll be forced to abuse my position and take advantage of you. I'm happy either way.'

Despite the irritating giggle Rinandor could not help liking him. He wasn't bad-looking in a skinny sort of way and he made no secret of the fact that he found her attractive, which helped, but as well as all that… You got the feeling there was nothing hidden about him. He was open and pleasant. The sort you trusted. And of course, in some ways that could be pretty dull.

'Don't you resent this at all?' she demanded. 'Here we are backtracking because they equipped this mission with lowest-cost junk. And it's you and me that are slogging our way to the ship to kick it back into life. Not them. It's never them, is it?'

'Depends who "them" is.' He burned another smaller patch through the undergrowth, partly as a marker and partly because he thought for a moment that something moved. But there was nothing there.

'Kley and Monly have my nomination,' Rinandor said. 'I think being in charge sort of makes them responsible. Or am I being disingenuous?'

Pertanor giggled again. 'If I knew what it meant I'd give you my opinion.'

'They didn't even know this jungle was here. I mean how efficient is that?'

'Yeah, that was weird,' Pertanor agreed. 'The nav data were supposed to be front-line. The latest available.'

Rinandor snorted. 'Like the rest of the kit they put together?'

'We should be nearly there by now,' Pertanor said. 'We've about covered the distance according to my baseline readings. What do you think? Can you see anything?'

They paused and peered around them.

'One patch of jungle looks pretty much like another to me,' Rinandor said, 'but a large OIG recon ship would be a useful clue that the calculations are correct, don't you think?'

Pertanor started forward again. 'It's got to be around here somewhere. It's just a question of getting the search pattern right.' He stopped abruptly.

Behind him, Rinandor almost stumbled into his back. 'What

is it, what's wrong?'

'Did you see that?' he whispered.

She peered past him. 'See what? I can't see anything,' she said. 'Is it getting dark already? How long is it to nightfall on this crapsoid?'

'Quiet!' he hissed.

They both stood quite still in the gloom under the jungle canopy. She still couldn't see anything but now she thought she could hear something. It was a slithering sound and it seemed to be all around them.

'The data on life-forms?' Pertanor said.

'What about it?' she asked, straining to hear and trying to decide whether the sound was getting louder.

'There wasn't any mention of dangerous stuff, was there? Squad snakes, anything like that?' he asked.

'No.' It was. It was definitely getting louder. 'But then…'

He finished the thought for her: 'There was no mention of this jungle, either.'

'I think now would be a good time to find the ship,' she said.

'Gets my vote,' he said. 'It's got to be close.'

'So is that… whatever it is… What do you think it is?'

'I think I'd rather not know.'

They started to walk again, Pertanor leading, Rinandor close behind him. They were continuing along the line of march that they had originally calculated should bring them to the ship if for any reason they lost electronic support systems. The slithering seemed to be keeping pace with them. They picked up their speed, moving as quickly as they could, but the jungle was too thick to let them run.

The Doctor's stroll through the pine forest was beginning to relax him. He had been hoping for a breeze but stillness brought its own pleasures. In the circumstances it was disappointing that one of those pleasures was not the sharp scent of pine sap mingled with the soft musty odour of loam, but sometimes things went that way. In fact the forest did not smell of anything very much, which did strike the Doctor as mildly odd, since it looked like any other collection of needle-leaved evergreen trees to be found on any number of similar M-class planets. Minor variations aside, it was a fairly routine evolutionary development, an unremarkable adaptation of a planet to standard environmental limits. And it should smell. There should be things visibly living in it too. He knew that these forests often did not abound in fur and feather. This was logical since the pines themselves were a response to marginal conditions, but tiny birds and small hardy mammals had usually adapted to the impoverished living and could be heard and occasionally even observed by the quiet walker. But not in this forest it seemed.

He wandered on through the gloom of the trees and as he got deeper into his thoughts he began to discuss with himself the differences between truth and reality. Like most people who spend time alone for whatever reason – in his case it was because he preferred to – the Doctor was in the habit of talking aloud to himself. It had been suggested to him once, at least once, that this was eccentric behaviour and he had considered that possibility. He had tried listening more carefully to what he was saying to himself and had concluded that most of it made sense at least to him, and since he was the one he was talking to there seemed no reason to be concerned.

'There must be objective truth,' he was saying now, 'which must exist outside ourselves. Reality exists within us. The world is what we think it is. How can it be anything else? But truth simply *is*. Unless I'm imagining everything. But if I am, then objective truth must still exist because I have imagined it to exist. True is different, though. If enough people believe something is true then it is true. That must be the basis of democracy, surely. But it's not the same as truth. Not necessarily. Not necessarily *not*, though.'

As he walked and talked in the smell-free, silent forest the Doctor was leaving a series of trails. Visually discernible tracks, scent in the air and on the ground, vibrations in the earth and on the air, infrared patterns, exhalation gases and pheromone traces, all lingering in the stillness; the options were many and varied.

Less intelligent predators tend to specialise in their prey and the way they detect and capture it. The creature that had been stalking the Doctor was unusual in this respect. For its huge size it had a tiny and very limited brain, but it was still a general hunter and it could have followed any of the different trails he was leaving, though not all at the same time. To switch between tracking modes was confusing for it and time-consuming, so it tended to pick one sort of trail and stick with that. Its purpose, the driving force in its dim control core, was to kill whatever it caught up with. For the creature, killing was not of course an idea it understood: killing was simply a process for improving its energy balance by absorbing the nutrients its quarry contained. Such simplicity put it among the most dangerous of predators; stupidly adaptable, mindlessly determined, pitilessly ferocious, it was a classic killing machine. With a little more intelligence its rise to dominant species on its home planet would have been irresistible.

'Can we deny the existence of something that has been thought of?' the Doctor now asked himself.

But before he could answer, something he hadn't thought of scuttled across his peripheral vision. He glanced back towards the movement. Deep among the trees and a long way off something was coming in his direction. Fascinated, he watched it methodically working its way forward. It was scuttling backwards and forwards like a hunting dog quartering the ground for a scent trail. Except that this was no dog. The Doctor marvelled at it. He could hardly believe what he was seeing. Surely it was too big to be what it appeared to be; an exoskeleton would not support a thing that size. Nowhere, as far as he could remember, had he ever encountered one that was taller than the TARDIS. Mallophaga could not grow to that size or move like that, so logically, whatever it was, it could not be a member of the order Mallophaga. But it certainly looked like one. Broad flat head with nasty-looking mandibles, long slightly flattened abdomen wider at the back end, legs at the front end. Yes it definitely looked like one.

'That can't be a bird louse,' he said aloud. 'What is it, I wonder?'

The creature stopped quartering abruptly and almost immediately began to move in a direct line towards him. It had reacquired the original vibration trail it was following. It had felt the Doctor speak.

'It does seem to have six legs, though,' the Doctor said. 'So if it's not a chewing louse of some sort, that could make it quick over the ground.'

With the location of its prey now identified and confirmed, the creature began to run. Its need to kill fast was an intensifying hormonal feedback loop, an unbearably deepening hunger, evolved to optimise the energy transfer. The longer it took to stop its target and absorb the nutrients the less benefit there was to be gained from the kill. There would come a point when pursuit cost more in energy than could be absorbed from the prey. The creature was not adapted to recognise that point and break off the chase. This was a predator that would keep on going until it reached its target or until it ran out of energy itself. Its options, though it did not recognise them as such, were to kill or to die trying.

It took the Doctor a moment longer to realise that the thing was coming after him. Then he, too, began to run.

Chapter Two

Kley checked the readouts again. There was still no sign of the systems coming back on line. They must have reached the ship by now, she thought. What was holding things up? They were both reliable enough, for toodies, and bright, particularly the girl. Both competent technicals. The girl lacked motivation but young Pertanor more than made up for that. He'd make a good SI. In fact she decided she would recommend him for the senior training school when they got back – that might embarrass Monly. Yes, Pertanor and Rinandor were a good pairing – that was why she'd sent them. It was the right decision. They couldn't fault her on that one.

'Chief?' Fermindor interrupted her thoughts.

'Yes,' Kley said, getting to her feet and picking up her field pack. 'It's time to move on if we're going to find the drop zone before dark.'

'I thought we were going to wait for them,' Sozerdor said.

'Or wait for the up-signal from the ship at least.' This from Monly, who smiled slightly and showed no sign of moving.

'We can mark the trail so they'll have no trouble catching up with us,' Fermindor said. He was already adjusting the straps on his own much larger pack and hefting it around on his back to make it more comfortable.

'Isn't it possible that will give our position away?' Monly asked, pointedly directing the question at Kley.

Belay got to his feet and brushed leaf litter and jungle mud from his fatigues. 'Only if he was behind us and was looking for us,' he said.

Kley couldn't resist adding, her voice heavy with irony, 'Whereas we're looking for him, and he's in front of us.'

'As far as we know,' Monly said evenly. 'Which isn't very far without the electronics, is it?'

Sozerdor said, 'I still think we should wait. It's better not to split your strength when things aren't going to plan.'

'It's not up for discussion,' Kley snapped. 'We're moving on. Come on, get on your feet. Let's go.' Even as she said it and they got up and began picking up their packs she knew the tone was wrong. She'd been to enough training lectures to know that was not the way to keep a team motivated and functioning at optimum efficiency. And it shouldn't have been necessary. This group profiled as the best available for a straight pursuit-and-capture mission such as this. 'Available' was the operative word here, but she'd been shown the psych numbers the computer had put together and they were good enough for this to have been flagged as 'a crack team of investigators' on the interworld news links. And they were 'led by an experienced and talented young officer in Chief Investigator Serian Kley' – she'd liked that, although it was a distortion. She wasn't young enough to be young and she'd been given a team-leader assignment too late for it to count, except against her if she made a mistake. Monly was the talented young officer. She almost wished she could hand over to him and see him fall on his smug *young* face, but she'd worked and waited for this chance, this half-chance, at promotion, and it was hers to use or lose.

'We're losing the initiative hanging around here,' Fermindor remarked.

Kley found she was grateful for the tacit support. 'All right,' she said, trying to sound firm and inclusive, 'I'll take the spot. Fermindor, you're rear cover. Make sure the trail is clearly marked. Sozerdor, you're left sight, Belay right. Don't let's miss anything. We know where he put down, we know we can find it in the dark if necessary. But don't let's make it necessary.'

Monly waited patiently for his instructions. If he was discomfited by being left out, which was what she intended him to feel, he was too well schooled to show it and his face was a study of calm confidence. 'Monly, you're backup,' she said finally. 'If I miss something or make a mistake I expect you to report it –' and she allowed a fractional pause before finishing – 'to me.'

'Rely on it, Chief Investigator,' he said.

When everyone had their kit strapped on and was in position they set off once again in a loose column following the line of march calculated when the full resources of the ship had been available. All the leadership decisions Kley had taken so far had been reasonable, based on her assessment of the circumstances.

Unfortunately she had no real idea of what those circumstances were. She was ignorant of how dangerous the fugitive they were chasing actually was and she was unaware that above the canopy of the trees winged predators were drifting on the rising currents of warm air.

The Doctor was tall and very fit for someone of his unusual age, but sustaining a flat sprint for minutes at a time still gave him no chance of outrunning a creature with six legs and a hunger that was growing more ravenous with every step it took. The Doctor tried sudden changes of direction but the creature could turn virtually on the spot and, as far as he could see, without any significant loss of momentum. It was too close now to be confused by the zigzagging and the Doctor quickly decided that the tactic was slowing *him* up more than the creature.

In places where trees had fallen there were patches of thicker scrub growing. The Doctor tried plunging through some of this, shedding the long coat as he went and scrambling under and over the trunks of the dead trees before bursting out and sprinting on across the more open forest floor. Eerily silent apart from the scrabbling of its legs and the rattle of its chitinous body parts, the creature ploughed through the bushes and, ignoring the discarded coat completely, it scuttled on. Relentlessly it strode over the fallen trees and by the time it reached the open it had gained even more ground.

The Doctor was tiring rapidly and it was clear to him that he wasn't going to be able to outrun the creature or confuse the trail enough to fool it. The lack of reaction to the coat suggested that it was not following his scent, so the chances were that it was following body heat or possibly sound. This did not seem a sensible time to stop and try to work out which, but on the other hand he knew he could not keep going for much longer. He knew too that running for your life was not conducive to rational thought and if he was going to have any chance of surviving this he needed to think rationally.

Ahead of him one of the larger trees looked climbable. Of course, if this monster was anything like the Mallophaga it could probably climb it too but it was possible that its weight might limit how far up it could get. Behind him he could hear the clashing skitter as the giant louse bore down on him. He flung his hat back over his shoulder in the forlorn hope that it might gain him a few extra seconds. There was no time left to consider the options because there were none.

The Doctor put on a final desperate sprint and leapt for one of the lower branches. It creaked ominously as he grabbed on to it. He jammed his feet hard against the trunk of the tree and pushed on upward. At first the branches were evenly spaced on the gradually tapering trunk and he could climb quickly, but that soon stopped and he was left with a wide gap. He stood on tiptoe on the branch he had reached and stretched an arm up towards the next. He was a long way short of touching it. The gap was impassable. Below him there was a tapping rattle. He looked down. The creature was feeling round the trunk of the tree with its front legs. Suddenly it reared up and lunged at where he was clinging. It could almost grab him from the ground – almost, but not quite. Deliberately and carefully it began to climb.

Pertanor stared at the flattened area. For a moment he forgot the noises that had been circling and gradually closing on them, as he tried to make sense of what he was seeing. Or rather what he wasn't seeing.

'This is the place, isn't it?' He started to run forward and then hesitated and walked very slowly out into the crushed clearing the landing had made. He put his hands out in front of him as though he was expecting to bump into an invisible ship.

'Somebody stole the ship,' Rinandor said disbelievingly. 'Is that possible? It can't be.' She took a couple of steps out from the edge and then just stood there.

'Do you think it was him?' Pertanor asked. 'Is he more than just a freako, do you think? Could they have got him wrong?'

'Surely not,' she said. 'They got everything else so right, didn't they?'

Pertanor had crossed the clearing and was peering into the jumble of jungle on the other side. He was still half expecting to see the ship hidden there as if by some amazing prankster. As far as he could tell the vegetation beyond the initial landing zone looked undamaged. He began working his way round the edge. 'He'd have to be fast and technically front-rank, and the take-off would have to have been suppressed. It would have been low and slow and in that direction.' He pointed in the opposite direction to the patrol's line of march. 'And where are the signs? I don't see any sign of that, do you?' He continued his methodical examination of the perimeter.

Rinandor dropped her equipment pack and rummaged around in it for her communicator unit. She had always taken a perverse pleasure in not keeping things neat and well ordered but there were times when it was a definite problem.

'What are you doing?' Pertanor said.

She finally found the palm-sized voice link and pulled it out of its dark-wrap. 'Time to tell our brilliant leaders that we're short one ship.' The light-sensitive aerial began to deploy.

Pertanor hurried back to her and clapped a hand over the activator before the unit could start tuning itself in to Kley's co-ordinator. 'What about the comm silence?'

'What about it?'

'You want to be accused of tipping the runner?'

Rinandor gestured around with her free hand. 'You don't think he knows about us already?'

'Come on, Ri, suppose this wasn't him.'

'Suppose it doesn't matter. Without a ship we can't take him.'

'What about his ship?'

'It's a write-off. You saw the orbit projections and the imaging.'

'So you trust the data on that, then.'

Rinandor pushed his hand away. 'I can't believe you're standing there making debating points.' But she put the communicator back in its pouch.

'Even if they got that one right,' Pertanor said, 'he'll have another ship hidden somewhere or else he'll have one coming for him. He's not suicidal and he's not stupid. That crash-down was part of his plan.'

'You've been thinking, Pe. It'll stunt your growth,' she said, and smiled. 'And all chances of promotion.'

Pertanor went back into the centre of the clearing, scuffed back the heat-shrivelled vegetation and kicked at the scorched soil. 'You don't suppose...?' he said.

'What?' asked Rinandor.

'Nothing. Stupid idea.'

Before she could tell him how irritating she found that sort of self-censoring, false-sounding modesty the noise of slithering pursuit suddenly got louder, much too loud to be ignored any longer. With it there was now a keening note pitched on the painful upper limit of audibility.

'That *is* a squad snake,' she said. 'That's the telepathic strike, isn't it?' Already her optic nerves were being triggered and agonising flashes were interfering with her vision. Soon the snakes, which had vestigial telepathic links and hunted in organised groups of up to a hundred individuals, would be in range and producing the fully disorientating sound that paralysed nerve centres in warm-blooded prey.

'Come on!' Pertanor grabbed up her pack and pulled her towards the far side of the clearing. 'Run!'

The five-foot-long snakes could spit nerve toxin as well as inject it through hinged fangs but in a straight chase they could not cover the ground as fast as a frightened quadruped of any reasonable size or even a terrified biped the size of a man. But a hundred snakes acting as one animal was a horribly efficient killer and if it managed to delay its prey long enough to surround it then a kill was inevitable.

'I can't,' she gasped, stumbling after him. Her legs felt heavy, achingly sluggish. 'They're all round us.'

'No they're not!' he yelled. 'Concentrate on running! Move!'

He shoved her into the jungle. She forced her legs to work, dragging and pushing one in front of the other. Pertanor tried to help, pulling and half carrying her away from the sound of the snakes. As they struggled on she wasn't sure whether they were really escaping or whether the snakes were driving them into some sort of supernatural trap. But gradually the keening did not seem as loud, the weakness in Rinandor's legs began to ease and she found she could move without Pertanor's help. Progress became faster and easier until she was almost running. There was no point in marking the trail since they couldn't double back through the snakes, and so they crashed on, following the easiest routes through the foliage.

They knew they were putting distance between themselves and the squad snake and they were beginning to come down from the fear-driven adrenaline rush when Rinandor tripped and fell heavily, twisting her leg under her. 'Pe!' she called out as she went down.

He turned and came back to her. 'Come on. You can't just lie there,' he said and tried to lift her to her feet.

The pain was immediate and agonising. 'Oh no. It hurts.'

'So does a squad snake. Come on Ri.'

He tried again, and again the pain made her cry out. 'You'll have to leave me here,' she said through gritted teeth.

'I wish you hadn't said that.' Pertanor stripped off his pack and dumped it and then helped her out of hers and threw that away too. 'You don't mean it and I wouldn't do it, so why should a beautiful and intelligent toody waste the time?' He leaned down close to her and pulled her arm across his shoulders. 'And you shouldn't waste the time either.' She tried to smile at his feeble joke. With a grunt of effort he heaved her upright. This time she did not cry out but her already pale complexion had turned white and her breathing was fast and shallow. Moving fast was not going to be an option.

Suddenly the keening of the telepathic strike became a nerve-searing howl.

The Doctor could see the hooks at the end of the creature's legs. Evolved presumably to allow the parasite to dig in and cling on to its host, they did not seem to have slowed this monster over the ground and now they were certainly helping it to climb. As he had reasoned, though, the sheer bulk of the louse was slowing its progress up the tree. Slowing but not stopping it. With five of its feet firmly hooked into the trunk it had extended a hard-shelled soft-jointed foreleg and was probing for him. The Doctor stamped down hard at the nearest gap in the exoskeleton of the leg, aiming at the centre of the fringe of wiry hair which partially protected the exposed muscle tissue. Taking care not to snag himself in the claw he kicked a second time at the same spot. The leg withdrew. The creature needed to be closer to make sure it could safely draw the prey into its paralysing fangs. With the sound of splintering wood it began disengaging each of its feet from the rough bark in turn and placing them carefully in a slightly higher position. It tested the grip of each of these new places before releasing any more of its existing holds. It struck the Doctor that for an animal that had developed to hunt this terrain the procedure was peculiarly tentative. It was something he would have to think about when he had more time. His immediate problem was that unless he could get higher up the tree himself he'd have no more time. Ever.

Standing precariously balanced on the branch with his back pressed hard against the trunk, he finished tying a knot into the end of his scarf which contained some odd coins, his penknife and the gold nugget he had kept because it was shaped like a duck. He tested the weight and looked up at the next branch, unreachably high above him, trying to estimate how much of the long woollen rope he would have to use. Ideally he needed to swing it in a tight one-hundred-and-eighty-degree arc or, better still, a full circle, but that would put it within snatching distance of the creature. He was still not certain whether snatching was part of its repertoire. He knew that it ran and turned quickly but that didn't necessarily mean its general reflexes were fast. Of course, hooks and woven wool were not a combination that required lightning reactions.

He decided to go for broke and began to whirl the weighted end of the scarf round and round, building the speed and gradually extending the circle towards the upper branch. When he had almost got the length right the creature below him responded to the vibrations in the air and prodded out a leg. Luckily this was intended to be no more than a warning to the unidentified flying outsider to keep away and was not a determined attempt to attack it. Nevertheless with the leg waving around in a vaguely menacing way the Doctor's room for manoeuvre had been severely reduced, so as the scarf swung up for the next pass he released enough to loop over the higher branch and was delighted to see the weighted end whip itself three times round the stem. But there was no chance for him to revel in this small triumph. Ominous clickings and scrapings among the branches below suggested that the creature was about to make dangerous progress in its relentless efforts to reach him.

Trying not to rush and get careless, the Doctor took a deep breath and tugged hard. The branch bent a little and the scarf stretched and slipped slightly. Given a choice no one in their right mind would do what he was about to do. But as the creature continued painstakingly to haul its ponderous bulk upward he had no choice. Keeping the tension on the scarf and reaching as high up it as he could, he prepared himself to climb. Abruptly, the noises from below stopped. He knew this was not a good sign. Quickly he launched himself off the branch and started to pull himself up, hand over hand, scrambling with his feet against the tree trunk in a frantic effort to take some of the weight off his fragile lifeline.

Almost immediately a pair of giant forelegs lunged upward, missing him only fractionally. Blindly feeling around, the creature found the dangling scarf. The hooks bit into it and began to wrench and tear. The branch to which the Doctor was climbing bent downward loosening the scarf, which was already stretching and ripping. He could feel it coming away in his hands. Glancing down, he could see the monster's powerful jaws opening and closing. He fancied he could see both acid and poison glistening and drooling as the inner-mouth parts twitched and quivered.

With a last desperate surge of energy the Doctor grabbed at the thrashing branch, heaved himself on to it and pushed in as close to the trunk of the tree as he could get. The scarf finally tore away and with it half the branch broke off and fell on to the creature below. Methodically disentangling itself, the insect ripped up the debris, discarding the pieces and ignoring them as it had ignored everything that had come between it and its prey, and set about the task of climbing higher.

The Doctor looked for his next handholds and footholds and discovered that the tree tapered rapidly from this point, and though the branches were closer together and easier to reach there were precious few left that looked as though they would take his weight. He assumed that meant the louse, or whatever it was, would be reaching its own limit fairly soon. Did that mean it would give up and go away? Or would it settle down to outwait him? Would the short-term memory of him fade if he could deny the thing the stimulus of vibrations or a moving heat source? *If* he could. And how long would that take?

He pushed on up through the branches until he could go no further. Perhaps something else would take its attention and draw it off. Except that he hadn't seen another living thing since this whole unfortunate episode started. It occurred to him that, though it did not seem likely, it was just possible he was the last live food left in these woods, and if that was the case the louse creature had no choice but to keep on coming.

With little optimism, the Doctor set about tucking and weaving the smaller stems and branches around himself in an effort to dissipate his body heat, disguise his autonomic vibrations and most importantly hold him in place if he fell asleep.

She was almost unconscious and that made her heavier. Pertanor hefted her arm slightly higher on to his shoulder and tried to jolt her awake. 'Come on, Ri. We must keep going!' he shouted above the screech that filled his mind and face with flashing agony and made him nauseous and aching to lie down, close his eyes and sleep. 'Come on, Ri!' he shouted again.

Rinandor mumbled something incoherent and slumped further into unconsciousness. She was more or less a dead weight now. The snakes were almost on them, and Pertanor was ready to give up. Dying accidentally on this undistinguished planet on this shambolic mission would be disappointing. No one would know about him. No one would mark his passing. His mother and sister would get nothing for his death. He wasn't ready to give up.

He stopped trying to drag Rinandor along and heaved her fully over his shoulder. He'd always liked the fact that she was well built, but then carrying her through dense jungle had not been a feature of his fantasy.

He staggered under the weight and shambled on. Through the whiteout flashes that were threatening to blank his vision he thought he saw a change in the leaf and liana patterns of the vegetation ahead. After all his efforts he decided it was probably a wave of snakes waiting for them. He could have been running round in circles – that was what they did to you, wasn't it? With an incoherent yell of anger and despair he ran at the place and crashed through it into a cool, shadowed pine forest.

The momentum carried him forward for twenty or thirty paces and then he fell in an ungainly tangle on top of Rinandor. As he lay on the ground, which was now covered in dry pine needles, and tried to understand how tropical jungle could change to temperate pine forest in the matter of a few yards a voice asked suspiciously, 'Who are you and what are you doing?'

'Squad snake,' he managed to gasp, looking for the source of the voice. 'Coming. Back there.' She was a few feet away. A skinny girl dressed in skins and crouched in a fighting stance, a large hunting knife held out in front of her. He was too shocked to be surprised. 'I don't think I can outrun them,' he said.

* * *

Leela had heard him coming long before he broke through the screen of plants. He had sounded as though he was running for his life and he might be carrying something heavy. All this was now confirmed.

'How many of them are there?' Leela asked.

'Never got to see,' the plump young man said. 'But they sound big.'

She checked the even plumper young woman. She was alive but obviously hurt in some way and in shock. Leela checked her for signs of the injury.

'She fell,' the man said. 'Her leg's broken.'

'No. I do not think so.' Leela could hear a noise now, a high-pitched whistle getting slowly louder. So that was it. They called it a squad snake here. She nodded at the dense wall of lush greenery they had run from and said, 'They hunt as a group? They work together, is that it?'

'A squad snake, yes,' he said.

Leela chopped a small branch from the nearest tree and quickly cut several small sharp stakes from it. 'What are you called?' she asked.

'I'm Pe Pertanor. That's Ri Rinandor.'

Why was he wasting time telling her the name of the unconscious girl? Leela wondered. She must be important to him. 'How long are the individual snakes, Pe-pertanor?'

'Just Pe,' Pertanor said and spread his arms to indicate about five feet. 'I'm guessing, though. Haven't seen any of this one.'

'Biters, spitters, or crushers?'

'All three usually.'

Leela took another branch and sharpened a longer spear. 'All right, Pe,' she said briskly. 'I am Leela. Take Ri-rinandor as far that way –' she indicated a direct line away from the boundary between forest and jungle – 'as you can carry her and then wait for me there.'

'What are you going to do?' Pertanor asked as he struggled to lift Rinandor on to his shoulder and get to his feet again.

'I am going to stop the squad snake,' Leela said, feeling that this much should have been obvious even to such a hopeless character, and set off for the place where the pair had smashed through the wall of vegetation.

'You won't be able to do that,' Pertanor said. 'Not without wide-beam burners.' But Leela had already gone, crossing the boundary into the jungle.

Pertanor looked off into the tranquil forest in the direction she had told him to go. It was possible, he thought, that she and this forest were both hallucinations, that he was already held by the snake, that this was his mind's flight from the moment of death.

Rinandor groaned. 'Are we still alive?' she whispered vaguely.

The telepathic strike was building up again. As hallucinations went, this one had some mundane details, Pertanor thought. 'Yes,' he said, 'we're still alive.' And he staggered off with her into the trees.

Leela ran through the warmth and humidity of the sudden jungle towards the sound of the snake. She knew the noise they were making was part of their hunting strategy and when it began to hurt her eyes she understood how they used it and how effective her counter-strategy would be if only Pe was doing what she told him to do. What she needed from him was a continuation of the same staggering, wounded-animal uncertainty which would keep the snake's hunger focused. By running directly towards them herself she expected to avoid detection long enough to do the necessary damage.

As the pain in her eyes became more intense Leela switched direction, running to the left and then stopping. She closed her eyes and screened out as much as she could of the mind sound and concentrated on listening to the snakes' physical movement through the jungle debris.

She knew this sort of hunting group would favour encirclement and would chase in a V-shaped formation, point first to begin with, the arms of the V folding forward the closer it came to its quarry. That way they could suddenly make their sound louder and the pain crippling as they closed the circle to make the kill. She hoped that this snake was confident enough of killing Pe and his companion to have reversed its formation so that the point was following.

As far as she could hear she had flanked the formation, which was not changing direction, so it had not spotted her yet. She opened her eyes as a grey-green snake passed within inches of her foot. She had not intended to get that close. It was as long as her outstretched arms and as thick as a man's wrist and instead of a normal serpent's narrow head it had a flattened-out face which was wide and raised above the ground. Its eyes were front-focused and its mouth was a gaping slash filled with moist fangs. At the top of the face was a single short antenna, which looked to be covered in vibrating slime.

Leela waited until she was sure that this was the animal at the extreme end of the formation before chasing it down and pinning it to the ground with a spear through the back of the head. Deftly avoiding the writhing coils and careful not to damage the antenna, she put her foot on the head, withdrew the spear and jammed one of the smaller wooden stakes through the same spot and into ground. Leaving the snake writhing and pulsing distress signals, Leela skirted the already slowing line and hunted down a second snake, which she dealt with in the same way. This was easier than she had expected.

The third snake turned on her. The venom came in a sudden cloud of viscous globules. She skipped backwards and it all fell short. Avoiding contact with the leaves where the deadly slime hung and dripped, she dodged and circled round the snake

31

looking for an opening, a chance to thrust the spear through the back of its head. The snake struck at her, missed but recovered its balance immediately. It rippled a coil, preparing for a stronger lunge. Leela realised that killing this one was taking too long. Around her others were turning in response to the arousal signals the snake was sending out. Leela threw the hunting knife, blade spinning horizontally, and severed the top of its head, abruptly ending the links with the rest of the squad snake. She snatched up the knife and stood listening. The nearest members seemed to be turning back to their original paths. This was not a clever animal but she had known that from the beginning. She must be on her guard, though, and not get too confident again. The stupider the animal the more dangerous it could be when it was hurt.

She moved on behind the line of the snake, which was hesitating, pain and confused reaction building in its collective nervous system. She was more careful this time, making sure that she was close enough to pin the member at the first attempt before committing herself.

When she had staked four more and killed ten outright Leela was satisfied that, for this squad snake, the hunt was over. The right flank of the formation, which had sustained all the damage, was wrecked and the left flank was instinctively folding round it in a tightening defensive loop. The hunting mind sound which sapped the will of terrified prey was gone and now was the time to destroy the snake for good. But that would take too long and she had more pressing problems. She ran round the collapsing animal and headed back to the temperate forest.

Rinandor stirred and woke up. 'What did you do?' she asked. 'The snake's stopped. It's gone. Where's the snake gone?'

'She killed it,' Pertanor said, unable to keep the astonished awe from his voice. 'With a bunch of sharp sticks and a knife.'

'It is not dead,' the thin aboriginal girl said. 'But it is in a lot of pain.'

'Thank you,' Rinandor said and smiled at her. She reached out a hand but the girl flinched back slightly. It did not seem to Rinandor that this was personal; it seemed more like a trained response, a conditioned reflex.

'It's all right, Ri,' Pertanor said. 'You're not hallucinating. She's real.'

'You have to think of anything that runs in a pack as one animal,' the girl said. 'It affects the way you fight it. If it is one animal you can see what it does and use that against it.'

'Leela used the telepathic spike. The bit that links it all together. It's so simple when you think about it,' Pertanor enthused.

'It's difficult to think about anything when you're scared crapless,' Rinandor said wryly.

'The Doctor says that is why fear is destructive,' the girl said. 'It gets in the way of rational thought and if you cannot think rationally you will always be afraid. He says it is a vicious circle.'

'So you are Leealor?' Rinandor asked, revising her first impression of the primitive-looking girl.

As she watched Ri-rinandor, Leela was suddenly aware that the plump young woman was looking at her with careful eyes. It was almost the look of a hunter. 'Leela,' she corrected her, unsure why she had lengthened the name and added an extra sound to it.

'Leela. Have you always lived here, Leela?'

'I do not live here. I travel with the Doctor,' Leela said guardedly.

'Thedoctor?' She pronounced it as one word. 'What does he do exactly?' She tried to get to her feet.

Pe-pertanor moved to help his companion, murmuring, 'Begins to sound like an interrogation, Ri. Do you think this is a good time?'

'Leela saved our lives,' she said. 'I'm interested, naturally.'

'The Doctor is just the Doctor,' Leela said. 'He travels in…' She hesitated. Something told her that these people would find it hard to believe in the TARDIS hut. 'He travels,' she finished lamely.

'And you travel with him,' Ri-rinandor prompted with a forced smile.

Leela wondered why the woman was feigning friendliness when everything about her suggested wariness. 'I am his student,' she said, using the term the Doctor had suggested was the correct way to describe their association.

'You obviously come from First Planet,' Ri-rinandor persisted.

'Do I?' Leela said.

'You have the name, you have the frame and you sound the same.'

It was an echo of the sort of chant used by the children of Leela's tribe to mock the privileged ones that they envied. Did she sound like one of these First Planet people, she wondered. She seemed to be able to speak their language. She had asked on one occasion how it was that the Doctor could speak whatever language was used wherever he found himself. The explanation was his usual stream of incantations and gibberish, which he made up on the spot no matter what the question was, because, she suspected, he did not know the answer and he wanted to keep her quiet. It seemed to come down to: the TARDIS does it; which was obvious nonsense. He might enjoy pretending that the travelling hut was the source of all his shaman's power, but how did it work when they were not in it? And how did it work on her? 'Is it important?' she asked.

'No, of course it isn't,' Pe-pertanor said, frowning at Ri-rinandor.

But the woman was not to be put off. 'When did you make planetfall? Was it fairly recently?'

'Rinandor, leave it, will you?' Pe-pertanor was showing signs of annoyance.

Ri-rinandor's smile remained. 'Leaving aside the question of what Thedoctor and Leela are doing here on this deserted crapsoid. Which happens to be an OIG interdicted planet...'

'Only because of the runner,' Pe-pertanor said, 'whose known associates do not include a toody called Thedoctor or a firster named Leela.'

'No lift-offs or landings are allowed without prior clearance from the Out-system Investigation Group,' Ri-rinandor went on. 'And I expect they've got a ship somewhere about. Or perhaps there's a rendezvous arranged.'

Leela watched the young man's expression change. He looked like a starveling who had noticed someone else with food. She decided she had wasted enough time on these people. 'Avoid the remains of the snake,' she said. 'It is still dangerous. The leg is not broken but you will need to walk slowly and use it as little as possible.' She started away.

'You're not going to leave us like this,' Ri-rinandor said.

It sounded like a threat to Leela. In her peripheral vision she saw the woman reaching for the weapon she carried in a holster at her waist. 'I have to look for the Doctor,' Leela said casually, and stepped to one side so that there was a tree between them. Keeping the tree in the line of fire, she loped away. She was fairly sure the handguns the two were carrying were short-range and ineffective. If they had had any real destructive power available to them they would have used it against the snake.

Chapter Three

It was becoming clear to the Doctor that the creature was not likely to give up and go away so he was going to need a new plan – or *any* plan – since all he had managed so far was *run away and climb a tree*, which owed a lot more to instinct than to intellect. He was also beginning to regret leaving Leela locked in the TARDIS. If anything did happen to him she could live a long time there of course, a full life span in fact, but sadly that was not the same as a full life. It was not a decision he had intended to take her on her behalf. Nor would he have done had he thought about it. Lack of thought was a regrettable feature of all his behaviour so far.

But all was not yet lost. The creature appeared to have reached the limit of its climb and was still not able to touch him. He was in no immediate danger. He had time to think. He set himself to analysing the situation and to finding the creature's weaknesses. The important point to remember, he reminded himself, was that any organism must be seen as part of the environment. Strength and weakness were not isolated conditions: organism and environment together created them. A fish might be huge and powerful but once out of water it was no match for the scrawniest of rats.

From what he had seen of this environment a creature the size of the one squatting below him on the tree should be constantly hungry. The fact that it had chased him with such single-minded ferocity suggested either ravenous hunger or aggressive fear. He was surely too small to be identified as a threat or a hunting rival, even by something as undiscriminating as a giant louse, so the probability was hunger. All things considered, given the amount of energy it must expend in moving as quickly as it did, there was a reasonable chance that the creature was living on the edge of starvation.

The beginnings of a plan began to take shape in the Doctor's mind. If he could persuade it to keep moving the creature might exhaust an already very small reserve of energy, thus weakening it enough to allow him to escape. Perhaps he could enrage it sufficiently to get it to keep climbing so that it fell off the tree and had to heave itself up all over again.

It struck the Doctor that as a plan it was not much more subtle than his first effort. This time what he had come up with was basically *call it names and poke it with a stick*. Simple plans were usually the most successful though. There was less to go wrong. 'Hey, you! Yes you!' he yelled. 'You're a lousy climber, aren't you?'

The creature stirred and clicked. Its whole body quivered and there were brief tearing sounds as it partially detached hooks from the tree trunk and then dug them back in again. It was a start, but the Doctor would need a lot more animation from it than that. He broke off a piece of branch and threw it down into what he judged to be one of its eyes. It had no visible effect. He tried again. There was still no response. 'I suppose you think you've got me trapped up here, don't you?' he shouted.

'That is what it looks like from down here,' Leela shouted back from the bottom of the tree.

The Doctor peered at her. The louse creature was ignoring her intrusion completely. But when he said, 'How did you get out of the TARDIS?' it began to quiver again.

'It has definitely decided it wants you or nothing, it seems,' Leela commented, searching the ground for something to throw at the animal.

'You haven't damaged the travelling hut, have you?' the Doctor asked suspiciously.

'I watched you,' Leela said, 'and I copied what I saw you do.' She found a piece of rotten wood and weighed it in her hand. It was too light and she discarded it. 'The TARDIS is a machine – there is nothing magic about it. And you can stop calling it the travelling hut. It is not funny to mock people's lack of knowledge, Doctor. Especially when you are stuck up a tree.'

'I think I may have underestimated you,' the Doctor conceded graciously with a vivid smile.

Leela did not acknowledge the apology. 'You underestimated the size of the predators,' she said.

'It is a big louse, isn't it?' the Doctor agreed. 'There's no obvious reason why it should be. In fact there are any number of reasons why it shouldn't be. If it wasn't there I would say it couldn't be.'

'That is what you did say,' Leela said raising her voice above the agitated clacking and rattling of the louse. Casting about she found the remains of the Doctor's scarf with the coins, penknife and gold nugget still in the knot. Individually they were too small for her purposes, but it did give her an idea.

'Saying I told you so,' the Doctor was saying and watching the effect the sound of his voice was having on the creature, 'shows a certain smugness, Leela. As well as being annoying, such self-satisfaction gets in the way of original thinking and you should avoid it as far as is humanly possible.' He waited, then went on. 'I wonder what else I have to do to annoy this thing enough to get it moving. It seems to be endowed with the sort of patience that the irritable would kill for. I was quite certain it was stimulated by my sound vibration patterns. Particularly my voice.'

Leela cut a straight branch and cleaned and sharpened it. 'It is conserving energy. I expect it gets cold here at night. If it comes from the jungle it is feeling the cold already.' Using threads from the torn scarf she carefully bound the coins and the nugget round the branch about a hand's breadth back from the sharpened tip.

'Jungle? Why should it come from the jungle?'

'Things grow larger in the jungle. Is that not so?'

'It doesn't result in gigantism. Not on this scale. Anyway, first find your jungle.'

'It is over there.' She waved a hand in the general direction she had come from. 'I found it while I was looking for your tracks.'

'It was probably just a patch of lush plants.'

'That is what a jungle is, surely?'

'What about the temperature?' The Doctor began to shake the top of the tree vigorously in the vague hope that he might convince the creature he was trying to escape. It remained doggedly unmoved.

'It was hotter than it is here.' Leela checked the balance of the tip-heavy throwing spear she had made.

The Doctor gave up the struggle to cause vibrations in the tree. 'It's no good. It looks as though I'm going to have to climb down and tempt it into action.'

'Do not disturb it. Let me try this first,' she called up to him, moving round to get a better angle. She targeted the more vulnerable soft tissue in the exoskeletal gap where a leg joint pivoted into the creature's main body section. Adjusting her hold so that the spear would carry point first, she threw, and missed. The wooden point bounced off the hard chitinous shell of the leg and the spear fell back to the ground. She tried again with the same result.

'If at first you don't succeed, try, try, try again,' the Doctor chanted. The creature quivered just a little at the sound of his voice.

A third attempt to spear the soft tissue failed.

'Then give up,' he said. 'There's no point in making a fool of yourself. Confucius.'

Leela threw away the spear. She took a pair of soft leather patches from her belt and laced them to her knees and began to climb up the tree.

'What are you doing?' the Doctor demanded.

'Killing it on the ground would have been easier,' she said, 'but it is not going to move so I will have to do it up there.'

'Leela, stop that, you stupid girl!' the Doctor shouted. 'Get away from that thing. You haven't seen what it can do!' He started to scramble down from his safe position at the top of the tree.

The creature, sensing that its prey was finally coming back into reach, raised itself slightly on four firmly anchored legs and stretched its two forelegs upward, probing and scratching and wrenching chunks of wood from the tree trunk.

The Doctor kept on descending. He had nothing that resembled a plan now other than to keep the louse's attention.

Leela kept on climbing. She calculated that if she could get on to its back the animal would be vulnerable to a close-range attack. The two front legs were mobile enough to pivot back to where she would be, but they would lack full strength working in that direction. She would prefer it not to go through its death throes halfway up a tall tree, but she had no choice about that. She did not have much time, either, for although she had planned that the Doctor should keep it occupied she had not planned that he hurl himself into its jaws.

Close up she found the monstrous louse was covered in tufts of strong wiry hair like tiny scrubland thickets. She had an idea that anything that might lurk in these would be larger and more troublesome than average lice. She must remember when the time came that such parasites were often at their most dangerous when the host died.

'Leela, I forbid you to do that!' the Doctor was shouting. He had reached the gap in the branches that had given him so much trouble on the way up and was finding the same difficulties coming down. 'We need to think what we're doing!'

Leela grasped the ends of a patch of hairs, put a foot on one of

41

the rear legs and hauled herself on to the animal's back. The rough surface of the chitin-shelled abdomen provided plenty of grip and she crawled up towards its head.

The Doctor had sat down on what remained of the broken branch and was working his way round into a position where he could hang from it by his hands and drop on to the creature. He was already perilously close to being within the grasp of the agitatedly scrabbling forelegs.

In its frantic eagerness to feed on the Doctor the animal was oblivious to Leela and she got to the end of the abdomen without much problem. There was a narrow cleft here which seemed to divide the main part of the body from a shorter but more powerful front part, which in its turn was separated from a small broad head by a series of much narrower clefts, little more than cracks. Leela pulled her hunting knife and looked for a place she could cut into with one stroke and destroy a vital centre; the brain would be best, but the cord of the spine would do almost as well. But the problem was not just to get at them – she had to decide where they were. She expected there would be eyes around this area too, a multiple set of them, which it would be sensible to avoid. Normal eyes were access holes through the protective bone to reliable kill spots, but on an animal like this the arrangement was more complex. With multiple eyes there was often only one hole and you couldn't rely on finding it at the first attempt. She stared at the bony chitin ridges behind the small head with its acid-loaded fangs and its clicking, quivering jaws. If she went for somewhere among those ridges she might be able to sever the brain-body links immediately and then she would have a chance to find a way to kill the brain before any defensive responses kicked in. But it was possible that those thin spaces between the ridges were just as strongly shelled as everything else, in which case she would be committed to a useless attack and she would waste all the advantages of surprise. Above her the

Doctor was busy lowering himself from the branch. He seemed determined to join in, despite the fact that being ripped to pieces was all he could manage to do from there. She had to decide what to go for. Now.

She leapt the last few feet and, holding the front ridge with one hand, plunged the knife in behind it with the other. She felt the tip scrape on the unyielding chitin. She was wrong: the crevices were not open down through to the soft interior organs. She planted her feet on the top edge of the front body, clasped her knees against the narrow ridges and this time, using both hands on the knife, she stabbed harder into the same place. It made no impression. She could not penetrate the tough shell of the exoskeleton. She dragged the knife along the crack, feeling for the weak parts she was still certain must be there. The ridges and gaps had to be for movement and that meant they had to be jointed or hinged or flexible – and that meant had to be weaker, if she could only find one of them before the animal woke up to what she was doing.

The Doctor, meanwhile, had come into the creature's range of perception far enough finally to drive it into a fury of action. With a shuddering lurch it stiffened its legs and pushed its body further away from the tree. Then, still firmly anchored in place, it rocked forward with a jerk, thrusting forelegs upward at the Doctor's dangling feet.

The suddenness of the animal's first movement took Leela by surprise. She lost her footing and began to slip but she had been trained never to lose her knife and she held on to it instinctively. It was twisted in the crevice and it was only this that stopped her from falling off. She scrambled back into position and as the animal ravened towards the Doctor she felt the ridged crevice widen slightly. It was stretching open. So that was how it worked: she had been right after all. She shoved the knife home and slashed the sharp edge through cartilage, strings and arteries, cutting first one way and then the other until nothing resisted the blade. A mixture of green and brown gore was welling up over the ridge as Leela clambered the last few feet and drove the knife into a soft notch at the back of the animal's head, just behind its mouth parts. She twisted the knife, working and stabbing until she was sure that if the brain was there it was mush. She jumped to the nearest branch then, and clung to it waiting for the twitching and thrashing that would tear the animal out of the tree and hurl it crashing to the ground. But nothing happened. There were no death throes. The animal simply stopped functioning as though it had been turned off. The hooks at the end of its legs remained set firmly into the tree, and it stayed stiffly where it was.

'Next time I tell you not to do something,' the Doctor said, lowering himself on to one of the creature's outstretched forelegs and using it as a ladder to climb down to the lower branches, 'you could at least pause for a *moment* before doing it.'

Leela smiled. 'I thought I should hurry. You looked as though you were planning to choke it to death with your foot.'

'Do you notice,' the Doctor asked, looking closely at the dead louse, 'that it seems to have no parasites, and apart from what you've done to it there are no signs of damage of any kind? It's perfect.' He climbed on down towards the ground. 'Are you coming, or did you want the head as a trophy?'

Leela looked at the animal. Youth could explain its condition. 'It was probably young,' she said.

'You equate youth with perfection.' The Doctor reached the ground and retrieved the remains of his scarf.

'Scars come with time,' Leela said, joining him.

'That depends,' he said.

'On what?'

'On how long it takes you.'

Leela decided he was being deliberately obscure. She collected the spear and practised throwing it so that it stuck into the ground and on her chosen target. 'Do you want the coins and the shiny pebble?'

'The wool might be useful,' the Doctor said, pocketing shreds of scarf. 'I don't suppose you can knit by any chance?'

'Knit?'

The Doctor nodded. 'I must teach you. It's very relaxing. It's an effect of the rhythm of repetitive actions. And I shall need a new scarf. How did you find me, by the way?'

Leela gestured at the fairly clear tracks on the forest floor. 'I tracked the animal that was tracking you. It was not difficult.'

'I expect you must have come across my coat and hat then?'

'No. How did you lose them?'

'It was by way of an experiment.'

'To see if you could run faster without them?'

The Doctor set out to follow the tracks. 'I'm sure we can find them,' he beamed. 'Then you can show me this jungle of yours.'

They stared at the devastated patch of deciduous forest. Everything had been blasted from the primary impact zone, leaving only a wide shallow crater of blackly scorched soil. Around the edge, trees had been flattened and burned. Further out those left standing had been stripped of leaves and the exposed side of the trunks charred. It had obviously been a much more major crash and burn than the initial data had suggested. So where was the debris from the downed ship? They searched as far as the undamaged trees and there was no sign of anything.

When they reassembled in the new clearing Fermindor said, 'I've seen emergency disposal outfits do a less thorough job.'

'Any guesses?' Kley asked. According to the book this was a time for including everyone, for keeping the dynamic of the team positive. Apart from which she was completely at a loss for ideas.

'We missed it. This isn't the drop zone,' Belay offered.

'So what is all this? A meteorite strike?' Sozerdor demanded. He was sweating, despite the drop in temperature there had been since they left the jungle and crossed into the temperate woodland.

'It's possible,' Monly said.

Kley ran a multiple-reference-point check on her wrist compass. 'These are the correct co-ordinates.'

Monly said, 'As far as we can tell without the base computer.'

Kley refused to be provoked. 'This is the correct terrain. It's what we've been expecting.'

'Finally, it does appear to be, yes.'

'The runner's hidden everything,' Fermindor said.

Sozerdor snorted. 'If he has we're going to need a bigger team.'

'Why do you say that?' Belay asked.

'Because *he's* obviously got one!' Sozerdor tried to laugh but it sounded nervous and forced. 'He couldn't do it on his own, could he? He'd still be burying the bits.'

'I mean,' Fermindor said, coolly ignoring the interruption, 'that he's faked this. He didn't lose it coming in. He made a controlled descent. He hid the lander. He set an explosion. You could get this effect without much trouble. You could do it all with a directed charge.'

'That could be it,' Kley agreed, trying to sound more confident than she felt. It was just about plausible. If you didn't think about the details too closely. I'll believe it if you'll believe it, she thought. I need time to get a grip on this. She could see that there was one glaring and immediate problem.

'Why?' Monly asked. 'What would he hope to gain?'

Kley nodded. For once it was a fair question. 'We'd spot it, wouldn't we?' she said.

'We just did, Chief,' Fermindor remarked flatly.

'As soon as we got here we'd spot it,' Monly agreed.

'Time?' Belay suggested. 'He gains time. It's a delaying tactic.'

'Time to do what?' Monly pressed.

The sudden possibility of humiliating disaster struck Kley in a sickening rush, like waking from a nightmare to discover you really were naked in a crowd. She caught Fermindor's eye and it was clear to her that the same possibility had just occurred to him. 'Is he that good?' she asked him. 'Could he really have planned to suck us in like that?'

'I'd say so,' Fermindor said. 'Unless you like coincidence as an explanation.'

Kley ripped open her backpack, took out her voice-link co-ordinator and waited in silence for the aerials to deploy.

'Is that a good idea?' Monly asked.

Kley ignored him and set the search for Rinandor's unit.

'We have an agreed strategy for this mission,' he went on. 'Comm silence was an essential part of it.'

'I just un-agreed the strategy,' she said. 'It's my mission, my responsibility, and it's my decision.'

'I'll try to remember that,' he murmured.

'See that you do,' she hissed, knowing he would and knowing he didn't mean what she meant. This would not look good on the mission report. This would look like a failure in the planning phase.

Rinandor's unit registered the acceptance alarm but she was not reacting to it. Wherever she was, her voice unit wasn't with her. What was she doing? Kley keyed Pertanor's unit. He did not respond either.

'Not a good idea, then,' Monly said. 'No advantage. Except to the runner. He should have spotted the signal without much problem. You might as well have stuck up a sign.'

'We'd better eat and rest up before we start back,' Fermindor said quietly.

Kley closed down the co-ordinator. 'Very well,' she said. 'We'll make camp in the trees there. Start back at first light.'

Already close to panic, Sozerdor seemed finally to realise what was happening. 'He's doubled back on us, hasn't he?' It was an accusation. 'It's such an obvious trap. You've led us into a stupid trap. I said we should have waited. I knew something was wrong. I knew it.'

Fermindor rounded on him angrily. 'You didn't know it, So. None of us knew it. Now shut your mouth.' He was slightly shorter than the older man and had not yet put on the extra bulk of age but there was no doubting which of them had the authority. 'We need wood for a fire,' he said and began gathering it.

Sozerdor set about gathering wood too. 'I did say we should have waited for them to come back,' he grumbled. 'I was right about not splitting our force.'

The fact that they were both Senior Investigators was just an accident of rank, Kley thought. Another triumph for the Promotions Board. She wondered how it was that some had it and some didn't, and whether she was one of the ones that didn't. 'Belay,' she said, 'will you sort out the rations?'

'You think that's why we can't contact the ship? The runner got to it?' Belay asked, picking up backpacks and taking them towards where the firewood was being stacked.

'Allocate minimum energy requirement,' she said briskly, then thought better of it. 'No, make that minimum plus a half. Allocate Rinandor's and Pertanor's and divide it among the others.' Toodies were less reliable than ever if their stomachs were empty. Better to have everyone sharp now. She would worry about conserving supplies when she had a better idea of what was really happening.

'Are you expecting to live off the land?' Monly asked from near the centre of the blast crater where he was scraping away at the burnt topsoil. 'Only I haven't seen much in the way of food sources, have you? Indigenous life forms are remarkably thin on the ground. Or in it for that matter.'

Monly was dead on cue and dead where he crouched. He didn't even have time to draw his gun.

The giant lizard had stopped riding the thermals above the jungle and gone into a long, gliding dive. At the last moment just above the clearing it folded its leg-webbing and hit the ground running upright on two of its four legs. It took Monly's head off with one powerful bite and with its front legs ripped him apart from neck to crotch.

Kley barely had time to register how badly she hated coincidence before a second lizard landed, and then a third. It was only a brief squabble over Monly's remains that delayed the trio long enough to let her snatch up the equipment pack and run for the cover of the trees, yelling at Belay, Sozerdor and Fermindor to take up defensive positions.

It was improbable, and it was in the wrong place – at least, it was not in the right place, which was almost the same thing – but it was certainly a jungle of some sort. The humidity was high. The foliage was lush. When they crossed the boundary, densely packed trees thickly overgrown with vines and creepers, the temperature change had been remarkable. There was something odd, too, about the way the boundary was not quite visible until you got close to it. Or until you knew what it was you were looking for. He would need to examine that again and try to be objective, though that would be difficult now he knew what it was he was looking for. 'You were right,' the Doctor said. 'It *is* a jungle. It shouldn't be here. Things don't work like this.'

Leela knew this was an unusual place but, young as she was, she had seen much more startling things that should not be where they were, or work the way they did. She felt the Doctor was being overdramatic. 'How does it stay warmer?' she asked. 'Would it be hot springs under the ground, do you think? Something like that?'

'Something like that. Where's all the life, I wonder?' It was like the pine forest. There were none of the smaller animals, insects and birds you would usually expect to see. And again, there was not much smell.

'Do you want to see the squad snake?'

'Not really. I think we should get back to the TARDIS.'

'Are we leaving?'

'I may have misinterpreted a problem with the sampling image locator.' The Doctor strode off towards the boundary.

'You do not think we should check on those people?' Leela knew from experience that he was no longer listening and that she might as well follow him because that was what he assumed she was doing.

'I assumed that the mismatch with the star chart was a malfunction but supposing it wasn't. Do you see what that means?'

'No.'

'It means this planet shouldn't be here,' he said triumphantly. 'Which puts a whole new slant on things, doesn't it? What were you saying about checking on those people?'

Pertanor was still annoyed with her. It was difficult to be truly angry with someone as attractive as she was, especially while she was leaning on him and he could feel the tantalising weight of her hip against his and the occasional brush of her breast against the side of his chest. He was still annoyed with her, though. He couldn't believe that anyone as bright as Rinandor could have behaved so stupidly. 'What were you thinking of?' he said yet again.

She stopped walking and turned to face him. 'Now look, Pe, I've said I'm sorry. I know it was stupid.'

'Stupid. That's the word I was groping for.'

'I think she and her minder are up to no good,' she continued, deadpan, 'and I doubt whether they would have helped us

50

voluntarily but… pulling a gun was possibly not the best way to make friends.'

Pertanor smiled and offered his shoulder for her to lean on again. 'I won't mention it any more.'

'Good,' she said. 'Because if you keep nagging about it I shall limp along without your help and you will lose the only compensation to have come from this whole sorry mess.'

'Which is what exactly?' he asked, his face an innocent blank.

Rinandor turned to lean against him and they walked on. 'The chance to get your body close to my body,' she said and let her hip move against his.

Pertanor giggled his slightly irritating giggle. 'I thought that was your compensation,' he said.

'Did I say it wasn't?'

He glanced around the darkening forest. In the steadily falling light the tall pine trees were fading to gloomy shadows. There was no sound, no movement except for wisps of thin fog which formed and sank slowly into the otherwise imperceptible hollows and slight depressions in the ground. 'We've got to find somewhere to spend the night.'

'Let's not get ahead of ourselves. The question I have to consider is, will you still respect me in the morning?'

'I meant the sun's going down, and who knows what horrors come out after dark?'

'I know what you meant,' she said. 'I was planning not to think about it until I absolutely had to.'

'I think you have to.'

'We could climb a tree,' she said.

'You can barely walk.'

'I can climb if I'm frightened enough.'

Pertanor shivered involuntarily. 'It's getting colder, isn't it?' he said.

'Are you sure you're not frightened?'

'Me?' he said. 'Frightened?' He giggled. 'I'm scared spitless. I'm this close –' he pinched his thumb and forefinger together – 'to screaming my lungs out.'

She stopped and turned to face him again. This time she put her arms round him and pulled herself against him. She rubbed her face against his. 'I could really get very fond of you,' she murmured.

Pertanor put his arms around her. The touch of her cheek against his was vivid, electric and feverish. He said, 'A fire.'

'Me too,' she whispered.

'I meant …' He hesitated.

'You meant?'

'I meant I'm afire,' he said.

She smirked. 'You're *so* easy to tease.'

'I know,' he said. 'But I think we should light a fire anyway, don't you?'

The Doctor was almost sure that this was the place where the TARDIS should be. Leela was adamant about it and he had no reason to doubt her skills as a tracker. So the TARDIS had been moved. But where to? And by whom?

'I left the door open,' Leela admitted, finding the only explanation she could think of that fitted. 'Someone must have got in and taken it.'

Recent events had made her cocky and the Doctor was inclined to let her feel the discomfort of failure, but since the failure was not hers he couldn't quite bring himself to do it. 'No, that's not it,' he said. 'It's been hauled away.'

Leela examined the area. It was getting dark now but any sign of the TARDIS being dragged off would be obvious. 'I don't see how that could be,' she said.

'Logically,' the Doctor said, 'it was taken straight down or straight up.'

Reflexively Leela looked up into the air and then, embarrassed, said, 'There might be marks on the trees,' by way of explanation. 'From…'

'From whatever lifting vehicle was used,' the Doctor agreed without looking up. He scraped at the soil with his foot in the place where Leela said the TARDIS had been standing. There was no recognisable impression that he could see but the soil had been disturbed. 'I'm inclined to think it went down.'

'How are we going to get it back?'

'We start by finding it.'

Distantly, among the trees, something grunted and howled.

'We had better find somewhere to shelter for the night,' Leela said.

The Doctor continued to examine the ground.

The howling was taken up by other animals. It sounded as though a pack was gathering.

'Time to climb another tree, perhaps,' the Doctor said. 'Somewhere well away from this spot, I think. Come on.' He began to stride away, but this time he checked to make sure she was keeping up with him.

'Do you think they will come back then?' she asked.

'Who?'

'Whoever took the TARDIS,' Leela said, just stopping herself from the further embarrassment of calling it the TARDIS hut.

'If they do, it won't be to apologise for the inconvenience,' he said.

'Does that mean you know who they are?'

'I don't know who they are, or what they are, or what it is they are doing,' the Doctor said. 'What I do know is that there will be a rational explanation for all this and if we live long enough we shall find out what it is.'

'You always think that,' Leela said. 'What would happen if you found something you simply could not explain?'

'There are a lot of things I can't explain,' the Doctor said. 'As I've told you, that does not make them inexplicable, merely unexplained.'

'But what would happen,' Leela persisted, 'if you were convinced that something was beyond all understanding? That it did not have an explanation.'

'Then I should know it did not exist. Can you track those two people you found? What were they called... um?'

'Pe-pertanor and Ri-rinandor. Yes I can track them.'

It was not bragging but a straightforward expression of fact. One of the things the Doctor had liked about Leela from their first meeting was her unaffected directness. It reminded him of himself. 'I want to catch up with them before it gets too dark to see.'

'Are you going to try to help them?'

The Doctor smiled. 'We're going to help each other,' he said cheerfully.

Pertanor had picked a spot close to a large tree. He reasoned it would be a source of extra firewood, and they could climb it if the flames weren't enough to discourage any night prowlers. When they heard the grunting and howling in the distance, he left Rinandor sitting propped up against the base of the trunk and rushed about gathering fallen branches and brush and stacking it all within reach of where the fire would be.

'Pity we lost both the packs,' Rinandor murmured.

'And the ship – don't forget I threw away the ship as well,' Pertanor muttered.

'I wasn't blaming you.'

'No?'

'I was just saying –'

'It's a pity I lost both the packs.'

'It was a casual remark. I was just making conversation.'

'If you hadn't pulled the gun on Leela she might have found them for us. Oh sorry. Just making conversation.'

She shivered. 'You can be very petty, you know.'

'Yes I can,' he said, taking off the jacket of his fatigues and draping it round her shoulders. 'When I'm hungry and scared and tired, I can be very petty indeed. I'm sorry.' She was still showing signs of shock, and it occurred to him now that he had no medical supplies of any kind if she really began to drop out of orbit. It *was* a pity he had lost both packs. 'I suppose this means sex is out of the question?'

She forced a smile. 'It could be a way of keeping warm.' Her shivering was getting worse and there was a thin slick of sweat on her face. 'I'm not cold enough yet, though.'

'You'd better give me back my jacket,' he said. 'And can I borrow yours for a while?' He began to lay the fire, working as quickly as he could. If he let her get any colder she could be in serious trouble. Heaping up bark and small sticks first, he then stacked the bigger stuff round it. At least it was dry. He checked the charge on his gun. There was just about enough left to start it all burning.

'We're not going to make it, are we?' Rinandor whispered.

'Sorry, didn't hear that,' Pertanor said.

'I said –'

'I know what you said. I just didn't hear it.'

'Oh rah, rah, rah,' she said and applauded weakly. 'I'm impressed. When you get out of the OIG you'll be running for office, will you? Or writing those inspirational thoughts they put on snack packaging?'

'I am going to live to get out then?'

'Clever. Scoring cheap points off a sick woman. Aren't you ashamed?'

The gathering pack of night hunters chorused distantly. He wondered how many of them there would need to be before they set off in search of food, and whether a small fire would be enough to put them off. 'Desperately,' he said. 'I can barely bring myself to look you in the breasts – *eyes*. Did I say breasts? I meant thighs – *eyes*.' He pushed the muzzle of the gun into the tinder and pressed the trigger. A small flame appeared on the edge of a piece of bark and began to climb and crackle through the smallest sticks. He holstered the gun and carefully fed more wood to the flame, watching with relief as the burning strengthened and the flame divided and multiplied. 'Besides, I intend to stay in. I told you I plan to be the first Director of the Group to rise from the ranks.'

'Skinny-dick started as an ordinary Investigator, didn't he? That's what he claims in every speech he ever makes.'

'He was a fast-track firster on the rapid-promotion programme – it doesn't count.'

Rinandor held out her hands to the fire. There wasn't much heat from it yet but the brightening light seemed to raise her spirits and her shivering lessened. 'I seem to remember some minor toody philosopher saying we should stop thinking like that.'

'Now who's scoring cheap points?'

'You're not a sick woman.'

'I could be if it meant getting out of here in one piece.' He put more wood on the fire. Rinandor already looked better, he thought. Of course, the warm, yellowy orange light could just be disguising her pallor, but she did seem to have stopped shivering. 'You feeling a bit warmer?' he asked.

'Yes.'

'Pity. Will you be all right, then, if I leave you and go and look for some more wood?'

'It's too dark,' she said. 'Anything could happen. You might get lost.'

Pertanor was elated. For a moment all he could think was that she was concerned for him. She did care. She wasn't teasing. 'I'm not going far,' he said. 'I'll keep the fire in sight.'

'We don't know what's out there,' she worried. 'You could get attacked. You could get eaten.'

He was about to reassure her with a witticism along the lines that getting eaten was the last thing he intended to do, when he heard the stealthy sounds of something approaching in the darkness, out beyond the reach of the light from the fire.

Chapter Four

The three lizards had attacked the defensive position running on all fours. They were slower than when they first landed and the trees seemed to confuse them. It was not until afterwards that Kley realised they were probably cold-blooded, and rapid cooling off in the temperate conditions might have had an effect. They were still fearsomely aggressive and gruesomely spattered with Monly's blood and body tissue.

At the first sight of them Sozerdor had panicked and wasted a full handgun charge and all the power in his auxiliary clip on the lead animal without hitting anything vital. It was lucky for him that as it opened its jaws for the kill Fermindor got it with a brain shot through the roof of its mouth.

It was lucky for everyone that the other two lizards immediately turned their attention to the corpse and tore into it with starving ferocity, ripping away ragged lumps of pale flesh and struggling with each other for possession of them. In these circumstances Kley, Fermindor and Belay had time to co-ordinate their shooting so that the kills were certain.

After that, they waited in the gathering darkness for the next attack. When that didn't come, they finished preparing their overnight camp, staying deep in the cover of the trees. They lit a fire, but decided against Fermindor's suggestion that they cook meat from the dead lizards; Sozerdor protested that Monly's guts were all over the place and they could end up eating bits of him.

'When we get back and I draw my twenty-five,' he said, 'I don't want to remember that I got there by snacking on my friends.'

Kley realised two things at that moment that she should have understood from the outset. Sozerdor had contract fever, and though he was a toody, with all the resentments against firsters that entailed, he thought of the dead second-in-command as a friend. Why didn't she know that? Why hadn't she been briefed? It was the sort of routine personality profiling that any team leader was given. She could have spotted the organisational weakness earlier, *would* have spotted it earlier and compensated for it, if they'd prepared her properly. In fact, she would have asked for a replacement before the mission lift-off. Was that why they didn't tell her? In case she asked for a replacement and there was none available? No, that wasn't it. All they had to do was refuse her request, they didn't have to leave her to find out for herself when she was up to her arse in carnivorous lizards. There was something behind it, something she wasn't getting. Or was she being paranoid?

Later when the four of them sat close to the fire eating their field rations Fermindor said, 'Since when was Monly a friend?'

'I was speaking generally.'

'I see.' Fermindor's voice was expressionless.

Sozerdor bristled. 'What do you mean by that?'

Fermindor shrugged slightly and continued to eat his rations in silence.

'I said what does that mean?'

'You were talking about superior officers generally, were you? I never thought of them as friends, that's all. Especially not him.'

'You wouldn't want to eat bits of them, though,' Belay mused aloud, apparently trying to head off a quarrel.

She was supposed to do that, Kley thought. She was meant to keep them from fighting among themselves, but simply didn't have the energy for it. The image of Monly, headless, blood spurting from severed arteries, guts spilling from his body, wouldn't leave the back of her eyes. The bickering among what was left of her command reminded her a bit of the lizards squabbling over his remains. She felt worse because she had

60

disliked him, and mixed in with the horror of his death and the fear there had been an exultant moment of relief. He wasn't going to undermine her any more. He wasn't going to make a report on her. He wasn't going to end up senior to her, giving her orders. So who's the failure now then, Monly?

'What did you have against him especially?' Sozerdor asked.

'He was routinely over-privileged, ambitious, greedy and ruthless, but apart from that not a thing,' Fermindor said.

'The young man is dead.'

'Might change how you see him, it doesn't change how he was.'

'I liked him,' Sozerdor said. 'He had a lot of charm.'

'He was good-looking too.' Fermindor's tone was still flat and expressionless.

'Always helps,' agreed Belay. 'Charm, confidence and good looks will take you a long way in this job.'

Fermindor threw his empty ration pack into the fire. 'I'll settle for a good, charmless, ugly professional who knows what needs to be done and gets on with it.'

'Like you, Fe, is that what you mean?' Sozerdor asked.

Fermindor smiled. 'At least I can shoot straight, So.'

'I was unsighted.'

'Had your eyes closed more like.'

'You'd all better try to get some sleep,' Kley said tiredly. 'I'll take the first watch, then you Fermindor, then Belay, then Sozerdor. One-tenth rotation each.'

They piled more wood on the fire, and the other three unrolled sleep bags and stretched out on their self-inflating relaxers. Kley, meanwhile, moved to the edge of the darkness and huddled down to listen, peering towards the crash site. She wasn't sure why she expected any attack to come from that direction. Perhaps it was the corpses. That amount of dead flesh must attract scavengers eventually. She strained to hear, though to hear what she wasn't sure. Chewing and crunching, perhaps, or the vomiting of digestive acid and the slurping up of the dissolving flesh? Before long, the stealthy sounds came shuffling through the dark and there were shadows moving wherever she looked. It took a conscious effort to keep her imagination from hearing and seeing all that she *expected* to hear and see. At least by the time it came to Sozerdor's turn on watch it would be getting light again. She couldn't trust his nerve to hold. In fact she wouldn't even have trusted a firster if they were coming up to full contract completion and a no-penalty discharge on twenty-five work bonuses. It was every career Investigator's ambition to retire with that sort of benefit package. So who was it who thought she could rely on someone like him for a mission such as this?

The Doctor offered his broadest and most beguiling grin to the woman Leela had introduced as Ri-rinandor. He thought that might in fact be two names, one personal, and the other perhaps patronymic or maybe tribal, given the similarity with the man's name and the physical characteristics the two of them seemed to share. Of all the culturally determined sensitivities names were among the most dangerous, he had found, with endless possibilities for misunderstanding and insult. He would have to wait until he heard how Ri-rinandor and Pe-pertanor addressed each other before he risked using a name, so in the meantime general charm was the best he could do.

The woman was clearly already suspicious of him and was not inclined to give away any useful information. The fact that she was suspicious was information of a sort, of course. 'Don't you find it fascinating,' he said, smiling widely into the firelight, 'that even the refusal to say anything must say something. If communication is possible then we may tell each other lies, but we can't tell each other nothing.'

'You sound like an Investigator,' Rinandor said, sounding very suspicious now.

'You're doing it again, Ri,' Pertanor muttered.

'Shut up, Pe, this is important,' she said. 'Is that what you claim to be?' she challenged the Doctor. 'An Investigator? Or is it what you used to be before you found Leela?'

'I'm an investigator of a sort, I suppose.'

'Of what sort exactly?'

Before the Doctor could think of a suitably anodyne response Pertanor cut in. 'I thought you were another predator,' he said. 'It was a serious relief when the noise turned out to be you and Leela.' He peered off into the darkness. 'Is she all right out there, do you think?'

The truth was, the Doctor wasn't confident about the way Leela had wandered off to see what was howling. 'I'm sure she is,' he said confidently. 'I'm only just beginning to realise how very good she is at that sort of thing.'

'Is that why you brought her here, Thedoctor? You know offworlds training is against Guild law, don't you?'

'Please, call me The,' the Doctor said taking a chance. 'I wouldn't dream of breaking the law, Ri. May I call you Ri?'

Rinandor nodded, puzzled. 'You're very formal,' she remarked. 'And – no offence – but you're also very thin for a toody.'

So the first syllable of any name is used as a standard diminutive and thin may be seen as an insult, the Doctor thought, and wondered in passing if these people might derive from a subjugated group. 'Perhaps I'm not a toody,' he said noncommittally.

'You think because your fighter is a firster you can pass too,' she mocked. 'It'll never happen, The.'

'Why would I want to pass?' the Doctor asked.

'Ambition.' She caught Pertanor's eye and smiled a little. 'Skinny toodies are noted for it apparently.'

The Doctor caught the look that passed between them and,

wondering what it meant he said: '"Let me have men about me that are fat; sleek-headed men and such as sleep o' nights. Yond Cassius has a lean and hungry look; he thinks too much: such men are dangerous."' It had been his experience that quoting Shakespeare, his favourite poet from his favourite planet, usually produced interesting reactions but in this case if he had wanted to boost suspicion into anxiety and hostility it seemed he could not have made a better choice. 'It's from a dramatic work by a poet of my acquaintance,' he explained. 'From long ago and far away.'

Rinandor stared at him in silence. Pertanor said, 'Of your acquaintance?' His voice was incredulous and sounded angry.

It struck the Doctor that 'long ago and far away' was perhaps not the ideal choice of words in the circumstances. 'His work,' he corrected himself. 'I'm acquainted with his work.'

Rinandor sighed. 'Do you take us for blasphemers or just for fools?'

'Was it something I said?'

'You know as well as I do there are firsters who'd kill you on the spot for speaking the text.'

Speaking the text? The Doctor would have been amazed if there was anything left that could amaze him. Shakespeare, he thought, or a coincidence: infinite monkey programmes on infinite monkey machines? And if it is the Bard of Avon then how long since the ancestors of their ancestors' ancestors left the home system?

'So how are we supposed to react?' Rinandor was saying. 'Are we supposed to report you? Is that what you're trying to find out?'

Sacred texts and paranoia. If they did originate from Earth they had brought their worst failings with them and nurtured them through generations forgotten and gone. 'Surely we're all friends here,' he said.

Pertanor giggled suddenly. 'You're a bold toody,' he said. 'Come on, Ri, you can't believe he's here because of us. I mean look at the state we're in.'

'Doesn't it strike you as peculiar that he doesn't care that we're Investigators? That he doesn't give a crap that he's crossed an OIG perimeter?'

'That was unintentional. I had no idea there was a perimeter in place,' the Doctor said, and wondered how he was going to find out what an OIG perimeter was.

'Was bringing a fighter here unintentional too?'

'You mean Leela? It was accidental more than unintentional,' the Doctor said. 'It was her idea to travel with me. She rather outgrew her background. She's quite a headstrong girl, you know.' He beamed. 'You could say she bullied me into it.'

Pertanor butted in. 'She is remarkable, isn't she?'

'Yes, I think she probably is.'

'But you're not managing and training her?' Rinandor persisted.

'Hardly.' The Doctor let his amusement show. 'I do my best of course. She's not the most easygoing companion I've ever had. She has the potential to be one of the most interesting, though.'

'The interesting ones don't last as long,' Rinandor said. 'But people like you make a lot more out of them, isn't that right?'

'People like me?'

'Admit it, The. You may as well,' Pertanor said. 'You are acting as the agent manager for a contract duellist.'

'And you've been caught breaking the law, which regulates that *profession*.' She said the word with such withering contempt that the Doctor aborted his embryonic plan to use the mistake to his advantage. But what should he replace it with?

Pertanor was saying, 'In strictly legal terms you and she shouldn't be here –' when in the near distance a sudden clamour of snarling and howling interrupted him. He hurriedly put another branch on the fire and stirred up a rising cloud of whispering sparks. 'But I'm glad she's around. And so is Ri if she's honest.'

65

The noises from the pack hunters stopped as abruptly as they had begun, and in the straining silence Rinandor said, 'If she *is* still around.'

She could hear them feeding on the carcasses and this time she knew it was real. Flesh tore greasily and sinews crackled as they were ripped and broken. Whatever was doing it grunted and fought short, fierce, snarling quarrels. Kley was certain her brain was enhancing and exaggerating what she was hearing but, compulsively, she checked the charge register on the power pack of her handgun yet again, just to be sure.

'You can't tell how big a thing is by the sound it makes in the dark,' Fermindor whispered behind her and almost got shot as a result of her startled reaction.

'Don't creep around like that,' she hissed. 'I might have killed you.'

'My turn on watch,' he murmured. 'Looks like you could do with a rest.'

'Did you hear what I said, Senior Investigator?' she demanded, the adrenaline rush overriding her carefully calculated rationality.

'Yes, Chief,' he said, keeping his voice low. 'I heard what you said. No disrespect, but does shouting seem like a good idea to you?'

'Is your gun fully charged?' she asked coldly.

'The backup pack is.'

'That's not what I asked you!'

'It's three-quarters charged with a full-strength backup pack, Chief Investigator,' he answered formally, though his tone made it clear that his opinion of her had changed for the worse.

As the shock subsided she regretted her stupidity, remembering the tutor who had told her that spoken words were, like death, irretrievable, and had then gone on to call her an uneducated lump. 'I'm sorry, Fe,' she muttered. 'That was stupid of me.'

It was the first time she had ever used his casual name and Fermindor didn't know how to react. He had a certain respect for her professional commitment and her lack of the sort of influential contacts firsters like her took for granted. But he had no particular wish to be on familiar terms with her. Obviously he was not even tempted to try calling her Serian. 'We're under a four-alarm decompression here,' he said. 'Bound to get cramps. For what it's worth you haven't missed a step that I've seen. Nothing that's happened can possibly count against you, Chief. Officially or any other way.'

She stared at him for a long moment. 'Thanks,' she said finally. 'I appreciate that. Now Monly's gone I'm promoting you acting second, full mission ACI contract credit.'

'If you think I'm up to it.'

'We both know you're up to it,' she yawned. 'I can't register it on the ship's computer so I'll make a note of it in my wrist log for now.'

Fermindor nodded. Assistant Chief Investigator. It was only an acting field promotion but it still felt pretty good to him. And, if he was honest, it felt like no more than he deserved.

Leela threw the dead animal down by the fire. It was almost as broad as it was long, with two wickedly clawed front legs slightly shorter than its four heavily muscled back ones. Its fur was mottled white-on-black, and it had a small head with large eyes, long ears and a mouth filled with row upon row of backward-angled, sharp-toothed ridges.

'Is that what was making all the noise?' the Doctor asked. 'Or is it just supper?'

'Both,' Leela said and settled down to skinning and gutting it.

'It doesn't seem to be adapted to run long distances,' the Doctor said.

'They jump,' she said. 'Very aggressive.'

'The eyes, the ears and the markings suggest it's almost exclusively a night predator,' the Doctor went on. 'I wonder what it normally feeds on.'

'I wondered about that too. There does not seem to be anything else out there. Nothing moving. Nothing alive. These things could have frightened everything off, I suppose.'

'It sounded like there were hundreds of them.' Pertanor couldn't keep the admiration out of his voice as he watched Leela chop off the animal's head and feet, cut sinews and rip off the thick pelt.

'Well, several anyway,' Rinandor said.

'It is another pack runner,' Leela said, carving chunks of meat from the carcass, skewering them on sharpened sticks and positioning them over the fire. 'This time there was one lead animal. It did the thinking for the others. When I killed it they gave up and scattered.'

'The lead animal was obvious?' The Doctor asked.

'Bigger than the rest.'

The smoke from the fat dripping into the flames was acrid but when the meat began to roast the smell of it reminded Pertanor and Rinandor of how long it was since they had eaten and how hungry they had become. They both inhaled the aroma with half-closed eyes and small smiles on their plump faces.

The Doctor was examining the animal's skin. 'Is this the summer?' he asked no one in particular.

'Climate data wasn't featured in any of our briefings,' Pertanor said, staring intensely at the cooking meat. 'Except to say that it wouldn't be a problem for us given the time scale of the mission.'

Before the Doctor could prompt further information from him Rinandor interrupted her partner. 'You expect us to believe that you came here,' she sneered at the Doctor, 'not knowing what season it was and what the weather conditions were going to be like?'

'Why not?' Pertanor remarked, not taking his eyes off the food.

'We did.'

'That's different,' she said.

'We weren't as well prepared as they were,' Pertanor said. 'Or as well equipped. Is that what you mean?'

'I mean we had a job to do. A *confidential* job.'

Now it was the Doctor's turn to try to distract Pertanor. He was not sure how committed the young man was to his service, presumably some sort of police group, and the mission that had brought him here, but confidentiality was not a concept the Doctor wanted him to dwell on. 'This animal,' he said, 'seems to be equipped for a climate that's a good deal colder than the one in which we find ourselves.'

'Maybe there is a cold area,' Leela said. 'Separate like the jungle is.'

'That's a good thought,' the Doctor said. 'It would fit the hypothesis. Though if that is how it all works the tests should not stray far from their base zones, not if they are going to be fully effective.'

'Are we supposed to know what you are talking about, Doctor?' Leela asked.

'I was thinking aloud,' he said. 'It's a bad habit of mine. And you can call me The again, by the way.'

'The?'

The Doctor nodded vigorously. 'The,' he beamed. 'Our secret is out, I'm afraid. But we are among friends.'

'I don't remember saying that you were among friends,' Rinandor remarked. 'Did we say you were among friends?'

Leela checked the meat. 'Are you hungry?' she asked.

'What do you mean by that exactly?'

'I mean the meat is cooked enough to be eaten,' Leela said, offering her a piece of the browned flesh on its charred stick. Rinandor accepted it with a show of suspicious reluctance.

Pertanor didn't wait to be served. He grabbed a stick and began eating the meat ravenously.

Leela gave the Doctor some. 'Why should I call you The?' she whispered.

'It's short for Thedoctor,' he muttered. 'You're a professional fighter, I look after your affairs, we're not supposed to be here.' More loudly he said, 'Thank you, Leela, but I'm not really hungry at the moment.'

'It is not as bad as it looks, The,' Leela said and began to eat the food herself.

'You're a sorry case, The,' Rinandor scoffed through a mouthful of food. 'Greed is making you into a skinny, lawbreaking blasphemer.'

The Doctor smiled. 'A skinny, lawbreaking blasphemer? That would be a bad thing, would it?'

Pertanor giggled. 'You have to enjoy a bold toody,' he chortled. 'I say if more of us were like The, then we'd be better off as a people.' He helped himself to more of the meat. 'There is nothing fundamentally wrong with greed.'

'If you're a firster,' Rinandor said, taking more food herself. 'There's no place for greed among us toodies. I mean let's be honest about this, Pe. Do you find thin people physically attractive?'

'Not really, but that's just a personal preference. I think we've got to be careful not to be prejudiced about body shape. It would be wrong to assume that all thin people are obsessively greedy, or selfishly aggressive. Leela's not like that, are you, Leela?'

Leela took what was left of the food and began to eat. 'I do not think so,' she said. 'Maybe you should ask The what he thinks of me.'

All three of them looked at the Doctor, who responded blankly. 'I'm sorry, what was the question?'

'Does body size affect the way you behave?' Leela asked.

'It helps to be taller if you want to see over people's heads. And it helps to be stronger if you've got to carry your own luggage,' the Doctor reflected. 'But then again, there are ladders and trolleys.'

'The question is body shape,' Pertanor pointed out, 'not body size. We're talking about being fatter or thinner.'

'Shape is in the eye of the beholder,' the Doctor said. 'Different gravitational conditions will change size and shape, as will climate and memory.'

'Memory?' Rinandor challenged.

'It's where appetites and attitudes come from.'

'Another philosophical toody,' she mocked. 'It *is* shape.' She looked at Pertanor. 'Get as thin as him and you'll be talking as much rubbish as he does.'

'It's getting lighter,' the Doctor said looking up and around and peering off into the trees. 'Of course. This system has twin suns, hasn't it?'

Rinandor wiped her mouth on her sleeve. 'I think your manager should eat something, Leela,' she said. 'Trying to switch planets is affecting his mind.'

'Switch planets?' Leela tried to keep the question casual. This was all getting way beyond her. She hoped the Doctor knew what was behind it, though judging by his expression and the way he was sitting and fidgeting she doubted it.

'You mean you hadn't noticed?' Rinandor smirked. 'I think that makes my point about firsters and toodies.'

It struck Leela that the trouble with casual questions was that the answers usually did not tell you much. 'The?' she said. 'Is there something wrong?'

'Apart from everything,' Pertanor giggled.

Leela had noticed before how the eating of food usually affected mood but she did not think she had ever seen it happen quite so quickly or so markedly as with these toody people. Perhaps they were right about the Doctor not eating, though. He did seem to be particularly distracted. 'The?' she repeated. Stupid name, she thought. She could not believe his plan required using such a stupid name, especially as she did not think he had a plan. And anyway she saw no reason why they had to pacify these two toody people. They were unfriendly and ungrateful. And they were unnecessarily plump.

'It would be useful to know if all the nights in all parts of this planet are as brief as this one,' the Doctor said. 'Unfortunately, without the TARDIS I have no way of getting the data or of making the calculations.'

'No problem,' Pertanor sniggered. 'Our reconnaissance data was unequivocal about that one.'

'Probably because it didn't make any practical difference to anything,' Rinandor laughed.

'So?' the Doctor asked.

'No, I'm Pe,' Pertanor said. 'So is with the others.' He hooted with glee. 'He's about as much use as a soluble space suit.'

'And as popular as a fart in an escape pod,' Rinandor added, almost helpless with merriment.

'It's important to know,' the Doctor said earnestly.

'About Sozerdor?' Pertanor seemed puzzled and then immediately suspicious. 'Why? Have you been lying to us? Are you a bony-brained liar?'

'Just tell the Doctor what he wants to know, will you,' Leela demanded. 'You people are not very clever, are you?'

'Typical,' said Rinandor. 'That is just typical. Never trust a friendly firster.'

'It's important to know about the dark periods on this planet, Pe,' the Doctor said, putting all the placatory charm he could manage into his voice and into his smile. 'There's something strange going on and if I can get enough information I can work out what it is and that will be good for all of us.'

Pertanor made a heroic effort to look dignified and sensible. 'The nights are always short, have always been short, will always be short. And that is the best irrelevant crap that money can buy,' he said, and promptly fell asleep.

The Doctor looked at Rinandor. 'Is that true?' he asked her.

'He said so, didn't he? You can trust my Pe. Even if he is a bit on the skinny side,' she murmured, as she too nodded off.

Leela felt distinctly odd. 'This is a very strange place,' she said. 'There seem to be only predators. That is not possible, is it?' She frowned and closed her eyes to think. After a little while, she opened them again. 'Unless they eat each other. Would that make sense, Doctor? Or should I say The?'

'Almost anything will make sense under the right circumstances,' the Doctor said. 'And unless you're careful you can convince yourself of all sorts of things without any evidence to back them up. For example, how is it –' He paused, and then raised his voice slightly. 'Are you listening?'

Leela opened her drooping eyelids wide. 'I am listening. I am listening.'

'How is it that specialist night predators have evolved on a planet with no real night to speak of?'

'I do not know,' Leela said, struggling to concentrate. 'How is it?'

'I don't know either.'

'So why bother to ask the question?'

The Doctor grinned. 'Only lawyers and policemen ask questions to which they already know the answers.'

'Like those two toodies,' Leela said and looked at the sleeping pair. 'They are what you call policemen, is that not so? Investigators? They are the ones who make sure everyone else follows the rules of the tribe?'

'Something like that,' the Doctor agreed.

'Do toodies only come in twos, do you think?'

'No,' said the Doctor seriously, 'but the names firster and toody

73

'must surely derive from one and two.'

'One and two what?' Leela asked, peering at him owlishly. 'Do not bother to tell me. You do not know. Do you know that you do not know more than you do know?'

'I do know that, yes. It's one of the things that make life tolerable.'

'Not knowing where no-night night predators come from makes life tolerable?'

'Knowing there's a question about them. Of course there is one obvious possibility.'

'Yes?'

'Yes.'

Leela yawned copiously. 'Go on then. Tell me what it is.'

'It would be better if you could tell me,' the Doctor suggested, hoping to get her to focus, and feeling anyway that this might be a good time for a lesson in thinking.

'No, it would not,' Leela said flatly, 'because you already know. You do not ask questions you already know the answers to unless you are a policeman or a lawgiver.'

'Lawyer,' the Doctor corrected her. 'And I forgot teachers; and that I keep underestimating you.'

'It is because I am younger than you.'

'It's possible that those animals haven't evolved here.'

Leela thought for a long moment. 'Why would anyone bring them in from the outside?' She closed her eyes again.

'Why indeed? That's a good question, Leela. We're going to talk about that and you're going to stay awake. Open your eyes now. Leela!'

Leela opened her eyes and sighed. 'I feel strange.'

'It was the meat,' the Doctor said. 'The possibility should have occurred to me but it didn't, unfortunately.'

'Have I been poisoned?'

The Doctor said, 'Those two just seem to be dozing, nothing

more than that. I think the three of you may be intoxicated.'

Leela sat up straighter. 'Intoxicated?'

'Something in the meat has affected your brain chemistry.'

Leela held up a finger and smiled. 'You do not know what it is and that makes life tolerable.'

The Doctor shrugged. 'Perhaps alcohol or something of the kind is a by-product of metabolism. Whatever it is, I'm sure the effects will pass. You already seem to be stabilising.'

Leela said, 'I did not get a chance to eat very much.' She peered at Rinandor and Pertanor, who were both snoring gently. 'Lucky they were so greedy.'

The Doctor stood up and stretched. It was already almost full daylight. 'They weren't greedy,' he said. 'According to their culture greed makes you thin.'

Leela got to her feet, rather shakily. 'What are the right circumstances for that to make sense?' she asked.

The Doctor was no longer listening. He moved to look more closely at the sleeping faces of Pertanor and Rinandor. 'It's possible those animals were never meant to be eaten by anything,' he said. 'It's possible they were designed that way.'

'Everything gets eaten by something,' Leela said. 'That is how it works.'

'It?'

'The world.'

'But supposing this isn't a world,' the Doctor said. 'Help me wake these two up.' He began to shake Pertanor by the shoulder. 'We need to find the rest of their unit.'

'Why?' Leela demanded irritably. 'Are these two not enough trouble by themselves?'

'I think they hold the key to what's going on here.' He began slapping Pertanor's face gently. 'Wake up, Pe. Come on, Pe. Wake up.'

Pertanor came to slowly. He sat up smiling. 'I feel wonderful,' he said, and then his smile vanished from a palely sweating face and he rolled to one side and vomited.

They were all dead. Dozens of them lay around among the torn-up remains of the lizards. They were all identical except for one, which appeared to be bigger than the others. Kley had never seen a fur-bearing animal with six legs before. 'Ugly brutes,' she commented, poking the large one with her foot. 'I wonder what killed them.'

'Eating lizard meat?' Belay suggested.

Maybe it was Monly, she thought, he was poisonous enough – and then she felt horribly guilty for thinking such a thing.

Sozerdor walked in a wary circle, keeping his distance from the carnage. 'It looks as though Monly might have saved our lives,' he said. 'What d'you think about that?'

'I think it'd be the first positive contribution he'd made to this mission,' Fermindor said. He holstered his gun, since it was obvious there was no longer any threat from these lifeless monsters. 'I'd like to know where they came from. There was nothing like this in the recon data, was there, Chief?'

Kley tried to remember precisely what the briefing *had* included, given that all she seemed to be finding was what it missed out. 'As far as I remember there was no mention of dangerous life-forms, jungles, or runners with carefully thought-out plans and powerful backup teams.'

'You don't think that's what he's got, do you?' Sozerdor directed the question at Fermindor but the potential to undermine her authority made no difference to Kley now. She was too tired for the niceties of command structure and organisational dynamics. She hefted the pack higher on to her shoulder and led off towards the trail that would take them back the way they had come the day before, back to the ship or whatever was left of it. She was conscious that all they seemed to be doing was running backwards and forwards along the same route without any really discernible purpose. The image of experimental animals in a laboratory maze suddenly came into her mind. That is definitely paranoia of the worst kind, she thought. I must get back in control of this. I must have a plan of action.

'Let's make sure we keep together,' she said, without looking back. 'We don't want to lose anybody else.' It seemed a feeble rallying call under the circumstances. She stopped and looked back as the other three fell in behind her. 'Guns to hand. Stay alert. What happened to Monly could happen to any of us.' She moved off again, staying in the cover of the trees as she skirted the edge of the empty drop zone.

Chapter Five

They were all dead. The squad snake was exactly where Leela had left it twisting round those painfully crippled members of the vestigial gestalt, but now there was not a single part of it left alive. 'I do not understand,' she said. 'Was it the shock that did it?'

The Doctor turned one of the snakes over. There was no sign of decomposition – indeed he could find none of the physical signs, not even the first subtle ones, that death normally produced. And yet there was no doubt that it was no longer alive. 'I think they might have served their purpose,' the Doctor said.

'And what purpose was that?' Rinandor asked. She was resting against Pertanor, one arm across his shoulder. When they had set off to retrace their trail she had declined the offer of a makeshift crutch, preferring to lean on Pertanor when the pain in her leg got too troublesome, which to their mutual and obvious satisfaction seemed to be most of the time.

'To kill us?' Pertanor suggested. 'They seemed to be very excited by the idea.'

'That must have been part of it,' the Doctor agreed.

'Only part of it?' Rinandor asked. 'What else was it all for?'

'That's what I hope to find out,' the Doctor said. He picked up another snake and examined it minutely. It was perfect and unblemished. Only the complete lack of any kind of animation confirmed it was dead. The Doctor had seen many creatures that routinely went into states of suspended animation to conserve energy, or to escape from predators, or to survive climatic catastrophe. He could affect a kind of physical shutdown himself, and knew how foolish it was to make assumptions about life and death, or anything else for that matter, on the basis of instinct or feelings. But despite all that he was certain this particular creature was never going to be revived. He dropped it to the jungle floor.

'You don't think we should try a couple of snake steaks, then?' Pertanor asked.

The Doctor smiled cheerfully. 'The venom is probably still toxic,' he said.

'I can't help feeling there'd be an opening in the snacks market for food with the sort of kick that six-legged thing packed,' Pertanor said and giggled. 'Or should that be kicks?'

'Now you want wealth as well as power?' Rinandor teased. 'I think you've got some firster blood in there somewhere.'

'What's wrong with wealth and power, Ri?' the Doctor asked conversationally as they waited for Leela to point out the path they should follow.

'That's what I say,' Pertanor said. 'What's wrong with wealth and power?'

'You have to sacrifice most of your life to get them and that shows a stupid lack of imagination. Besides, if you're not a firster it's a waste of effort to begin with.'

The Doctor wondered again how rigid the system had to be to produce attitudes like that, or whether perhaps Rinandor was simply one of those stubbornly difficult outsiders you come across from time to time. The sort of person he had himself been accused of being, though quite mistakenly of course.

'So which is it: a waste of time or a waste of life?' Pertanor asked.

'Isn't it the same thing?' Rinandor said.

'Not necessarily,' the Doctor murmured.

Leela had stopped listening and had turned her full attention back to the trail these irritating people had left. So far it had been as easy to find and to follow as she had expected it would be. Not too much time had passed since it had been crushed out by two terrified, plump and clumsy people in desperate flight. There had been no extremes of weather to obliterate the tracks or obscure the damage to the foliage. The fact was it needed no skill to follow such a trail – a child could do it; the Doctor himself could do it. The skill lay in noticing what neither the child nor the Doctor would have noticed: that there was something not right about it. As far as Leela could tell, what she was following was a perfect and unchanged trail. It had not deteriorated at all, not even in the smallest ways. It was as though Pertanor and Rinandor had run through no more than an hour before. Apart from the squad snake and herself, nothing had crossed this trail, nothing had stirred small shiftings of soil, no sap had risen to slightly lift some parts of squashed ground plants, no broken stems of taller bushes had withered significantly. Leela thought about telling the Doctor that there was something wrong, but he seemed so interested in his conversation with the two toodies that she was reluctant to interrupt with something that would probably sound silly and unimportant. She did not want to look as if she was trying to force them to pay attention to her.

Leela signalled the three of them to follow and, setting a relaxed pace, walked along the trail which, according to what Pertanor had said, would lead first to the clearing that no longer contained their grounded spaceship. She felt that the Doctor could have told them that the TARDIS had also disappeared, but when he did not she had to assume that he had a reason of some sort.

Despite the slow pace, Leela had got some distance ahead of the others when she saw the water, dark in the brightness of a wide clearing. She approached it carefully. The water looked clear but the angle at which the light was striking it made it difficult to see below the surface. There was a small island in the middle. Nobody had mentioned a lake lying directly across the trail she was following. Rinandor had mentioned losing equipment packs but she had said nothing about leaving them on an island in the middle of a wide expanse of what looked like very deep water.

Leela bent down and put her hand in the motionless liquid. It was just warm enough to be difficult to feel: blood warm, she thought, or was it the same temperature as the heavy damp air?

In the black depths, something stirred and drifted up towards the vibrations moving on the surface.

There was nothing left of the route they had marked through the jungle growth. It seemed to stop at some invisible dividing line. One moment it was there, and then it was gone. On one side of the line it was easy to see the trail: it was almost a pathway. On the other side it simply faded away: everything they had broken and scorched had grown back and healed over. It was as if nothing had ever passed that way before.

'They couldn't have found us even if they were looking for us,' Sozerdor whined.

'Stop talking like an idiot,' Fermindor said flatly. 'They had the co-ordinates, same as we did. They didn't need a trail, or weren't you paying attention? We were just trying to make it easier for them to catch up.'

'But they didn't catch up, did they?' Sozerdor was triumphantly gloomy.

Kley adjusted her wrist compass reference points and checked that she was tracking correctly. 'We'll probably come across them,' she said, realising as she said it that it was not the most well-chosen of phrases and that someone was bound to pick up on it.

Sure enough Sozerdor grizzled, 'Why is that not a comforting thought?'

'You're not here to be comforted!' she snapped. 'Shut up and do your job!'

'I see,' he moaned. 'Everyone's decided to pick on me, have they? It's not my fault it's all gone wrong, is it? I didn't get us into this mess, did I?'

'No, and you're not going to get us out of it either,' Belay said. 'Be quiet, So, you're not helping.'

Fermindor walked up and back along the border between trail and non-trail. He was looking for the kink in the original line of march which had to be the explanation for its sudden disappearance.

Kley watched him for a moment and then said, 'We didn't deviate.'

'Maybe the soil changes here,' Belay said. 'Special growth hormones, or… or…' He shrugged helplessly.

'Maybe it isn't real,' Fermindor said. 'Maybe the runner's messing with our minds.'

'How would he do that?' Kley said dismissively.

'Yeah, what is he?' Sozerdor demanded. 'A superbeing? Mighty-firster, Lord of the Runners?'

'He's a toody,' Kley said.

Fermindor stopped and turned to look at her. 'This runner's a toody?'

'Yes.'

'We weren't told that.'

'What difference does it make?' she asked, knowing suddenly that it made a serious difference. Toodies would understand another toody better than she did, wouldn't they? Was that the difference it made? Or was it that they didn't instinctively despise a toody? Underestimate a toody?

Fermindor frowned. 'I don't know,' he said. 'If it doesn't make a difference why weren't we told?'

'*Because* it doesn't make a difference,' she said. 'He's a runner. A rogue weapons tech. That's all that matters, isn't it?' How bad could it be? How badly had she underestimated this runner?

'But you were told, Chief,' Fermindor persisted.

'I'm in command of the mission,' she said.

'You didn't think it was important to give us all you had on the runner we were chasing?'

Sozerdor and Belay were both staring at her now. The fact was she hadn't checked on the team briefing because there hadn't been time, and she had been told that Monly had taken care of it. She was tempted to bluff it out. The truth would surely destroy what little was left of her authority. She hesitated, but then she had to acknowledge to herself that lying took more energy than she had left. 'I thought you knew,' she said. 'It was supposed to have been covered in the briefing.'

Ironically it was Belay, a firster himself, who voiced the thought that was in all their minds:'What else haven't they told us?'

'I didn't tell you because I didn't know,' Pertanor protested.

'It wasn't here before,' Rinandor said.

Leela prowled round the edge of the lake trying to see how deep it was and whether there was anything living in it.

'Leela?' the Doctor called to her.'Those equipment packs aren't worth the risk. Stay out of the water.'

For once Leela agreed completely with what the Doctor said, if not with the way that he said it, and although she disliked being told what to do she had no intention of going into this lake to prove a point. While she was, with some reservations, prepared to accept that Pertanor and Rinandor believed what they were saying, her immediate problem was that it couldn't be true. This lake had been a lake for a long time. The jungle clearing it was in was not a new one – the trees and general vegetation showed that – and the bank at the water's edge was weathered and had been colonised by small bog plants. As far as she could see the island looked well established too. Plant growth correctly developing from water's edge to high point showed clearly that this was no small hill left above the waterline of an overnight flood. Even if there was any hint of a reason for a flood, which there was not. And there tossed down in the middle of the island, in the middle of the lake, were the two discarded equipment packs which the couple admitted belonged to them.

'There can't be anything in the water,' Rinandor said.

'Are you sure about that?' the Doctor asked.

'It's only just happened. They don't come complete with wildlife.'

'They don't come complete with convenient islands either,' the Doctor said, watching Leela cutting lengths of tropical vine from a tree at the edge of the clearing.

'It's not exactly convenient,' Pertanor said. 'If we want those packs back I'm going to have to wade for them.'

'You'd have to swim, I think,' the Doctor said. 'Not a good idea under the circumstances.'

'I can do that,' Pertanor said defensively. 'I can swim.'

'It could be that swimming is what you're being invited to do,' the Doctor said. 'It would be far more sensible to wait here. Leela seems to have a plan.'

'What would you do without her?' Rinandor said scathingly.

'Think more. Run less,' the Doctor said and smiled, leaving her uncertain whether she had been insulted or not, leaning as she was on Pertanor to take the weight off the painfully aching leg she had twisted running in mindless panic.

At any other time, Leela would have been sure that Pertanor and Rinandor were lying. If she was reading the signs correctly, and she knew she was, then the couple had run into the water on one side of the lake, reached the island, shed the cumbersome packs and plunged on, leaving the water on the other side. But why should they lie? Why was the trail so unnaturally perfect? And when they fell across her path a little while after their swim, why were they not even slightly wet? When the air was warm and full of moisture like it was in this jungle area you do not dry out quickly after a full soaking. She finished knotting the lengths of vine together and coiled it by running it through her hand and round her upper arm.

'If we can find a suitable planet I must take you sailing,' the Doctor said as he approached. 'You've obviously got an aptitude for rope work.'

'I am going to try to throw a line over those equipment packs,' Leela said.

'A running loop might be helpful,' the Doctor suggested.

'A loop!' Leela said wryly. 'Did you think I was going to throw it and hope it got tangled in the straps?'

'Sometimes,' the Doctor said, 'it's the obvious ideas that get missed.' He took the coil from her and held it so that she could fashion a lasso at the more flexible end of the knotted vines. 'You should never be afraid to state the obvious,' he went on. 'If people know it already they are pleased to think they're clever. If they don't know it already they're pleased to think you're clever. Either way they're pleased.'

Leela finished the loop and took the coil from the Doctor. 'You do talk rubbish,' she said smiling.

'After we go sailing I'll introduce you to some revered prophets, gurus and religious figures worshipped by millions who make that sort of rubbish sound like transdimensional engineering manuals.'

Leela circled the lake looking for the best throwing position. There would not be much advantage in it because the lake was uniform but she wanted the highest of the banks that was nearest to the island. As she walked and checked the angles she was forced to revise her opinion. There would not be any advantage in it because, unlikely as it seemed, there was no highest bank and every curve and bend looked to be the same distance from the island. Leela had seen optical illusions before, but this was not a trick to baffle the eye and fool the head: this looked a lot more like a careful plan.

'That isn't going to work,' Rinandor remarked as Leela walked past where she and Pertanor were sitting on the spongy ground. Leela would have ignored her but Rinandor said, 'Did you hear what I said? That is *not* going to work.'

'Then we will have to go on without them,' Leela said.

'There's food and painkillers in those packs,' Pertanor said. 'I shouldn't have dropped them both.'

'It was that or drop me,' Rinandor said. 'I think you made the right choice. I like the way your mind works.'

Leela walked on until she reached the Doctor again. He was sitting on his haunches peering into the water. He did not look up as he said, 'No good place to throw from.' It was not a question and he did not sound surprised.

'Do you think this is real, Doctor?' she asked.

'Oh, it's real,' he said. 'The question should be: is it really what it looks like?'

'Is it really what it looks like?'

The Doctor continued staring into the water. He couldn't see anything lurking but logic said it was there. He made up his mind. 'No.' He stood up quickly. 'It's a trap. We're leaving. Now.' He took the coiled vine from Leela and tossed it away. 'Rinandor, Pertanor!' he called. 'Time to move on.' He gestured for them to follow, adding, 'Keep well away from the water!' before taking Leela's arm and hustling her towards the trees. 'Come on, Leela. Come on. Whatever it is, it's probably amphibious.'

Leela pulled her arm away, stubbornly refusing to be rushed. 'What is? What are you doing?'

'If I'm right,' the Doctor said, still trying to urge her on, 'something wants to know how resourceful we are – or how resourceful *some* of us are, Leela, especially you. I'm not sure about that yet. What I am sure about is that it's ready to kill us all in the course of its researches.'

He tried to take her arm again, and again she resisted. 'If you are right, how will running away help?'

'By keeping us alive,' the Doctor said.

'Yes, but for how long?'

'For now will do – for now.'

Leela drew her long hunting knife to make her point. 'You have to face an enemy if you want to survive,' she lectured.

The Doctor strove to be patient. He knew she was just repeating what she had been told but he had thought her more intelligent. 'You have to find them if you want to face them,' he said. He gave up trying to hurry her to the trees and strode on, relying on her impulse to finish the argument.

Leela sheathed the knife and loped along beside him. 'You don't find them by running away,' she challenged.

'We're running away from the experiment, not the experimenter,' the Doctor said as they crossed into the trees.

It was then that they heard the scream from the lake behind them.

'Did you hear that?' Sozerdor stopped and held up his hand. 'Listen. In the distance. Very faint. That was a scream, wasn't it?'

He's doing it again, Kley thought. We've had this before and before and how often before. The laboratory maze was back in her mind. 'Keep it moving, Sozerdor,' she said, pushing on through the increasingly dense vegetation.

'I heard a scream.'

'Stop obsessing about dying,' she said wearily. 'The only person who doesn't know you're dead is you.'

'What's that supposed to mean?' he demanded.

'It means if this place doesn't kill you,' Fermindor growled, 'I will.'

'I heard it too,' Belay said. 'I can still hear it.'

Kley stopped now and they all listened. Very faintly, in the far distance, someone was screaming.

'Can you make out where they are?' Fermindor asked.

Kley checked her compass. 'I can't even make out where *we* are,' she said.

Rinandor screamed again and kept on screaming as Pertanor was dragged back under the water. The Doctor retrieved the vine-stem rope but by the time he reached the bank there was no sign of the young man.

'Do something,' Rinandor sobbed. 'It's killing him!'

'What was it?' the Doctor shouted at her.

'I don't know,' she wailed. 'I didn't see it. It was waiting under the surface.'

Leela took the vine from the Doctor and looped one end of it round her waist and handed the other back to him. Before he could argue about it she had stepped into the water and started wading out. 'If it wants to know about me then I will show it.'

'Whatever this one is it'll be driven by hunger, Leela,' the Doctor called to her as he paid out the crude rope. 'It's looking for a meal, that's all. But its real purpose, the reason it's been put there, is to see if you can kill it before it kills you.'

'Hurry up!' Rinandor screamed 'You're wasting time. Stop wasting time!' She limped round the bank towards the Doctor. 'He's still alive. You can still save him!'

Leela unsheathed the knife again and waded on through the deepening water which stayed just warm enough to feel as though it was not there at all. Suddenly she felt the lake bed drop away from under her feet. She ducked her head below the surface, then lifted up, took a deep breath and arched over and downward.

'Keep your eyes open and don't be long down there!' the Doctor shouted after her and she heard his voice distorted and rippling, the weight squeezed out of it by the water. 'I hate swimming!' were his last recognisable words but they had little meaning as her concentration focused on diving down.

Her momentary impulse was to keep her eyes closed, but then 'Keep your eyes open' swirled into her mind, and she opened them quickly to find herself swimming down in a column of light surrounded on all sides by shadows, deepening to abrupt blackness.

She recognised immediately and without needing to think about it that the lake must be a squat bottle shape, with most of its volume hidden in darkness underneath the banks. The light was coming from the comparatively narrow neck of the bottle where the surface of the water was. Directly in front of her, the island was a rock pinnacle rising up from the gloomy depths. She kept on swimming downward. Where was Pertanor? There was no sign of him. There was nothing. Nothing moved in the smothering emptiness of the blood-warm water.

Panic struck at her without warning. She needed to breathe. Horrors lurked in this darkness. She needed to breathe. Unimaginable things were behind her. She needed to breathe. Pertanor was gone and she needed to breathe. *She needed to breathe*.

She turned towards the surface. And then she saw it. Something moved under the shelf of the bank which had been at her back. The shock of it went through her like a jolt of electricity and the panic turned to fury. She swam at the movement with her knife held out in front of her. There was nothing in the dark she could not kill, nothing in the dark like the furious fear, and she found it and she grabbed it and it struggled weakly, and she realised it was Pertanor. Without thinking she dragged at him, swimming hard for the light and the surface. His unconscious body moved easily at first and then tugged to a stop. With panic gone and fury fading, Leela found she really did need to draw breath soon. But now she could not move Pertanor. Why could she not move Pertanor? And

90

then he did start to move, but away from her, away from the surface, and down into the dark.

When she saw why it was happening the panic almost took her again. Pertanor was being dragged inexorably downward, drawn by a broad, pinkish ribbon of slowly contracting flesh which was wrapped round his right leg, totally enveloping it. It was a tongue. Leela slashed at it with the knife, cutting deep into it, and cut again and again and the water was filled with blood and lashing and the tongue whipped away.

Leela pulled Pertanor free and swam for the surface, towing him by the collar of his tunic. The skin of light seemed too far away ever to be reached and breached. Her need for air was a painless ache which emptied her chest and filled her bones and hollowed out her skull. She reached for it, and reached and reached and reached.

Below her in the darkness something huge shuddered and raged upward, hungry mouth wide.

The Doctor was conscious that the vine rope was cumbersome, and he had been doing his best to feed it out quickly enough to avoid hampering Leela's swimming. At the same time there was no point in having it tied to her at all if he left it so slack that it gave no indication of what was going on down there below the water. At a pinch he felt he ought to be able to haul her up and out if she got into serious trouble. On the other hand he could put her into serious trouble himself if he started hauling at the wrong time. *In extremis*, if there was absolutely no alternative, he would have to swim and use the rope to guide him to her, but he preferred not to think too closely about that. He had seen straight away from the movement of the rope that the lake was probably tear-shaped: wider at the bottom than at the top with undercut shelving and banks. He hoped Leela spotted that the thing would have places to hide which were not obvious from the surface. *The* thing? Was it likely there would be only one? A shoal of fish would prove nothing. A lot of smaller amphibians would compete among themselves and in a lake this size it would have shown. No, this was a static trap; a test like this called for one animal.

The Doctor was still trying to reason out what it was they were facing when the rope went slack suddenly. He waited for a second or two. Nothing happened. He waited for a few seconds more. The vine drooped away in the cloudless water until it disappeared out beyond the edge of the shelving bottom. It wasn't moving. He made up his mind: she had been under too long, and he started to pull it in. Relieved to have made the decision to get her out of there he hauled rapidly hand over hand but as fast as he did so, it wouldn't go taut. It seemed he was dragging nothing but wet vine from the lake.

'Where are they?' Rinandor keened, staring intensely at the water as if she thought she could draw them back up into the air by will alone. 'Where *are* they?'

Then, like an answer, the water erupted and Leela was gasping on the surface and struggling to get Pertanor's face in the air. 'It's coming after us,' she managed to shout. 'Help me get him out!'

The Doctor ran backwards holding the vine rope, and Leela clung on to Pertanor as they were both pulled across the surface. A wide pink worm flicked at them and missed as they passed and rolled into the shallows. While Leela was staggering to her feet, Rinandor rushed into the water, heaved the unconscious man on to the bank and immediately started to work on resuscitating him.

The Doctor trotted back to where Leela was standing breathing deeply, trying to get her head clear and her strength ready. 'How big is it?' he asked, urgently.

Leela cut the slimy vine off herself with the knife she had been holding all this time, even when she was swimming out the last of her breath. *Your knife makes you a warrior. Lose it and you are not a warrior, nor have you ever been.* She knew it was primitive nonsense – the Doctor told her it was primitive nonsense and so did her head – but her hand would never drop the knife by accident. 'I do not know,' she said. 'Bigger than that thing that chased you but slower, I think.'

'If that was its tongue,' he said, 'that won't be slower. We have to move. Get in among the trees.'

'Maybe it is not a problem now we are out of the water,' Leela suggested hopefully, following the Doctor to where Rinandor was frantically trying to revive the unresponsive Pertanor.

'Wake up, Pe. Come on, toody, stir your outrageous skinny bones,' she was muttering as she worked. Pertanor was breathing but barely. 'You're not going to die on me. Not here, Pe. Not on this miserable crapsoid.'

'We can't stay here,' the Doctor said to her. 'It'll be safer in the cover of the trees.'

Rinandor shrugged off the Doctor's hand as he tried to get her to stand up. 'You go ahead. We'll follow.'

'We tried that,' the Doctor said. 'It's why we're in this mess.' He made a more determined effort to get her on her feet. 'There's no time for this.'

She resisted. 'Pertanor will die!' she shouted at him, twisting away.

'He will if we don't get him away from here,' the Doctor said calmly, and, deciding that it would make better sense to concentrate his attention on the more reasonable of the two, he pushed Rinandor firmly to one side and set about lifting Pertanor.

Leela had to prevent her from attacking the Doctor. 'You can't do that!' Rinandor protested, hysterically.

There was an element of wry truth in that, the Doctor thought, as he staggered under the dead weight of the plump young man. It suddenly looked a lot further to the trees and it would have been difficult enough even without Rinandor lunging past Leela and making grabs at him. But then when she actually managed to get hold of the unconscious Pertanor it became impossible. 'Leela,' the Doctor grunted, 'get her off me.' Stumbling to his knees he noticed with a lurch of understanding that Leela and Rinandor were beside him with Leela half supporting, half restraining the distraught young woman and shepherding her towards the trees.

The Doctor twisted round to look. In the middle of the lake a huge squat head had emerged from the water. It seemed to be a vivid purple but, as the Doctor watched, the colour quickly changed to red and then to orange and then to yellow. Faster and faster the rainbow waves washed over and through the animal's skin. It was oddly compelling. The Doctor stared. Only the animal's eyes remained unchanged. They were black and opaque, like gaping tunnels of darkness. The Doctor felt himself drawn to them. There was something there that murmured of rest and peace.

Abruptly the animal rumbled with pain and the low-frequency sound waves it used to panic and sap the will of its prey moved into the fully audible range.

'Doctor!' Leela shouted as she pulled her knife from the amphibian's tongue, which was wrapped round Pertanor once again, this time round both his legs. But this time the tongue did not bleed copiously and, despite the evidence of pain, it was not withdrawn but kept its grip on Pertanor and kept reeling him in towards the cavernous mouth. A mouth that looked wider than the huge head and gave on to a monstrously flexing gullet.

The Doctor woke from his trance with a start and found himself being dragged over the ground as he held on grimly to Pertanor. He wondered at this animal's single-minded pursuit of its original prey, if that was what it was. Like the louse. Was it coincidence, evolutionary refinement, or strategic choice? He dug his heels in and tried to slow things down. 'The end Leela,' he yelled. 'The nerves are in the end!'

Leela slashed the edge of the knife across the end of the fat, encircling worm and the amphibian reared up out of the water, twitching its head and scrabbling and splashing with its stubby front flippers. It stopped retracting its tongue for a moment, sending a muscular spasm along the whole length of it, but still it did not let go of Pertanor.

With silent ferocity Rinandor threw herself on to Pertanor's legs, clawing at the folds of the tongue, trying to prise them loose with her hands. It was futile and she made it more difficult for Leela to work with the knife but her weight and determination gave the Doctor a chance to let go of Pertanor. He rolled clear, scrambled to his feet, and sprinted away.

'Come back, you coward!' Rinandor screamed after him.

The Doctor reached the bank where the discarded vine rope lay. Close up the amphibian's changes of colour were hardly discernible under the blue-green sheen of its skin. The animal was bloated, so bloated it seemed impossible that it could fit into the lake at all, and the thought struck the Doctor that it might actually be stuck in the surface bottleneck. He jumped up and down and waved at it and shouted. 'Hey! Big mouth! Over here!'

One of the matt-black eyes swivelled to look at him. The darkness in it was so profound, the Doctor knew that it had to be the animal affecting his perception. It was not what he was seeing but the way he was seeing it. Seemingly out of nowhere a tongue flicked towards him. The Doctor flung himself to one side, falling hard and knocking the breath out of himself. So much for exclusivity. The tongue missed him. It flopped and curled on the bank and then began to retract. The Doctor sat up and stared. The animal had two tongues – at least two. He snatched up the rope and ran back to where Leela and Rinandor were struggling with the other one.

'Tight as you can and as close to him as you can,' the Doctor instructed, handing Leela one end of the rope. 'A running loop would be best.'

Leela pushed the vine round the tongue and began to make the noose just beyond Pertanor's legs. The tongue started to retract again.

'No! Oh no! No!' Rinandor yelled and scrambled for a purchase with her feet.

The Doctor took the other end of the rope and ran for the nearest trees. 'And stay alert,' he shouted over his shoulder. 'It's got more than one tongue!'

Leela tightened the knot as the Doctor slogged across the open ground dragging the rope behind him. To reinforce it, she hurriedly cut a thread of leather from her tunic and bound the trailing ends.

The Doctor reached the first tree with just enough rope left to throw a loop round the trunk and tie it off. He would have preferred to use a thicker specimen with a stronger stem but they were all further away and he knew the vine rope would not reach any of them. Already, with the amphibian's tongue contracting, the rope was tightening up. He started back, shouting 'Cut the end again!' as he ran.

Leela pulled back the folds in the tongue. Rinandor grabbed them from her and pulled back hard so that the slightly narrower tip was fully exposed. Leela plunged the knife in and twisted it.

This time the animal let out a gurgling roar of pain and anger. It shook its head violently from side to side. Yanking on its trapped tongue, it heaved itself out of the deep water altogether. Its monstrous low-slung body was supported on ten legs, the front and rear pairs of which were flippers. It lifted hugely over the shallows and waddled on to the dry land. The mouth gaped and bubbling gusts of air and water droplets belched towards the Doctor and the others. The Doctor noticed that the creature's breath had no real smell.

Leela stabbed the tip of the tongue in a second spot, and pushed and twisted the knife as deeply as she could. The animal lurched into ponderous action. The second tongue flicked out and caught the Doctor round the ankle. He kicked at it with his other foot but the grip merely tightened. A third tongue flashed at Leela, who ducked to one side, slashing her knife down the pink blubbery flesh. Missing Leela, it found Rinandor and clamped itself bloodily round her waist.

Now the animal began to plod towards the place where the other tongue and Pertanor were being held fast, while at the same time it dragged the Doctor and Rinandor to its open mouth. All three of them would soon be devoured unless Leela could do something to stop it.

'Rinandor,' the Doctor said, 'dig your heels in. Fight it as much as you can. We have to leave the rope alone. It's going to break if we hold on to it too.'

'I can't,' Rinandor gasped, her face screwed up against the pain in her leg. 'I'm sorry. It hurts.' She closed her eyes and her face went slack as she passed out. Reacting to the sudden relaxation in its prey the animal began to pull her in faster. The Doctor lunged after her and grabbed her under the arms. He lost ground in the manoeuvre and, when he dug his heels in and strained against both tongues, he found resistance more difficult.

Leela could see no other choice. She ran straight at the animal, jumping over a fourth tongue and skipping round a fifth as they lashed out. The animal's vast mouth loomed above her. Leela trusted that the vine rope and the tree it was tied round would stay tight enough to limit the animal's head movements. Her final leap depended on the thing not rearing any higher. She lengthened her stride, balanced her last few steps, bounded high on to one of the animal's front flippers and with a grunt of effort threw herself upward, reaching for the outside edge of the top of the mouth.

She got her hand over the rigid cartilage of the lip and on to skin above, but found it was too slippery to grip. She had been expecting that, and she clawed her free hand and dug her fingernails in to give her a brief purchase. As she lost her hold she pivoted, and used her other hand to stab the knife home as far up as she could get. She slapped both hands on to the hilt of the knife and steadied herself. For a moment, she hung with her legs swinging in the open mouth. Enraged, the animal tried to bite down on her but with its tongues still extended it could not close its jaws. It tried to toss its head back and dislodge her so that she would drop into its throat, but the trapped tongue stopped it. By the time it had adjusted one of its free tongues to swipe Leela from its lip, she had hauled herself up and was temporarily out of reach. She repositioned the knife and climbed further up.

The Doctor and Rinandor were very close to the mouth. Now she was on the head, Leela realised that her plan went no further than that. She had no idea what she should do next. Compared with the louse, the amphibian was soft. Cutting into it was not nearly as difficult. But it was bigger and much fatter. Striking through to reach something vital would be almost impossible. Even if she picked the right place to work on, by the time she stopped this thing it would already have swallowed the Doctor and Rinandor. They were going to be eaten alive unless she did something very quickly.

One of the eyes swivelled its eerie blackness towards her. For a moment Leela felt herself unbalanced, giddily drawn into it. She was lost. She was falling. She pulled the knife out of the head and as she plunged downward she slammed it into the dark. Water gushed from the eye, the dizzying blackness emptying away. Leela found herself hanging by the knife again. She scrabbled for a toehold. The animal swatted at her with one of its feet. She regained her balance and leaned in on the knife. The blade slid through tissue and membrane, and Leela pushed it further in until her arm had sunk up to the shoulder through the eye socket. As the knife hit the brain, the animal gave a series of shudders and then sagged heavily into the fading twitches of death.

Leela pulled her knife from the mess, and climbed down from the dead monster. She was tired now and there was no sense of victory, no feeling of elation as she went to the lake to wash herself.

'There might be more of them, Leela,' the Doctor shouted, extricating himself and Rinandor from their respective tongues.

'I do not think so,' Leela answered.

'Neither do I,' he agreed. 'I'd say that was a pass, but be careful anyway.'

'What do you mean that was a pass?' Rinandor asked, groggily.

'I think we're in some sort of test programme,' the Doctor said.

Rinandor smiled. 'In the unlikely event that we were,' she said, '"pass" would be on the generous side, don't you think, as grades go?'

'We're still alive,' the Doctor said. 'No thanks to you two. What was he doing in the water?'

'He felt bad about losing the packs,' she said. 'He thought...' She shrugged and shook her head.

'He thought you'd be impressed,' the Doctor finished for her.

'I was,' she said, crawling towards where Pertanor lay.

The Doctor nodded. 'Stupid behaviour seems to be a universal problem with people in your situation,' he said, not unkindly.

'People in what situation?' Rinandor demanded, reaching Pertanor and stroking his face, gently.

'Pair bonding,' the Doctor said. 'Sexual selection? It's basically instinctive. Such hormonally-driven responses seldom involve rational thought or intelligent behaviour in my experience.'

Rinandor looked back at him. 'You are a very weird toody.'

'That is very true,' the Doctor said.

'*Are* you a toody?' she asked, seriously.

The Doctor thought he recognised another universal: the police interrogator's switch of emphasis. Maybe that was instinctive too.

Before he could answer her, Pertanor groaned and then sat up coughing weakly.

'You're still alive,' Rinandor breathed. She was grinning broadly.

'I did a stupid thing didn't I?' Pertanor croaked. 'I can't believe I survived that. Some people are too stupid to live.'

'Leela saved you,' Rinandor said. 'She saved all of us.'

Pertanor caught sight of the dead amphibian for the first time. 'It was that?' he gasped. 'She killed that?'

Rinandor took his hand and stroked it. She could not stop grinning. 'I think I'll make a special effort to be nice to her from now on,' she said. 'Annoying her doesn't seem like a promising survival strategy.'

The Doctor was examining the giant carcass for evidence of its origin. Six legs and four flippers. In all his travels he had not come across any of the creatures they had so far encountered. The aggressive use of subsonic waves. A suggestion of tele-hypnotics. The lack of odours. The sheer size of the thing... And perfect. These were all functioning adult specimens by the look of it. How many individuals reached that stage of maturity in perfect condition? Could it be that these things were engineered? Could it be that this whole *world* was engineered?

He looked up to find Leela walking towards him carrying the two equipment packs from the island. 'How did you get those?' he asked.

She dumped them down. 'I swam across.'

The Doctor sighed. 'Does that seem like a sensible thing to do?'

Leela looked at the dead monster. 'I wanted something real to show for killing it.'

'A trophy, is that what you mean?'

'No. Trophies are for children and fools.' She frowned. 'A warrior is weakened by death without purpose.'

The Doctor smiled and said, softly, 'Another entry from your trainer's little red book?'

'It was only looking for a meal,' Leela said, staring up at the animal's ruined eye. 'You said so.'

'I didn't want you to be afraid.'

'I know that.'

'Fear gets in the way of thought. It can get you killed.'

Leela nodded. 'It did help. The thought that it was just an animal looking for food did help. But now it is dead and there should be a purpose.'

'You killed it to save our lives,' the Doctor said.

'That could have been done by keeping away from the water as you told us to do.'

'But we didn't, so that was a reason.'

'Yes,' Leela agreed. 'That was a reason.' She picked up the packs and took them to where Rinandor and Pertanor were recovering. 'But these are a purpose. There is a difference you know.'

Unable to resist, the Doctor said, 'No, there isn't. Not in this case.' But he was quite relieved to have the comment drowned out by the delight of Rinandor and Pertanor at seeing the packs.

Chapter Six

Long before Kley had managed to get any practical sort of fix on it, the screaming had stopped. They all had their own ideas about what direction it had been coming from and how far away it was; and every one had been different. With a show of authority Kley had picked a direction that matched their line of march and the others followed her choice without much argument. She had given up all hope of identifying any of the marked trail, and had simply continued pushing on through the thick jungle vegetation in as straight a line as she could manage. The idea of finding some part of the original path again on the other side of the local anomaly – which was due to ground water conditions, plate tectonics, lizard droppings, or something else they were in no position to analyse – vanished as she realised that this might as well be a whole new jungle. Kley had fought off the panicky thought that they had been transported somewhere else, and that they were now so far beyond lost that the word was meaningless. She had been waiting for Sozerdor to pick up on this idea, but he seemed content that they were making progress back towards the relative safety of the ship, and he had been mercifully quiet. She was reluctant to call a halt for a meal in case this gave him in particular a chance to think about what was happening. But there had been no choice, and so far there had been no problem.

'I think it could have been an animal we heard,' Belay said. He took a swig of water and then shook his canteen. It sounded almost empty. 'Or a bird, maybe.'

'There aren't many of them around here, are there?' Fermindor said, tossing an empty ration pack into the bushes. 'I haven't seen a living thing without a root since we got back into this miserable jungle.'

'And you're complaining?' Sozerdor said. 'After the lizards and those other things I'll be happy if we're the only free-moving life left.'

Belay shook his head. 'Something alive made that noise.'

'Not necessarily,' Kley said. 'It could have been non-organic.'

'Non-organic?' Belay asked.

'It could have been anything,' she said.

'For example?'

'For example,' she said, 'it could have been…' And then found she could think of absolutely nothing that it could have been. She shrugged vaguely. 'It could have been…'

'It could have been a steam vent,' Fermindor supplied.

'It could have been a steam vent,' she agreed, wondering whether he had left her hanging there for a moment longer than necessary just to make it clear that he was better at all this than she was.

'A steam vent.' Sozerdor smiled mockingly. 'Have you seen any steam vents? As we tramp backwards and forwards through this nightmare have you seen the smallest sign of a steam vent?' He was still smiling.

Kley was struck by how much more controlled he seemed to be. He must feel that the probability of survival is improving, she thought, now that they were going back. 'You heard that wheezing noise before, didn't you? Maybe that's what it was.' Another stupid mistake, she thought, as soon as she said it.

Belay was chuckling. 'That was a rat fart,' he said, but then stopped smiling.

'Do you think it was her?' Sozerdor asked. 'Screaming? Do you think it was Rinandor?' This time the question was put directly to Kley.

'I don't know,' she said tiredly, 'any more than you do. I suggest we get back on it and try to find out.'

As the others got slowly to their feet, Kley checked the co-ordinates again. She glanced back the way they had come. The trail they had left was so clear and obvious to the naked eye. She stared at it half expecting to see it disappear as she watched.

'Chief?' Fermindor said.

Kley turned and moved to lead off. 'Sorry, Fe. Let's get on it.'

If Belay and Sozerdor noticed the breach in command formality and the failure to maintain firster-toody etiquette they were both too diplomatic or too tired to react.

'Do you want me to cut trail?' Fermindor asked. 'Might be better if you saved your strength.'

'I'm all right,' she said. 'Stay close, though. If something comes at me suddenly I'm not sure how fast I'll react.'

'Don't worry,' Fermindor assured her, and strapped his handgun higher to make sure he could reach it quickly.

That was how it was that Fermindor almost got his throat cut after he took a shot at the girl who stepped out of the tangle of vegetation just ahead of Kley.

The Doctor was not entirely sure whether Leela would have killed the second-in-command of the patrol if he had not stopped her in time. She had been holding the man from behind with her knife at his throat. She was frightened and angry and reluctant to let him go.

'Shooting at someone without warning is cowardly,' she had said loudly in his ear. 'And you have the Doctor to thank that it is not the last stupid thing you will ever get the chance to do!'

It was fortunate that the man was, as far as the Doctor could see, one of those tough-minded professionals who are comfortable enough with themselves not to carry a grudge. And when the man told her, 'You took me by surprise,' this was clearly intended as an explanation, not an excuse.

'Do you kill everything that surprises you?' Leela had

demanded, still tense.

'On this planet we do!' the woman in charge of the unit had interrupted, angry herself. 'We've already lost one man. And jumping out at an OIG patrol on an interdicted planet may get you shot or it may get you arrested but what it won't get you is prizes for intelligence.'

With some of the misunderstandings sorted out, the reunion with Pertanor and Rinandor had still been marred slightly, and things didn't improve when they finally made their report.

'He can't have stolen the ship,' Sozerdor protested. 'Can he?'

Exhaustion rolled over Kley like a suffocating cloud. 'Does it matter?' she said. 'We're trapped here. For whatever reason.' If she could just lie down, she thought, and sleep for a while, perhaps she could think of an answer. 'I'll have to send a help call. Get them to pull us out.'

'Can you do that without your ship?' the Doctor asked.

No she couldn't. Of course she couldn't. Find somewhere unobscured and set off a low power general distress beacon – that was the best she could do. Kley closed her eyes and took a deep breath. 'Why should that concern you?' She opened her eyes and gave him a hard stare.

'We're as trapped as you are,' the Doctor explained. 'Our ship has disappeared too, you see.'

Sozerdor dropped his pack and sat down on it heavily. 'You know why all this is happening, don't you?' he said. 'It's because of me. Those bony-brains will go to any lengths to avoid paying me my benefits package.'

Kley looked at him. He was smiling. He was actually smiling. She smiled back. 'Maybe if we shot you?'

'Too late, Chief,' he said. 'I don't know what the plan is, the big plan I mean, but I don't think it involves any of us drawing contract bonus credits on this one.'

'I take it you can't send a signal?' the Doctor said.

'Distress beacon,' Fermindor said. 'No real power. Can't get it off-planet or even do a surface uplink to one of the orbiters. Open ground might help. Somewhere high and wide preferably.'

'You have satellites up there?' the Doctor asked.

'Low-orbit microbeacons,' he said. 'Most of them will have burnt up by the time we find this runner and stuff his guts into a disposal sack.' He looked at Kley. 'That is what we plan to do, isn't it?'

'Yes,' she said, trying to sound as positive as he did. 'Never mind the big plan, our aim is to finish what we started. Are we all agreed?' She glanced round at them. 'Are we all agreed?' she repeated, more urgently.

The other five members of the team nodded solemnly.

'We don't have to vow eternal comradeship or mingle blood or anything do we?' Rinandor said drily.

Pertanor smiled. 'I thought we did that already,' he whispered to her and was foolishly pleased at her blush.

'Now that we've settled that,' Belay said, 'the pressing question becomes: how do we find him?'

'He's run rings round us so far,' Sozerdor agreed.

'Thedoctor has some theories, don't you, The?' Pertanor said.

'Leela does the work, The does the theorising,' Rinandor said.

Kley shed her pack and the others followed her lead. Everyone flopped down and sat in various states of weariness. 'We're open to suggestions, Thedoctor,' Kley said.

The Doctor sat down cross-legged on the ground. 'First tell me, how much do you know about this runner of yours?' he asked.

'He's a weapons technologist,' Kley said.

'That's not normally illegal, is it?' the Doctor said.

'Not in itself.'

'So what has he done to annoy the authorities?'

Kley frowned. 'It's a little more serious than that.'

The Doctor nodded.'Obviously.'

'He's wanted for unauthorised experimentation,' Kley said, picking her words carefully.

'And that means, exactly?'

'It means exactly what it says.'

'It doesn't exactly say anything.'

'It means he developed a series of weapons which were strictly forbidden by arms-limitation treaty.'

No one noticed Leela step into the dense cover of the surrounding jungle and slip stealthily away to check on the sounds only she had heard.

This conversation was like pulling teeth, the Doctor thought.'By himself?' he said.

Kley looked genuinely puzzled.'I don't understand.'

'Was he a one-man research facility or was he part of a team?'

'I don't know,' she said.

'And what kinds of weapons did he develop?'

'I don't know that either.'

'Yours not to reason why, yours but to do and die?' the Doctor murmured and then asked more loudly, 'Shouldn't you know these things?'

'We were all badly briefed,' she said.'My team didn't know it was a toody we were chasing.'

Pertanor sat up.'He's a toody?'

'Doesn't that make you proud,' Sozerdor said. 'We're being crapped on by one of our own.'

'He's a psychotic pervert,' Fermindor said,'but at least he's *our* psychotic pervert.'

'Maybe if we'd known,' Rinandor said to Kley,'there might have been something we could have told you about him.'

'That thought had occurred to me too,' Kley agreed.

The Doctor was watching the two women now and comparing them. The leader, Kley – the shorter name was clearly important – was slightly taller and had slightly thinner features. But then everything else, it seemed – her hair, her uniform fatigues, even her boots – was deliberately styled to make her look thinner and taller. Objectively there was very little physical difference between her and Rinandor. The inflexions of their speech, their accents, might have been different, but inevitably his ear was imperfectly tuned to such subtleties. He would like to have asked what 'firster' and 'toody' really meant and whether his theory that it referred to the time when their system was originally colonised was reasonable. But there was other information that he needed to glean, and while these people might co-operate with a civilian who knew nothing of the work of professional investigators, an alien who was totally ignorant of the underlying culture might have a more difficult time. No, on balance this was probably not the occasion to indulge his general curiosity.

'I forgot to ask you,' the Doctor said to Rinandor. 'When you were attacked, were you examining the ground where the ship disappeared? When the snake attacked, I mean.'

'They were hunting us before that.'

'Well, they were following us more than hunting us,' Pertanor said.

Rinandor smiled. 'I felt hunted. I still do.'

'But when we were actually attacked,' Pertanor said, 'I was looking at the ground, yes. I had the weirdest feeling that the ship had been…' He hesitated as if at a loss for the appropriate word.

'Swallowed up,' the Doctor supplied. 'What about you?' he said to Kley. 'Were you in a clearing made by a vanishing ship?'

'Monly was. Dead centre. Dead being the operative word in the event.'

'When I examined the place where ours disappeared,' the Doctor said, 'a pack of aggressive carnivores began to gather.' He looked to Leela for confirmation and was irritated to see that she had wandered off on her own again. Had he not made it clear to her that she was a key element? That whatever was doing this might now be focusing on her?

'I was attacked soon after I first landed,' he continued. 'But that was routine, I think. I was alone so I was treated as a test subject.'

'Alone?' Rinandor said. 'What about Leela?' She looked round. 'Where is Leela?'

'What do you mean "a test subject"?' Fermindor asked. 'What is it you're saying?'

'Did your runner come here deliberately, do you know?' the Doctor asked. 'Was he trying to throw you off? Did you chase him here, or were you just following him?'

'You didn't answer Fe's question,' Kley said. 'What are you saying?'

The Doctor got to his feet. He must look for Leela. 'I'm saying that if your runner is a weapons technologist, he's picked an interesting place to run to ground. I think that we're all stranded in a weapons development facility of some sort.'

The two tall, heavy-set warriors were making no attempt to be quiet. The deep-chested grunts and guttural noises must be speech, Leela assumed, except that they did not seem to be paying enough attention to each other to be saying much. The men, if that was what they were, had green skin, hairless and smooth, the same dark shade of green as the large fleshy-leaved plants that dominated the jungle thicket in which she was crouching. Their heads were bald apart from a crest of bright yellow spines, which they raised and lowered as they gurgled and snorted. Their arms were long and seemed to have double elbows, their upper bodies were wide and powerful and their legs were long and muscular with narrow three-toed feet, which were bare. They wore what looked, from where Leela was, to be woven metal body armour. They carried short-shafted spears and had small round shields clipped to their forearms. It was this combination of weapons and their uncaring loudness that left no possible doubt in her mind that these were raider-warriors rather than hunter-warriors.

The two of them were standing by what might be a shaft which emerged among a small outcrop of rocks in a jungle clearing of the sort Leela had quickly learned to mistrust. As she watched, a third warrior climbed out of the entrance and then closed a cover over it. His crest of spines was white, but in every other respect he was identical to his two companions.

The three warriors swaggered down from the rocks and stood forming a half-circle at the centre of a natural arena of flat grassy ground. They continued making the strange noises and raising and lowering their head crests but to this they now added the occasional clash of spear on shield. Leela quickly recognised that what they were doing was offering to fight. But they were ignoring each other and there was no one else around, so who could they be challenging? The ritual display of aggression went on, but still they ignored each other and still no one came. Then the warrior with the white spine crest turned and looked at where Leela was concealed. She could see his eyes clearly, vivid yellow slits with narrow black irises, staring directly into her eyes. He knew she was there. He struck his shield with the flat of his spear blade. There was no mistaking it. He was challenging her to fight. She stared back without moving. She could see no reason to accept the challenge. He had nothing she wanted. There was nothing she needed to prove to anyone, least of all herself. If he knew she was there and was determined to fight her, let him attack across the open ground so she could see him move. The warrior stared for a moment longer, then turned slightly and repeated the performance, staring at a new spot in the dense shadows of the jungle vegetation. His companions began to perform similar threatening stares at particular places at the clearing's edge. It struck Leela that perhaps this was a religious ceremony. The warrior cult trying to show defiance and scare off the demons that lurked in the trees. Warrior cults were stupid like that. She remembered her own initiation into the sacred mysteries of the warrior gods. She had been proud to be initiated and more than a little ashamed that it proved impossible for her to believe in the sacred mysteries. When she had tried to explain how she had felt to the Doctor, he had made her learn off by heart: 'Useful, convenient or pleasurable behaviours become habits, habits become rituals, rituals become superstitions, superstitions become obsessive compulsive disorders, obsessive compulsive disorders become religions.' She did not fully understand what it meant but the Doctor seemed to believe it had mystical powers, because he said she should repeat it to herself whenever she was tempted to stop thinking and give in to mindless mumbo-jumbo – it would protect her.

Without breaking cover, Leela stood up and, very stealthily, ghosted through the thicket to find a new position. Maybe when these warriors had finished making themselves feel stronger and safer they would go back into the shaft in the rocks, and she could get a closer look at it. This might be exactly what the Doctor was hoping to find.

'Excuse me?' she heard his voice say from the other side of the clearing. 'Uh, I couldn't help noticing that access port.' He was striding forward, smiling, his hands held out in clear view, palms upward to show that he was not armed. 'Would you mind very much if I had a look?' Leela reached for her knife. What did the Doctor think he was doing?

All three warriors turned to look at the Doctor. They fell silent as he walked past them and stepped up into the rocks. He was already examining the cover on the access port when they seemed to recover from their surprise and started banging their

112

spears on their shields and grunting fiercely. The Doctor ignored them and pushed open the cover. He peered into the opening. To Leela's surprise the warriors lost interest in him and returned to challenging the unseen enemies.

It came as a relief, but no real surprise, to the Doctor that the aggressive-looking bipeds were not really interested in him. He had kept the distance between himself and them wide enough to allow him the chance to dodge and run if he had seriously miscalculated the situation, but he was fairly confident that if he did nothing to trigger their threat responses they would ignore him. The response to Leela would be different, of course. It was possible, probable in fact, that they were waiting specifically for her. He wondered how she was supposed to be lured to them. Leela was aggressive by nature and training, but she tried to be rational and controlled, and she wasn't stupid. How was she to be brought face to face with these characters? Unless that was the test. To see if she was bright enough to avoid an unnecessary fight. But then how would they know she had declined the fight rather than simply missed it, simply not been aware of it in the first place?

Then another thought occurred to him: suppose *he* was the bait. Suppose this rather crudely designed access shaft was set up to lure him in, and he was set up to lure her. For a strategy like that to work it would have to be clear from a distance that he was in serious danger. One or all of the spiny spear-bangers would need to be creeping up on him or something of the sort. The Doctor stole a glance at the three fighters. They appeared to have forgotten about him altogether, and were practising some sort of martial exercise ritual.

He decided to go with his original plan and ignore them and concentrate on what he hoped might be an access route to whatever was controlling the systems that had taken the TARDIS.

He was bothered by the idea that taking ships was not a targeted procedure to trap them on the planet, but was a routine process with a completely different purpose.

He set about analysing what he had so far. It was not promising. The entrance was disappointingly simple, little more than a manhole set in the rock of a crumbling limestone outcrop, which jutted out of the soil at an angle of about forty-five degrees. The outcrop looked real enough but oddly out of place, like a very good museum exhibit. The manhole cover was not locked, nor was it protected in any standard way, though it was cold to the touch and unexpectedly heavy. The shaft was a narrow tube which went straight down into darkness. It seemed to be wide enough for a man to move through, but there were no mechanisms, no ladders or ropes, so there was no way of doing it unless you were prepared to climb down with your back braced against one side and your legs pushing against the other. The Doctor leaned in and felt the lining of the shaft. It was cold, like the cover. Whatever it was, it wasn't limestone. He hunted round in the tumbled rock and found a small piece of loose shingle. He reached back in to the shaft and used it to scratch at the surface of the lining. It made no impression but, more strikingly, it made no sound. He tapped the rock against the lining and there was nothing, a dead and deadening silence. Apparently the material was tough and readily absorbed certain wavelengths. He dropped the rock down the shaft and, as he expected, it disappeared soundlessly into the dark.

Leela could not decide whether the Doctor knew the warriors would not attack him or whether he was just trusting to his luck. 'Trust to your luck and be glad you're alive, and march to your front like a soldier' was a chant of Kipling the storysinger that he liked to speak. It seemed like a strange choice for a shaman whose power came, he said, only from understanding things. You could

114

not understand luck. There was no explanation for it.

'*But what would happen if you were convinced that something was beyond all understanding? That it did not have an explanation.' 'Then I should know it did not exist.*'

She must put that to him next time. She watched him poking about in the mouth of the shaft. Did he know that was where the warriors came from? Yes, he would see that even if he had not seen it happen. He must not take too long scouting the hole, she thought. If those three finished before he did and they wanted to go back… Walking past them was one thing, but standing in their way could be a dangerous mistake.

It was then that Leela noticed that their movements were changing. All three of them had their crests erect and they had lowered their spear blades into what looked to her like a first-attack position. They were all looking in the same direction, but luckily it was not at the Doctor or at her. At least, she thought it was lucky – until she saw what it was they were looking at.

The Doctor decided to finish his investigation of the access shaft. He needed a route into the subterranean levels but one that did not require prodigious gymnastic feats or suicidal plunges. Hearing that the sounds the warriors were making had altered, he stood up, and dusted himself off, and prepared to charm his way back into the shelter of the trees. The warriors had their backs to him and for a moment or two he couldn't work out why.

'Friends of yours, Thedoctor?' Kley shouted as she led the patrol into the clearing. They paused just clear of the trees and spread out in an untidy line. Fermindor and Sozerdor stood either side of Kley with Belay at one end of the line. At the other end of the line was Pertanor with Rinandor standing inside and slightly behind him. They had all drawn their guns, though this was largely for effect since only Kley, Belay and Fermindor had fully functioning power packs.

'If you back away slowly,' the Doctor called, trying to keep his voice flat and relaxed, 'back into the trees, without alarming them, I may have a chance to leave without finding out how good they are with those spears.'

'Don't worry about that,' Fermindor called back. 'We'll cover you, come on!'

'Please, do as I ask. Go back.'

Kley took a step forward. 'Those spears against these guns? Not a problem.'

The warriors were silent, rocking backwards and forwards slightly on the balls of their feet, swinging the spear tips through small, tight arcs.

'We don't need a confrontation,' the Doctor shouted, climbing slowly down from the rocks. 'I can handle this.'

Kley stood her ground. 'They may be able to tell us something about the runner.'

'No,' the Doctor shouted. 'That's not what they're for.' He was stepping down behind the warriors now and though he had left himself plenty of room to escape it was clear he was not going to need it. They were focused and poised and about to strike and there was nothing he could do about it. 'They're getting ready to attack,' the Doctor shouted. 'There may still be time.' But he knew that it was already too late.

Leela stayed hidden and watched as the stupid investigators refused to listen to the Doctor again. They were too confident that their weapons would give them an unbeatable advantage in a fight. Leela doubted whether they had ever faced warriors. There was no unbeatable advantage when you faced fighters like those three unless you used it immediately. When they were dead, *then* it was unbeatable.

Taking care not to give herself away she slipped closer to where the investigators were standing. As she expected, they were not ready when the attack came.

The three warriors sprang forward simultaneously. They moved with startling suddenness, perfectly balanced on their powerful legs. The spears were carried horizontally at waist height braced by the upper elbow joint, the lower elbow joint flexing to drive up or down with equal power. The forearm shield was carried higher, in front and to one side of the face.

Kley braced herself and fired at the lead warrior. The shot hit him squarely in the chest. It barely slowed him down. She fired again, hitting him in the chest again. She fired again and again. Almost too late she realised that the woven metal tunic was more than just primitive body armour. 'Aim for bare flesh,' she shouted and shot at his head. The forearm shield absorbed the energy of the shot in a frosty blur. She had used up the full handgun charge. The gun was dead.

The Doctor could see immediately that the warriors had divided their attack. Two of them were heading for Kley and the third, the white-crested one, was going for Rinandor. It wasn't much consolation that he seemed right about the focus on Leela. It looked as though these three had been primed to recognise and attack females. 'They're targeting Kley and Rinandor!' he yelled, running towards the fight.

The two warriors were almost on Kley when Belay dropped to his knee and, firing low across the line of charge, hit the second one in the leg so that he stumbled and fell. The leading one sprinted the last few steps and then, skidding low and ducking to the right, lunged upward at Kley's unprotected side. Fermindor was firing at the white-crested warrior in an effort to stop his run at Rinandor. Too late, he realised that Kley's gun was empty and tried to snatch her backwards out of reach of the spear thrust.

Shouting with incoherent rage, Sozerdor flung himself in front of the spear, grabbing and scrabbling for the haft. The warrior drove home the blade. It struck deep into Sozerdor's stomach. With a snarl Sozerdor put his arms round the warrior and pulled him close. The green head nodded and then lifted, raking crest spines through the flesh of Sozerdor's face. In a delirium of pain and fury Sozerdor head-butted him. The warrior ripped the spear sideways and out and when it was clear slammed it up through the side of Sozerdor's ribcage. He head-butted the warrior again and again. As he died he was shouting, 'You stupid savage, I was so close – who sent you to take it away from me?' at the expressionless face, but the warrior did not understand him, and no one else heard the roaring of the whispered words.

At the other end of the line, the white-crested warrior plunged towards Rinandor. Unarmed, Pertanor pushed her behind him and dropped into a ludicrous crouch to face the pitiless fighter.

Leela ran from cover at an angle. She had seen the warrior's eyes and she was confident that he did not see well at the extremes. His was the predator's sight: narrow and forward-fixed. At the flat run she hit him hard and low, kicking his legs out and knocking him down. He recovered instantly, twisting as he fell and stabbing at her with the spear blade. Leela dodged the blow and rolled to her feet. The warrior was up almost as quickly. He circled, shield raised, spear poised. Everyone else was gone from his attention. This was his purpose. Killing Leela was what he was here for.

The warrior's blade stuck for a moment in Sozerdor's ribcage and he had to break the bones to pull it from the corpse. The dead man's embrace made it more difficult but it seemed frustration was not part of the warrior's make-up. So he simply wrenched until it was clear and then shoved the dead man backwards out of the way.

The warrior Belay had hit had somehow pulled himself upright and was hopping forward, intent on killing Kley. Belay shot him in the other leg. As he went down the warrior threw the spear with fierce strength in Kley's direction. The spear hit Sozerdor's collapsing body. Belay shot the fallen warrior in the head and then found it was his last shot. His gun was empty.

Fermindor fervently hoped that he had two shots left because he knew that to stop the thing he would *need* two shots and he would need to get them right. Fermindor fell backwards as the warrior leapt high over Sozerdor's body, spear raised, Kley within reach. Fermindor fell backwards as the warrior crashed over him and from under the shield arm he fired upward at the warrior's chin. The shot tore out the bottom of his face and the leap became a tangled sprawl. Fermindor kicked out with both legs and heaved the warrior's body to one side, then lunged at the spear arm and held it down with his own body. Reaching over with the gun, he jammed it into what was left of the warrior's face and blew his head to fragments.

The fight had been abrupt, brutish and so short that it was over before the Doctor could reach it and try to intervene. Only Leela and the white-crested warrior were still on their feet and in combat by the time he got to the shocked survivors. Sozerdor was obviously dead but the others seemed to be dazed but otherwise more or less unhurt. He helped Fermindor and Kley stagger clear of the mess, saying, 'I'm going to need your help to stop that.' He jerked a thumb towards Leela and the remaining warrior.

The warrior feinted right with his spear and at the same time threw a kick from the opposite direction, a perfect low, flat arc with his left leg. It was like a lethal dance step made possible by his double elbow joint and his perfect balance.

Leela pirouetted away and slashed backhanded with her knife at the warrior's ankle tendon, nicking it but not damaging it enough to slow him up. He circled to the left, looking for the weakness. Leela circled with him.

The Doctor was shedding his coat. 'I'll put this over his head and shoulders. Each of you grab an arm and the other two get his legs.'

Kley stared at him blankly. 'I got Sozerdor killed,' she said.

'Possibly,' the Doctor said brusquely. 'I don't want the same thing to happen to my companion.' He glared round at the others. 'So do you all know what you've got to do?'

Leela had been taught to hide her thoughts and feelings as she fought. Circling warily she tried to hide them now, but she was beginning to lose confidence. The warrior's face gave nothing away. His expression was blank no matter what was happening. He showed no surprise, no fear, no tiredness. There was not the slightest flicker of a clue for Leela to pick up on. His attacks came without warning; her attacks were countered without reaction. The only recognisable intention this alien fighter showed was a silent, obsessive determination to kill her. She had been combat-trained by the best and most talented in the tribe but they were human, as she was. This warrior was *not* human as she was. *Looking. Always looking. Look for the opening. Look for your opponent's fear. If you cannot find fear look for desire. Both are weaknesses that can be used against them.* What good was that to her here in this fight? This warrior had no fear, no desire. Unrelenting aggression. Nothing except to kill her. To kill her for no clear understandable reason.

Then she saw it. He wants to kill me. That was his desire. That was his weakness. How much of a weakness was it? How badly did he want to kill her?

The Doctor realised he'd have to help Leela by himself. These people weren't up to it. The danger was that if he distracted her without slowing the warrior up there was a good chance of getting her killed, but he couldn't just stand by and do nothing. The fight was fast, as Leela and the warrior circled and struck at one another, and already they were moving out across the open ground.

The Doctor went after them.

The warrior had been driving Leela back steadily into the grass arena. She was giving ground faster than necessary because she wanted to be sure that none of the survivors got in the way. The warrior tried a variation on the feint and kick – this time both came from the right. She parried the spear with her knife and stepped inside the kick, punching at his throat with the stiffened fingers of her free hand. He dodged the blow and she ducked under his shield arm and, skipping round behind him, slashed her knife at the back of his neck. He leapt forward to avoid the pass and whirled to face her, and they were circling again. Leela's confidence was coming back. He was quick but not as quick as she was. He was stronger, but he was not clever. She was convinced now that part of the reason he showed nothing was because there was little to show. As they circled, she glimpsed the Doctor hurrying towards them carrying his coat like a hunting net. She knew she could not wait any longer. She had to finish this. She half turned away and caught her foot in the rough grass and stumbled. The warrior saw the weakness he had been waiting for. His reaction was stunningly fast. Committed completely to the kill, he launched himself at Leela. Powerful lunge and fierce spear thrust were part of the same fluid action. The ferocious speed and strength of the attack were irresistible.

The Doctor was running. He was still some distance away from them when he saw the warrior suddenly overwhelm Leela.

'No!' he bellowed helplessly. 'Leave her alone!'

Leela had guessed the warrior could not resist the stumble. That was the weakness she had probed for and prepared for. She was sure he would go all out for the kill then, because the kill was all he desired. Time the stumble right and she would know the moment and the direction of the attack – and she would know he was unbalanced and she would know there was no way back for him.

So, although the warrior's response was blindingly quick, Leela was fractionally quicker. She was balanced and turning and already inside the line of the spear thrust. This time she made no attempt to parry it, but chopped straight at the wrist with her knife. The hand was severed and it hit the ground still gripping the spear. The warrior's momentum carried him crashing into Leela and they both fell heavily. Defeated but still lethally determined, the warrior tried to stab his spines into Leela's throat as he smashed at her head with his shield. Without hesitation, Leela drove the blade of her knife into the back of his chin and up into his brain.

'Are you all right, Leela?' The Doctor examined the warrior's corpse, then pulled it away. 'Are you hurt?'

'I do not think so,' she said, closing her eyes and taking a couple of deep breaths before sitting up slowly. 'He was strong, though.'

'What a mess,' the Doctor sighed. 'What a cruel and unnecessary mess.'

'Where did he come from?' Leela asked.

The Doctor helped her to her feet. 'There's an access shaft over there.' He nodded towards the rocks.

'I know where he came from,' she said irritably. 'I meant –'

'You meant where did he come from?' He shrugged. 'I don't know whether they're taking them or faking them.'

'What does that mean?' Leela tore a handful of grass and began to clean her knife meticulously. 'Our tribe's shamans talked in riddles. It made them sound wise. The more nonsense they talked the more powerful they became.'

But the Doctor was not listening closely enough to recognise the criticism. 'I can't totally rule out anything yet. However, assuming these things are not all indigenous it seems unlikely that they're being brought from other planets, or even other parts of this planet, and simply let loose to run around here waiting for the opportunity to jump out and attack people. But if they're not taking them then how are they making them?'

'You said "faking them".'

'Same thing.'

Leela found that the knife blade had lost its edge in some places. 'I need to sharpen this,' she said.

They walked towards the rocks, leaving the investigators to recover. 'Are they cloning from original templates?' the Doctor mused. 'And if so, where would they get them from? There would have to be a bank somewhere. Unless they're specifically engineering them one by one.'

'Who is this *they* you keep talking about?'

'Exactly,' the Doctor agreed. 'And how do they know where to set up their creations? Does your presence trigger it automatically or are they directly targeting you?'

'Why are you so sure it is me?' Leela flared.

'It's something to do with weapons development.'

'All I have got is a knife.'

'I think that might be the point,' the Doctor said thoughtfully. 'Of course I could be completely wrong.'

They reached the limestone outcrop. Leela sat down by one of the larger pieces of tumbled rock and set about honing the damaged blade. 'So what you are saying is,' she said, carefully spitting on the metal, 'you have no idea where he came from.'

The Doctor smiled a depressed smile. 'Before he came out of that shaft?' he said. 'None at all.'

Chapter Seven

They sealed Sozerdor in a tagged seek-bag and left him for autolift by the search-and-retrieval ship when it came, if it ever came.

Kley was full of agonised remorse. 'This whole mess is my fault. I should have pulled us out at the first sign that there was something peculiar going on.'

'That would have been more or less immediately,' Fermindor said. 'You couldn't have done that. No team leader could.'

'It was already too late anyway,' the Doctor said matter-of-factly. 'Once you started there was no going back.'

Leela was beginning to feel the effects of the fight and a combination of shock and suddenly aching bruises was making her tense. 'If you had listened to the Doctor you could have avoided that battle,' she said.

'And Sozerdor would still be alive,' Kley said. 'That is what you're thinking, isn't it?'

'No,' Leela said, not very convincingly. 'Nothing is achieved by thinking such things. The lesson to be learned is that the Doctor is a clever shaman whose advice is usually worth listening to.'

'Shaman?' Belay said.

'I admit it. I am a bit of a showman,' the Doctor said quickly, 'and that does sometimes make it difficult for people to take me seriously.'

'We're ready to listen to you now,' Fermindor said. 'Isn't that right, Chief?'

Kley nodded tiredly. She seemed ready to listen to anything or anyone. Just so long as she didn't have to think any more. 'So what is your advice, The?'

'Be with you in a moment,' the Doctor said.

* * *

The Doctor clambered up over the rocks to the access shaft and looked down it again. As he expected, the visible section was getting narrower. He reached in and felt the side. It was soft to the touch, and warm. Too late to use this as an access route. He climbed back down to where the others were waiting.

'What do you suggest we do now?' Kley asked.

'Nothing,' he said.

'Well that was worth waiting for,' Rinandor commented, her voice heavy with sarcasm.

'I suggest,' he continued imperturbably, 'we find somewhere in the shade and we make ourselves comfortable and sit and wait for something to happen.' He looked around for a suitable spot and pointed to a large frond-leaved tree at the edge of the clearing well away from where the fight had been. 'How about over there?' He picked up Sozerdor's equipment pack and strolled towards the tree. Leela walked beside him.

After some hesitation, the others straggled after them.

'I'm impressed,' Rinandor announced loudly.

'Shut up, Rinandor,' Kley said.

'I should stick with the showmanship, The,' Rinandor continued even more loudly. 'I can't see you making it as a chaser.'

'I said be quiet!' Kley snapped. 'Do I have to remind you that I am a CI and I am the team leader here?'

'No. I think perhaps I have to remind *you* of that,' Rinandor snapped back. 'Why are you trailing along behind him? Why are you giving so much respect to that... that... duellist's agent?'

'Is that what she is?' Fermindor asked. 'A contract duellist?'

Pertanor said, 'We're not absolutely sure.'

'Yes we are,' Rinandor chided.

'We think she might be, yes.'

'I wish I'd known.'

'Would it have made a difference?' Belay asked mildly.

Fermindor grinned ruefully. 'She'd have scared the hell out of me even more than she did.'

Kley said, 'And he's running her? Illegal offworlds training then.'

'She saved our lives three times,' Pertanor said. 'Rinandor and me.'

'She did,' Rinandor said. 'But *he* didn't.'

'She seems to think a lot of him,' Fermindor said. 'Respects his opinion.'

'She's young,' Kley said.

The Doctor and Leela were sitting under the tree when the others got to them. The Doctor had stretched out and closed his eyes. Leela had opened Sozerdor's equipment pack and was eating a ration concentrate biscuit.

Kley frowned and said, 'Those are for personal emergency use.'

'Your friend does not need them any more,' Leela said reasonably.

'In which case we divide them up,' Kley said, sitting down heavily. 'That's the rule.' She couldn't believe how absolutely exhausted she was.

Leela tossed her the uneaten portion. 'I have already taken my share.' Then seeing the expression on the woman's face she said, 'You should eat some now. For your personal emergency.' She shook Sozerdor's canteen. It was less than half full. 'How much water are you all carrying?'

'We were expecting to find some,' Fermindor said. 'But so far…' He shrugged.

'There's the lake,' Rinandor said. 'We found a lake, didn't we, Pe?'

'I'm not sure. I think it might have found us,' Pertanor said.

Rinandor chortled. 'Yes, of course it did.'

'And I'm not sure we could find it again.'

'We were stalked by a pond,' Rinandor sniggered. 'Pursued by a puddle.'

'It won't be there now,' the Doctor said without opening his eyes. 'I don't think drinking it would have been a good idea anyway.'

'Why not?' Rinandor demanded. 'Could it be because you forgot to take any?'

The Doctor opened his eyes and sat up. 'Somehow I doubt whether it was water.'

'It tastes fine to me,' Rinandor said, producing her canteen and opening it with a defiant flourish. 'Score another one for the showman.'

She raised the canteen to her lips but before she could drink from it Leela leaned back and stretched out her leg. She flipped the canteen out of Rinandor's hands with her foot and caught it neatly. 'If you will not listen to the Doctor,' she said, 'then listen to yourself. Do you not remember the effect the meat had on us?'

Rinandor stared at Leela with owlish concentration. 'That could have hurt,' she said finally.

Kley asked, 'What is the matter with you, Rinandor?'

Rinandor yawned, lay down and curled up. 'I hate it when people I don't like are right,' she muttered as she went to sleep.

'Rinandor?' Kley said. 'Rinandor? Is she sick?'

'She will be,' the Doctor said. 'When she sobers up.'

Pertanor took the canteen from Leela and poured the contents away. He took his fatigue jacket off, folded it and put it under Rinandor's head. 'Why is this happening to us?' he asked looking at the Doctor. 'Why is this place so weird. And why is it so different from what we were told to expect?'

Why indeed? the Doctor thought, and it occurred to him that this was a team of people drawn from the ranks of what was apparently an elite law-enforcement organisation. And yet they appeared to be poorly briefed, poorly trained and poorly equipped, and they seemed to lack any basic resourcefulness. It was almost as though they were administrative personnel who had suddenly found themselves transferred to operations.

'Why are there so few of you?' Leela asked.

'We're chasing one man,' Kley said. She had eaten some of the concentrate as Leela had suggested, and was already looking better. 'It's the sort of job where you send in a small fast group to grab him before he knows you're there; or you send in an army. There's no middle ground.'

'It looks as though an army might have been a better choice,' Leela said.

'What's wrong with your team?' the Doctor asked.

'Nothing's wrong with it.' Kley glared at him.

'Two dead, one drunk, no communications, no functioning weapons, no ship. A well-oiled machine is not the metaphor that leaps immediately to mind,' the Doctor said, hoping to provoke her into openness.

'Whereas you have no ship, no communications and a functioning knife,' she said. 'Or have I missed your point?'

'The point is we are not chasing anybody,' Leela said.

'You shouldn't be here at all,' Fermindor commented.

'Why have you been given such poor weapons and equipment?' the Doctor asked. 'I thought OIG was an elite force.'

'It's all I could afford,' Kley said. 'It took me a long time to get this chance and I needed to score here. Are you satisfied?'

'I'm not sure I quite understand,' the Doctor said, at a complete loss.

'I needed to make a success of this mission. So I had to keep the budget as low as I possibly could.'

'Is that why none of your equipment is rechargeable?'

'It *is* rechargeable,' she said. 'It's mostly reconditioned but it's not complete rubbish. Anyway, without the ship what are we supposed to do?'

'That would be the cheapest way, I suppose,' the Doctor agreed tentatively. 'To use the ship's power plant.'

'Even top-of-the-range energy converters don't give you a gun that charges in the field so if you're relying on the ship's power plant for them –' she shrugged – 'why not for everything else? It seemed like a good cheap idea at the time. Turned out to be just a cheap idea.'

Fermindor grunted. 'We all stood to benefit. Extra bonus credits, better career prospects, stuff like that. We all had our reasons.'

'Maybe it would be useful if we examined what those reasons were,' the Doctor said, making an effort to sound detached and objective and avoid the obvious reaction.

It came anyway. 'You first,' Kley said.

Which was it, the Doctor wondered: did the suspicious become policemen or did policemen become suspicious? He didn't want to waste time on the wrong end of an interrogation, particularly when there was a reasonable possibility that they were all being closely monitored. He decided to let them go on believing what they thought they already knew. 'Ah, well, Leela is going to be a very important duellist,' he said. 'I was looking for a place to sharpen her skills.'

'Why contravene the rules?'

'Ambition.'

'Isn't that unusual in a toody?'

'I don't think so. And under the circumstances I wonder that you still do.'

Kley fell silent. He was right of course. Weird but right. How could she have said that? They were chasing a toody. Fermindor was a better investigator than any firster she had ever worked with. Pertanor was ambitious. Rinandor was brighter than she was herself. How could she have said that? Was she really that stupid? 'Am I really that stupid?'

'I don't know,' the Doctor said. 'Only you can tell really. It's a difficult concept I think. As far as I can see it's memory that makes intelligence. Short-term behaviour modification built up by trial and error or pain and pleasure stimuli can look like intelligence but it isn't.'

Kley said, 'It was a rhetorical question. I was just thinking aloud.'

'I apologise,' the Doctor said, and smiled. 'The subject interests me.'

'Why did you come to this planet?' Fermindor asked.

'Pure accident,' the Doctor said and smiled more broadly.

'Your turn,' Leela interrupted.

Fermindor said, 'I like being an investigator. I'm good at it. It's what I do. I get bored when I'm not doing it.' He took a small swig from his canteen. 'This has been a bit more extreme than the usual assignment. But like they say: if you haven't got a sense of humour you shouldn't have joined.' He did not smile.

'I can see why you chose him,' the Doctor said to Kley.

Kley looked at the short, heavy-set man who was now her second-in-command, as he should have been from the beginning. 'Fe would have been my first choice, had I been given a choice.'

The Doctor kept the question casual. 'You weren't given a choice?'

'The team was assembled in a hurry. The computer profile was appropriate for the job. The psych numbers were fine.'

'But the job wasn't what you expected, was it?' the Doctor suggested.

She shrugged helplessly. 'Who could have known?'

'Who indeed? Not the computer certainly.'

'Did you feel that?' Leela got to her feet. 'The ground is shaking.'

'Are you sure?' the Doctor asked.

'It is stopping now.' Leela knelt and rested first her forehead and then her ear on the ground. 'It is very faint. It is a sort of creaking sound. It may be coming from the rocks.'

Belay watched her admiringly. 'If you ever wanted to sell shares in her,' he said, glancing at the Doctor, 'I'd be very interested in taking an option on any part that was available.'

Leela sat back on her heels. 'What did you say?' she demanded of the thin, pale young man who was smiling at her. She rested her hand on the handle of her knife.

'It was intended as a compliment, Leela,' the Doctor said. 'I think you have an admirer.'

'I have a reasonable amount of money saved,' Belay said. 'That's why I volunteered for this assignment. The payments were better than average.'

'Because the costs were low,' the Doctor said. 'Or because the risks were high, which may be the same thing of course.'

'I'd say she was a worthwhile gamble,' Belay said. 'In fact there are some people I know who might be interested in buying her contract outright. If you wanted to take a guaranteed early profit.'

The Doctor thought for a moment, looking suitably serious. 'If we get out of this alive, we'll discuss it.'

'Leela has a lot of potential,' Belay said. 'And I've seen some of the best kills, I mean actually seen them in the flesh, not just on screen. I've been to major fights, seen big-league players, and she moves like the best of them.'

'I think I have heard enough of these... compliments,' Leela said pointedly. She stood up and stalked off into the clearing.

Kley stood up too. 'Why are we sitting around here?' she said without looking at the Doctor. 'What are we doing? Is this your master plan, Thedoctor?'

'Do you have an alternative?' the Doctor asked politely.

'"Do nothing" is your brilliant strategy?'

'You've been running around,' the Doctor said, 'chasing someone you haven't seen, who is doing something you haven't understood. You're out of ammunition and before long you'll be out of food and water. My advice is to stop confusing movement with action and simply wait for him to make the next move.'

'So you think the runner is responsible for everything that's happened,' Fermindor said.

'He has something to do with it, certainly.'

'Yes, but what?' Pertanor asked, inhaling deeply as though he was suddenly short of breath.

'That's what we're waiting to find out,' the Doctor said, stretching out and closing his eyes. He was a little tired himself now. It seemed to be getting hotter. He really should have checked the movement of this planet in relation to the positions of both the suns nearby. It could get hotter still, especially if there was some sort of focusing effect on this area. Perhaps a heat-retaining gas layer.

Kley sat down again with a heavy sigh. 'Suppose he doesn't make the next move. Suppose he doesn't do anything at all.'

'He'll have to do something' the Doctor murmured drowsily. 'I think we have something he wants.'

'Any chance you might tell us what that is?' Kley asked and then yawned.

But the Doctor was asleep.

Kley looked across the clearing at Leela who was standing close to the rocks. She was quite still, staring at the ground. Kley remembered what the Doctor had said about the attacks in the open areas where the ships had vanished.

Fermindor snorted. 'The strategy is developing. It's gone from "do nothing" to "do nothing and sleep".' He took another small sip from his canteen. 'Is it getting hotter?' he asked no one in particular.

'Leela?' Kley called. Maybe this wasn't where a ship had vanished but then again maybe it wasn't so different. 'Leela?' she called again, but the girl ignored her and continued to stare at the ground. 'Leela!' she shouted more urgently. 'Get off the open ground!' This time the girl gestured at her to be quiet. Kley was too tired to get to her feet again. She looked up at the clear cloudless sky. There was no threat that she could see in that bright emptiness out beyond the unmoving tree fronds. She listened. Apart from her companions, nothing else stirred. Nothing seemed to be moving anywhere. Not a rustle, not a murmur, not a click. Automatically she pulled her gun and checked it again, just to be sure. It was dead. It was useless. Like her.

She put the gun back in the holster. Out of the corner of her eye she saw a movement. A jolt of shock thrilled her sharply awake. She gasped for a hollow breath as she looked up, momentarily alert. Leela was running towards her. Kley tried to get to her feet, tried to understand what it was the girl was running from. Fermindor had turned to see what it was she was looking at. Now Pertanor and Belay were turning too. And then Leela vanished. One moment she was running straight at her, sprinting, face clenched, arms and legs rhythmically driving, and then she was gone. How? What had taken her? Where was she?

Then she saw it. Slashing black and ripping hugely through the flat ground towards them, falling in on itself, collapsing in a monstrous V-shaped slice, point rushing at them, pointing the way for the ever-widening all-swallowing crack which came carving through the surface to drop them into a churning, falling maelstrom.

The Doctor woke to total darkness. Only the sound of his own breathing told him he was still alive and that he was probably conscious. If this was a dream or a hallucination he decided that it would make little difference to his actions, so he would lose nothing by dismissing the possibility from his mind. If he was unconscious he would wake up in due course and in a new set of difficulties. If he was not unconscious then he was already in trouble.

A more thorough exploration of his situation suggested that the air was breathable and the ambient temperature was tolerable, but that all he seemed able to move were his hands and feet. He thought about this for a while, listened to the whisper of what was possibly an air-conditioning system and then, since there was nothing much else he could do, he cleared his throat and said, 'Hello? Is anybody there?'

Someone cleared their throat and a voice said,'Hello? Is anybody there?'

The Doctor waited a moment and said,'I'm the Doctor. Who are you?'

'I'm the Doctor. Who are you?' the voice said.

'Lights?'

'Lights?'

'And God said:"Let there be light",' the Doctor proclaimed. 'And there was light. And you could see for miles.'

'And God said:"Let there be light", and there was light. And you could see for miles.'

An automatic response of some sort, then, the Doctor thought, but was it a recorded playback, or a more complex simulation?

He tried singing and was entranced to hear how sweetly tuneful the copy seemed to be. He made animal noises and was disappointed to think that if the voice was copying him exactly, then his talent as an impressionist was limited. Finally it occurred to him to wonder what would happen if he spoke over the other voice as it was repeating his words. Could whatever it was unscramble the two lots of speech or would it simply ignore the interruption? Its reaction might give him some notion of the mechanism and the purpose the repetition was serving.

Needing something fairly long and mildly coherent he recalled part of a speech he had once given at a symposium on 'The Question of Fear'. Let's see what it makes of this, he thought as he began, vaingloriously, 'Death is the question that cannot be answered. It does not follow that because a question *cannot* be answered it *has* no answer. But an unanswerable question is frightening because it hints at the failure of reason: the denial of cause and effect. If your world lacks cause and effect then you are doomed to be a victim and fear is all you can expect. You must tremble and bow down. Do not look, do not ask, howl down anyone who does. That is why the supernatural is terrifying: it has no causes, it has only effects. Madness is terrifying for exactly the same reason.'

He had been rather proud of that argument, which was probably the reason he still remembered some of it, and he was briefly tempted to listen to himself uninterrupted as the voice repeated, 'Death is the question that cannot be answered. It does not follow that because a question *cannot* be answered it *has* no answer –'

'But, soft! what light through yonder window breaks?' the Doctor declaimed over the sound of his own speechmaking. 'It is the east, and Juliet is the sun!'

The copy voice stopped speaking abruptly and after the briefest of pauses a new and different voice said, 'You have a robust attitude to blasphemy, Thedoctor.'

'I hope so,' the Doctor said. 'How much of William Shakespeare's work have you people forbidden to be spoken aloud? You do realise it was written for precisely that purpose. To be spoken aloud, I mean.'

'What are you talking about and what sort of a name is William Shakespeare?'

'Yes, I should have known. How can you have a flesh-and-blood author for a holy text? It would tend to undermine the supernatural aspects, wouldn't it?'

'Yes, I should have known. How can you have a flesh and blood author for a holy text?' the copy of the Doctor's voice repeated. 'It would tend to undermine the supernatural aspects, wouldn't it?'

It was impossible in the functionally perfect darkness for the Doctor to judge the distance or the direction of his tormentor. In fact, he was not even sure whether he himself was being held down on a horizontal or a vertical plane and whether the orientation was upside down or downside up. Although he strained and flexed in every way he could think of he was also quite unable to break free of the total-body restraints. He decided therefore to make a virtue out of necessity and wait in contemplative silence for the runner's next move. It had to be the runner of course. He had made the same culturally predetermined assumptions about names and called him Thedoctor, and he had the same religious taboo as the other toodies. But what was it he wanted? The Doctor had assumed that Leela was the key: that was what he meant when he told Kley they had something the runner wanted. Odd, he thought, that what in other times and places would be called a fugitive from justice was called a runner by these people – even he himself now thought of him as the runner. You ended up missing things when you started accepting other people's assumptions. It stopped you asking your own questions. So what was it he was missing? Surely the point about this runner was that he was not running. All along it was *they* who had been running.

'Thedoctor?' the runner said. 'You can speak now. That part is finished. I am satisfied that the narcotic has been fully metabolised. You are rational. The algorithms are acceptable.'

The Doctor remained determinedly silent. A narcotic gas, presumably, he thought, seeping out at ground level. Lying down had been a mistake.

'Come now, Thedoctor. The relationship between memory and intelligence interests me too.'

It gave the Doctor a moment's small satisfaction to have it confirmed that he and the others had been closely monitored. It would be interesting to learn more details about that, he thought. Was it vision as well as sound? Everywhere or just the chosen test sites?

'It needs an intelligent mind to appreciate what I have done,' the runner said, managing to sound arrogant and just a little peevish at the same time. 'I had hoped yours was such a mind.'

The Doctor resisted the urge to be flattered. This man was clearly interested in something more than erudite conversation and the chance to show off to an intellectual equal. He wanted something that he had not yet managed to get. After the flattery would come threats.

Sure enough, the runner said after a longish pause, 'If you are no more intelligent than the others then I can see no reason to keep you alive.'

And then, thought the Doctor, he would try blackmail.

'They are alive at the moment but whether they stay that way will depend on you. Perhaps you'd like to pick which of them I kill first?'

And finally perhaps a demonstration of some sort.

'I don't think you believe me, do you, Thedoctor?'

Abruptly the Doctor was conscious that whatever was holding him was tightening inexorably and it was becoming increasingly painful.

'Do you feel that?' the runner asked. 'Can you imagine it getting tighter and tighter and tighter until you are a crushed and liquefied mess?'

It didn't take much imagination as the pressure increased on every part of the Doctor's body. The pain came in excruciating waves and it slowly blotted out everything else, and just when it seemed he could stand no more, the pressure was released and the pain subsided.

'Now.' The runner's voice was little more than a whisper and sounded close to the Doctor's ear. 'Shall we decide which of them is going all the way to the squelch? Let's start by considering the options.'

Hanging in the darkness, a holographic image of Leela formed directly in the Doctor's line of vision. She was suspended immobile in a coruscating column of yellow and white light. Bands of twisting brightness pulsed slowly up and down the column. It reminded the Doctor of a lights-and-illusion conjuring show he had seen used to dupe people on a planet where the original colony had collapsed into primitive barbarism. Though the image was bright in itself, the coherent light generating it cast no glow into the surrounding darkness and gave the Doctor no hint about his own situation.

'One,' the runner said.

On the column, the twisting bands visibly contracted. Leela's fingers twitched and her eyes opened wider. Her mouth formed an oval of mute pain, a silent scream.

'Two,' the runner said.

An identical column of light formed beside the first. In it, Kley was suspended. Her eyes were shut and her mouth was firmly closed.

'Wake up!' the runner commanded, and the bands expanded and contracted in sharp, teasing spasms. Blood showed on Kley's mouth. She had obviously bitten into her lip but she did not open her eyes. The Doctor saw the blood trickle down on to her chin and decided that they were all, including him, being held in the vertical position. He was not sure whether knowing that would be of much use but the acquisition of knowledge was never worthless. Thinking always mattered.

'Three.' A third column contained Pertanor. He was glaring into the middle distance. He appeared to be straining to turn his head. Was that because he could see, or were they all imprisoned in the same darkness?

'Four.' Rinandor was still unconscious in her column. 'Perhaps I should kill her first,' the runner said. 'Before she starts to vomit all over herself.' It struck the Doctor then that whatever had caused this couldn't have happened long ago. The effects of drinking the liquid from the lake would be short-lived and they didn't seem to have worn off yet.

There were four columns now standing side by side, rippling

and sparkling round their isolated and more or less agonised prisoners. It was beginning to look to the Doctor like a rather macabre art exhibit.

'Five,' said the runner, and Belay was added to the line-up. His eyes were open but they seemed to be unseeing, darting unfocused this way and that. He seemed to be speaking or, perhaps, shouting. The Doctor looked along the line. He was convinced now that they were all in the same darkness as he was in.

The runner said, 'I think the girl would be an ideal candidate myself. I think that's the one you would find most stimulating. Yes I think the girl. But the choice is yours. Which one of these would you like me to squeeze the life out of?'

There was one missing, the Doctor realised. Where was the second-in-command – what was his name…? Fermindor, that was it. Where was Fermindor? Why was he not a candidate? If he was already dead would the runner not have used his death to demonstrate his ruthlessness? Did he imagine the omission would go unnoticed?

'All this just to get me to speak?' the Doctor said. 'Or was there something else you wanted from me? I'm afraid my capacity for applause is somewhat limited in these circumstances. I could shout bravo from time to time. Would that do?'

The runner's voice was once again close to his ear, little more than a whisper. 'Tell me what you know,' it murmured.

'I've always found that what I don't know is much more interesting,' the Doctor said. 'Isn't that your experience?'

'Tell me what you know or pick four survivors,' the voice whispered.

The Doctor had never taken his eyes off the five tormented images. He was finding it increasingly disconcerting to be able to see them so clearly but to have no light at all by which to see any part of himself. 'You can stop whispering,' he said. 'I'm totally disorientated, as you must know, so it's an unnecessary elaboration of your threat-and-torture techniques – which, I'm sorry to have to tell you, do rather lack subtlety. If you're serious about becoming a brutal psychopath I think you need to do some more studying. Sadly there are no established courses that I'm aware of – *Fiend Six Six Six: Barking for Beginners*; *Psych O-One*, that sort of thing – but I can recommend some classical sources, some unholy texts as it were. History is full of role models for you. It's a crowded speciality. For an amateur like yourself it will be a difficult field in which to make your mark.'

The runner's voice did not change in any way as it whispered, 'No survivors, then.' The bands contracted on each of the light columns and within them the victims' faces contorted with agony. Even the unconscious Rinandor was reacting.

The Doctor struggled to think of some way to stop what was happening. 'What is it you want to know?' he asked, doing his best to keep the tone of the question calm and matter-of-fact.

The runner's voice became normal and conversational, matching the Doctor's tone. 'It is one of the great disappointments faced by all rational beings, that they will never know everything there is to know.'

'That's not a disappointment,' the Doctor said. 'It's the consolation for being alive.'

'There *is* no consolation for being alive,' the voice said.

The torture of the prisoners was reaching a climax. It looked to the Doctor as though the images might be getting bigger. Was it his imagination or was it a deliberate ploy?

'If you kill them,' the Doctor asked, 'what hold will you have over me?'

There was no response from the runner. The Doctor watched the images expand and blink out of existence as each of the prisoners reached the point of death. He was left finally with the utterly blank blackness.

Then the voice of the runner said, 'You carry the past inside you. Every time someone dies there is less of it. Death is essential. If everyone lived for ever, the past and the present would be the same.'

If this madman has killed them all, the Doctor thought, he has his justification ready and prepared. A weapons technologist would always need reasons. At some level, everyone needed reasons for everything. This was a rationalising madman, but how rational was he, and how mad?

'Our essence is change,' the voice went on. 'We are movement. Being out of balance is life. Perfect balance. Stasis. That is death. Life yearns for perfection. Death is perfection. Do you understand?'

Quite mad, the Doctor realised. There was a good chance they were all dead by now. 'If you've killed everyone,' he said, 'how do you expect to make me do what you want?'

In the darkness a new column materialised. It was the same as the others had been but this time it contained the figure of the Doctor himself. 'The brain goes last,' the voice said. 'You will be able to see yourself die.'

'I take back what I said earlier,' the Doctor said, waggling his fingers and watching the image carefully. 'You may have a natural aptitude for unpleasantness.' There seemed to be a very slight delay between the movement of his hand and the response of the image. It was hard to tell for certain because the range of possible movements was so limited.

'Unpleasantness?' the voice sounded genuinely offended. 'You underestimate me, Thedoctor. Unpleasantness does not begin to describe what is about to happen to you.'

'I'm prepared to take your word for it,' the Doctor said, moving his fingers, first one hand and then the other. He was almost sure there was a delay. He tried closing and opening one eye and then the other. The delay was barely perceptible but it was there. What sort of technology was it that could not deliver an instantaneous holographic image? Unless it was a virtual image, constructed and manipulated separately and slaved into whatever he was contained by. Perhaps that was what he was being shown all along, he thought hopefully. Perhaps the pictures of the others were just images of pain, manipulated and exaggerated for his benefit. 'Tell me what it is you want me to say and I'll say it.'

'That's the problem with interrogation,' the voice of the runner said. 'How can you trust what you are told when eventually all you are told is what you want to hear?'

'Well it helps if you ask questions,' the Doctor said. '"Tell me what you know" doesn't really offer much in the way of guidance to your victims. I am at a loss to understand why you killed those people if all you want is a debate.' It seemed to the Doctor that the runner was wasting time for some obscure reason of his own. The delay between his movement and that of the image might have become very slightly more marked too. He had been watching his virtual lips as he spoke. They were definitely out of synch with what he could feel of his mouth. It was as though someone was getting overconfident and careless, or else they were trying to make sure he had noticed that there was a delay.

The runner's voice was now replaced by the Doctor's. 'Don't you find it fascinating,' the voice said, 'that even the refusal to say anything must say something? If communication is possible then we may tell each other lies but we can't tell each other nothing.'

'Should I be flattered that you paid such close attention to all my conversations?' the Doctor asked.

'I wouldn't be,' Fermindor said from somewhere between him and the image of him. 'That crapwit is crazy.'

There was a sudden flash of white in the Doctor's eyes and he thought he saw the glowing column of the holographic image gather itself into a whirling ball, which dissipated into a cloud of bursting pinpoint fragments of blazing light.

The image of the Doctor stood blinking in the brightness before it, too, faded, leaving the Doctor standing blinking in the brightness.

He looked round. He was in a tall, tubular chamber made out of an opaque, waxy-looking material which was a deep yellow flecked with tiny particles of sparkling crystal. The chamber was perhaps three metres in diameter and four-and-a-half metres high. Access appeared to be a circular hole in the floor, which looked barely large enough to have allowed the stocky Fermindor to squeeze through it.

'Have you seen any of the others?' the Doctor asked.

Fermindor shook his head. He looked quite unscathed and remarkably rested and healthy. 'Listen, I only fell across you by accident,' he said. 'And I don't want to rush you, but I think we should get out of here before it realises what I did.'

'It?'

'I think this whole place might be alive.'

The Doctor touched the wall. A hint of static prickled vaguely across his hand. 'What did you do?' he asked.

'I pressed that.' Fermindor pointed at a dark patch about the size of hand on the wall beside him. 'It brought you down from there.' He indicated a place halfway up the wall. 'You were stuck there, staring at nothing and talking to yourself.'

'Talking to myself?'

'Loudly. That's how I found you.'

'You were passing.'

'Yes, and I'd like to get back to it.' Fermindor grabbed the Doctor's arm and propelled him towards the hole in the floor. '"Stop confusing movement with action" – that's what you said, wasn't it? Well stop confusing standing still with surviving, that's what I say.'

The Doctor allowed himself to be pulled down into the hole, which was a tube lined with the same material that he had seen in the shaft in the rocks. The tube sloped down at a steep angle, and the Doctor noticed that the unexpectedly slow slide through it seemed to be controlled by extra but heatless friction.

The tube gave on to a larger, semicircular passageway brightly lit from below by a glowing floor. By the time the Doctor slid out and got to his feet, Fermindor was waiting impatiently to set off. 'Why that way?' the Doctor asked.

Fermindor shrugged and said, 'I was following the light.'

As if on cue a pulse of extra-bright light moved along the floor and disappeared into the distance. The Doctor glanced back in the direction from which it had come. It was definitely darker that way. 'How far have you walked?'

'I don't know,' Fermindor said. 'And before you ask, "I have no idea" is the answer to your next question, whatever it is. I woke up in a heap somewhere back there, feeling worse than I've ever felt in my life. Walking in that direction –' he pointed in the direction the pulse of light had gone – 'makes me feel better. Walking in that direction –' he jerked a thumb over his shoulder – 'makes me feel worse. I am walking in *that* direction.' He pointed and started to walk. 'I see no virtue in feeling crappy,' he said over his shoulder. 'You must make up your own mind. But do it quickly. Things keep changing round here and none of them seem to be for the better.'

The Doctor put his hand inside the tube from which they had just emerged. It was getting warmer and softer to the touch and it was already narrowing. After thinking about it for a moment or two, he could find no compellingly logical reason to go in the other direction so he set out to catch up with Fermindor. He had the strong feeling that this was what he was being encouraged to do, but he would need more to go on before he could decide if and why this might be.

'Fermindor,' he called. 'I have one or two more questions that maybe you *can* answer.'

Chapter Eight

A towering pillar of rock pushed steadily up in the middle of several square kilometres of wind-carved and dust-blasted open desert ground, and settled in place with titanic groans and shudders. In the centre of the pillar, the modified unit rose through a narrow shaft and emerged high above the surrounding country. Once the device was in position the access shaft narrowed to become a wire-thin link with one of the smallest of the power sources far below the planet's surface. The unit's control programme had been adapted to uplink with any available orbiter, as well as to scattercast direct pulse-plasma signals. Its power had been boosted to the limit and all its signals were stronger and more coherent than specification. Once it had been activated it would be only a matter of time before a search-and-retrieval ship responded to this second-hand, standard-issue distress beacon and came looking for the OIG team led by CI Serian Kley and consisting of ACI Monly, SI Sozerdor, SI Fermindor, and Investigators Belay, Pertanor and Rinandor.

Leela found the voice of her captor ingratiating and threatening in equal measure. Bullies like that were common enough in her experience, wheedling and intimidating by turns, and she had never had any trouble ignoring their attentions. Avoiding this one was more of a problem, though, since he had hidden himself in the darkness and someone had bound her so tightly that she found herself completely unable to move. From the sound of him he was enjoying himself and she had no intention of adding to his pleasure by speaking to him or acknowledging his presence. All she could do was wait and then, when something changed, she would take whatever opportunity came with it to escape.

'Why won't you speak to me?'

Leela had discovered that counter-attack came naturally to her.

'I can make you tell me what I want to know.'

Her strength as a warrior had always been based on speed rather than physical power but recently she had come to realise that it was quicker still to wait and see what happened and react to it.

'Thedoctor has already told me all I need to know, so it's of no importance. But it is rude not to answer when I speak to you.'

Leela wondered where the Doctor was and whether he was a captive too.

'I hate rudeness. It's unnecessary. It makes life so stressful, so graceless.'

If he was, she had no doubt he would be trying to work out where he was being held and what was happening and who was doing all this – and why. He did so much of that sort of thinking that he tended to miss the opportunities when they came because he was not paying attention and he was not ready.

'I will hurt you again.'

Leela had no intention of making that mistake.

'I will hurt you very badly.'

Leela waited to see what would happen.

Kley kept her eyes tight shut. She could not move. Spasms of ferocious pain shot through her without warning. She had obviously been injured in the earthquake and now she was trapped in some sort of air pocket. The chances of rescue were zero. She knew that if she opened her eyes she would finally lose her mind and she would scream and she would never be able to stop screaming. The whispering continued.

'Talk to me... Tell me... Pain...'

If she listened to the whispering – or, worse still, if she spoke to the whispering – she would be lost. She bit her lip again. It didn't hurt enough to make the whispering go away.

Pertanor had peered about in the darkness and shouted Rinandor's name a few times but there was no response. When the reason for that became clear he shut up as he had been trained to do. The psycho toody could rant and threaten as much as he liked, Pertanor was not about to start chatting to a runner who had probably already killed Rinandor and the others. How could a toody *do* something like that?

Belay kept talking to the runner. Negotiating would have been easier face to face but the important thing was to keep talking. He couldn't work out what it was the runner actually wanted. Basically he just seemed to want to talk but there had to be more to it than that. If he kept talking he would find out eventually, and besides, the psychology of captor and captive was such that the former found it more difficult to kill you if you kept talking. Belay hardly noticed when the runner stopped prompting him to speak.

Rinandor remained unconscious throughout the first phase of the process. With her brain chemistry already affected, the narcotic gas that had knocked down the others had a massively increased effect on her.

'Amnesia?'
  'Well, what would you call it?' Fermindor said reasonably.
  The Doctor strode on. They seemed to be getting nowhere. 'I'd call it odd,' he said. The passageway felt endless and, since it seemed to curve slightly to the right as they walked, it looked endless too.
  'There are more things in heaven and earth,' Fermindor said,

'than are dreamt of in your philosophy.'

'Horatio,' the Doctor said absently. '"There are more things in heaven and earth, *Horatio*, than are dreamt of in your philosophy."' He was still trying to find a rational explanation for the fact that Fermindor could remember virtually nothing of how he came to be running around loose, so he missed the significance of the casual blasphemy. When he did realise he said, 'You're not a devout man then, Fe.'

'Neither are you, The,' Fermindor said confidently.

Was this a clumsy attempt at intimacy to boost the Doctor's confidence, or to divert his attention away from other questions? The Doctor smiled at him and he smiled back cheerfully. 'If we get out of this alive,' the Doctor said, 'what do you plan to do?'

'Retire,' Fermindor said without hesitation. 'With the best contract bonuses and personal-injury package I can sue out of them.'

The Doctor nodded knowingly. 'The standard front-line ambition.'

'Every Investigator's dream,' Fermindor agreed.

But not Fermindor's dream as far as the Doctor could remember, so what had happened to the man to make him so different? He slowed his pace slightly and dropped back a little so that he could see if there was anything strange about his walk or general movements that might suggest he was injured or drugged. The Doctor hated it when he knew something was wrong without quite knowing why.

From time to time as they had been walking a pulse of brightness in the floor had overtaken the Doctor and Fermindor and raced on ahead of them, gradually disappearing round the long curve, the glow slowly dissipating until it was completely gone, leaving only the uniform underfoot lighting to illuminate the way. There seemed no predictable pattern or regular timing to these pulses, and now, behind them, there was another sudden increase in the light level. The Doctor glanced back to see the wave of light sweeping along the passageway above the silent pulse. He increased his pace and the light passed and rushed on. The function of the light pulses interested him, and he found himself actually hurrying after this one in the hope of seeing it do something different or change in some way. Ahead of him, Fermindor had speeded up too. That was when the Doctor thought he knew what the pulses were for and he stopped walking. 'Fermindor?' he called. 'Wait a minute.'

The other man stopped and turned. 'What is it?'

'I'm getting tired.' The Doctor yawned as if to emphasise the point. 'How about you?'

'We've got to keep moving.'

'Yes,' the Doctor said. 'I think that's the point.' He glanced back into the darker distances of the passageway behind them. 'And any second now we're going to be encouraged to do just that.'

'What are you talking about?'

'This,' the Doctor said as another pulse of light flowed through the floor.

'Come on, let's go,' Fermindor urged, taking a couple of anxious steps after the departing light.

'Interesting,' the Doctor said. He could feel it himself, the same impulse to move on. There was, it seemed, some frequency within these pulses which interfered directly with the brain's electrical activity. 'Move along, follow me, keep up. That's what it's saying.'

'You're not hearing voices, are you?' Fermindor asked nervously. 'I thought we could help each other but if you're hearing voices we're in real trouble.'

'The next one will be even more intense,' the Doctor said. 'Universal non-verbal movement instructions? All-purpose crowd control? What's it really for, I wonder? It can't just be for us.' The next pulse came and as he had predicted the Doctor found that the need to follow it was much stronger.

'We have to go!' Fermindor almost shouted. He was fidgeting, agitatedly hopping from one foot to the other.

The Doctor hesitated and then said, 'All right.' They immediately set off at a brisk pace. Fermindor relaxed at once and the Doctor was irritated to find that although he knew they were being manipulated he still felt better the faster they walked.

It gave the impression that it was a huge dome-shaped space, but it was impossible to tell for certain how large the chamber was because most of it remained in total darkness. Occasional prickles of energy sparkled and flickered briefly across the vast open plain of a gradually revolving floor on to which, from hundreds, perhaps thousands, of channels, waste materials of all kinds poured continuously. Anyone watching long enough and concentratedly enough might catch a glimpse in the lightning flashes of the slow vortices swirling around the distant centre, each one drawing down a different constituent as the debris was steadily reduced to its basic elements.

At the edge of this colossal recycling machine the TARDIS was turning slowly in a small eddy of its own, enveloped and lit by a strobing blaze of plasma ball-lightning. It stood out from everything else because it was the only thing that was continuously lit and because it was the only thing of any size that remained in one place, showing no sign of collapsing in on itself and falling smaller and smaller as it separated down and down into the basic molecular structures of its usable elements.

The Doctor stood in the glowing-floored gallery to which the light pulses had finally drawn them, and looked down on the fitfully flickering darkness. He assumed the narrow ledge, protected and enclosed by a colourless and diamond-hard moulded plate, was intended as a viewing gallery. It seemed unlikely that it was for tourists, so presumably the idea was that technicians could monitor the processes and make appropriate adjustments, but there were no controls of any kind that he could discover.

'What *is* that?' Fermindor asked, indicating the TARDIS, which was almost directly below them.

'How would I know?' the Doctor said. He peered at the wall, which seemed to be made of the same material as the cell from which Fermindor had released him. He was hoping to find control pads like the one Fermindor had used, but there were none that he could see.

'This doesn't look like a way out to me,' Fermindor said. 'I was hoping there was going to be a way out here. Can *you* see a way out here?'

'Only as recycled molecules. Does being part of a pack-hunting snake or a psychedelic toad appeal to you?'

'Are you sure that thing isn't a way out?' Once again Fermindor drew his attention to the TARDIS. 'There's something very peculiar about it.'

'Like what?' the Doctor asked.

Fermindor hesitated. 'Uh…'

'Yes?' the Doctor pressed.

Before Fermindor could come up with an answer, there was a movement at the entrance to the gallery and Belay staggered in looking dishevelled and out of breath, but otherwise unhurt and robustly healthy. 'I thought nobody else was alive,' he gasped.

'I expect you heard us talking, didn't you?' the Doctor said. 'As you were passing?' He smiled, but the wryness was lost on the other man.

'No,' Belay said shaking his head vigorously. 'I followed the light.'

'How did you escape?' Fermindor asked.

'I don't remember,' Belay said earnestly. 'I woke up.'

'In a heap?' the Doctor suggested, still wondering whether he was he being unnecessarily suspicious.

'And it seemed like a good idea to follow the light,' Belay finished.

The Doctor stared down at the TARDIS. He was beginning to feel outmanoeuvred, as though he had no choice but to go along with the two of them. To go along with the three of them, really, since the runner was in the background of all this. These two seemed open and sincere. They believed what they were saying. It might be naive of him, but he was ready to believe them too.

'What is that?' Belay asked. He was looking at the TARDIS.

In the lightning-sparkled darkness it was true that the TARDIS stood out, vividly. And it was true that the Doctor had been looking directly at the TARDIS. But, coming into all this for the first time, was the TARDIS really what you would look at first? And was that the question you would ask?

'Too quick,' the Doctor said. 'Too obvious.'

'Too many?' the runner's voice suggested.

Looking genuinely alarmed, Belay and Fermindor searched around for the source of the voice.

'Two of them was over-egging the pudding a little,' the Doctor said.

'Over-egging the pudding? Is that in the sacred texts?'

'No.'

Fermindor said, 'Who are you talking to, The?'

'It's your runner,' the Doctor said.

'My runner?' He clearly had no idea what the Doctor was talking about. 'What runner? Where is he?'

The runner's voice said, 'There you are, you see? I delayed things for as long as I could but there still wasn't long enough for a full... briefing.'

'I thought you were deliberately wasting time,' the Doctor remarked.

'You probably noticed you were walking in a circle too, didn't you? It's my experience that people are more inclined to trust something they have had to work for, or in this case walk for. I underestimated how suspicious you are and I gave you too long to think, didn't I? You have some very un-toody-like traits, Thedoctor. You remind me a lot of me.'

Belay had turned on his heel and was leaving the gallery. 'I don't know what's going on here but I want nothing to do with this.'

Fermindor went after him. 'Belay? Where are you going? Come back here. That thing is the way out, you know it is.'

'What makes them think that what appears to be an indestructible box is the way out of here?' the Doctor asked.

'First thing I put in,' the voice said. 'It's always difficult to get the levels in the right order. Particularly when you're having to rush. The directives become distinctly unsubtle. You have no choice but to fall back on to the crudest basic drives. That will be why their approach was so obvious. It's disappointing, but not disastrous.'

The Doctor went back to looking down at the TARDIS. It was safe for the moment. It was too large to move away from the coarse material reduction at the perimeter. If he could find a way to reach it, then he might find that the power being poured at it in a futile attempt to break it down would make getting on board problematical, but there was bound to be a way round that. To his surprise, he saw light suddenly spill from an opening in the chamber wall and two figures stepped into view at the edge of the processing floor. He hadn't noticed before, but there seemed to be another narrow ledge running round the bottom of the chamber slightly above the roiling mass of the recycling. This ledge was obviously not enclosed by a clear protective plate like the gallery was, because pieces of debris had been tossed up on to it. Belay and Fermindor were pushing them back into the churning turbulence as they made their way to the TARDIS.

'What are they doing?' the Doctor asked.

'Following orders,' the voice said.

'To commit suicide?' The Doctor's voice was low and hard.

'In a way.' There was a distinct chuckle in the voice. 'I suppose that *is* what they've been instructed to do.'

'You find it amusing?' the Doctor demanded. He banged on the clear sheet and yelled, 'Belay! Fe! Get away from that!'

'They can't hear you,' the runner said. 'And even if they could they wouldn't pay any attention to you. You can't argue with a basic drive, especially a crude one.'

'Of course you can!' the Doctor raged.

'You really think so?' the voice said. 'What a disappointing life you must have had.'

The Doctor could see in the harsh plasma flashes from the continuing assault on the TARDIS that Belay and Fermindor were approaching the place where it was nudging against the ledge. 'I'll make you a deal,' the Doctor snapped.

'I'm listening.'

'First stop them. Call them back.'

'I can't do that.'

'You're going to let them die?'

'You said it yourself: they're going to be recycled molecules. No perfection here, I'm afraid. Nothing dies. Everything is born again. But first, a small experiment…'

As the Doctor watched, Belay reached towards the TARDIS. The power arced into him and he disintegrated, blowing apart in a heavy cloud of falling droplets. Most of him collapsed into the soup on the floor but where droplets touched the plasma ball they too blew apart.

'That's your idea of an experiment?' the Doctor shouted, furiously.

'Half an experiment,' the runner said. 'Keep watching.'

It was as if Fermindor hadn't seen what had just happened to Belay. He backed away along the ledge a short distance and then he ran forward a few paces and jumped towards the top of the

TARDIS. For a split second he seemed to reach over the searing power of the strobing light, then his legs touched it and he was gone, the cloud falling over the plasma as each droplet blew apart again and again and again.

The Doctor was appalled.

'That must have hurt,' the runner's voice said.

Cold rage left the Doctor momentarily speechless. Finally, shaking his head as if dazed, he muttered, quietly, 'You're a truly perverted individual.'

'Isn't that what I tried to tell you?' the runner said. 'I tried to tell you that. You don't listen, do you? So anyway, now that I've got your full attention, what exactly was this deal you wanted to make with me?'

The Doctor could not make up his mind whether the man was being serious. Could he be stupid as well as insane? He stared down at the unaffected situation far below. The gap in the chamber wall was closing up. The power that battered at the TARDIS continued unabated. He stared round the gallery. How did the runner know exactly what was happening all the time?

'Face to face,' the Doctor said emphatically. 'I only make deals face to face.'

'Are you impressed?' the runner asked.

The Doctor stayed calm in the face of this new turn in the conversation.

'With what?'

'With this. It regularly remakes everything, more or less from scratch. It sterilises as it goes to remove the biological contamination brought in by the subjects.'

'Subjects?' the Doctor asked. 'As in "experimental subjects"?'

'It's a remarkable piece of machinery,' the runner went on, ignoring the question. 'It retrieves all materials falling on the surface, meteorites and the like, and breaks them down, storing the materials for later use.'

157

'That's what happened to the ships,' the Doctor said.

'Yes. Bit of a problem, that. Your own vessel seems to be the only exception.'

'My vessel?'

'Don't be coy, Thedoctor. I saw you come out of it. You and your fighter.'

The Doctor snorted derisively. 'Out of that? Are you serious?'

'I saw you.'

The Doctor thought he heard uncertainty in the voice. 'I don't think so,' he said, scornful and dismissive. 'I'm terribly claustrophobic. I can't imagine getting into that box, let alone travelling in it.'

'How did you get here then?' the voice challenged.

'The same way you did,' the Doctor said. 'And this monstrosity ate the ship so we're just as stranded as you are.'

'No.'

The Doctor stuck his hands in his pockets and strolled towards the entrance to the gallery. 'If you're that convinced,' he said. 'I admit it. It's my ship and I'm giving it to you. Now it's your ship. Where shall we meet to discuss the deal I have for you?'

'Shall I tell you what's happening to it?'

'The deal?'

'The box. It seems to be time-shifting very slightly. Backwards and forwards. Fascinating protective mechanism.'

The Doctor glanced down at the TARDIS. If you knew what to look for there was a tiny slippery shimmer that could be detected on the sharper, more clearly defined edges. If you saw it you might interpret it correctly as the runner had. Insane, then, and homicidal, but not stupid. 'Interesting theory,' he said.

'It's taken a while to find the key to it,' the runner said.

The Doctor grinned mirthlessly. 'In other words you haven't. And you won't. My guess would be that it's randomly phased.'

'I don't care if that's a ship or the box you keep your currency and a change of clothes in – I want that time-shifting device. Do you have any idea of the sort of battle system I could develop out of that?'

'Let me guess,' the Doctor said, strolling out of the gallery. 'The tomorrow-the-world sort.'

'Leela? Are you there?'

It was the Doctor's voice in the darkness. That did not mean it was the Doctor. Mimicking a voice was no great trick. Leela had known warriors who did that to amuse a hunting party at the night's fire. There were even animals and birds that did it to fool their prey.

'Leela, where are you?'

Leela tensed slightly, ready for the change in what was happening and her chance to get free as a result of it. She closed her eyes and held them tight shut for a long moment, then opened them wide in an effort to catch some glimmer through the darkness. There was nothing to be squeezed out of the blackness. She narrowed her eyes now, but kept them open. If light came suddenly it would be blinding. She took a couple of deep breaths. She was ready.

'Leela?'

The Doctor's voice was becoming irritated.

'Leela!'

Abruptly the cell was bright with light and as she had expected she was blinded by it, her vision filled with flashing yellow and behind that, the reflection of the blood-red at the back of her eyes. At the same time she was released from her bonds, and muscle twitches and small spasms swept through her.

'There you are,' the Doctor said.

When she could see more clearly Leela recognised that the room she was being held in was too small for her captor to have hidden in the darkness, so it was just his voice that had been there. The Doctor was standing by a hole in the floor and smiling at her cheerfully. He looked very relaxed and fit. He pointed. 'This is the way out,' he said. 'Shall we go?'

Leela moved quickly towards the hole. There was something missing, but she was not going to waste time on it. She drew her knife and dropped two-footed into the hole.

Out in the passageway she said, 'Where were the ropes?'

'Ropes?' the Doctor asked vaguely.

'I was tied up.'

'Oh that. It was direct interference with the nervous system. Complete override of muscular control.'

'How did you untie me?' Leela said looking up and down the passageway.

'I switched it off. It was an electrostatic charge. Do you understand what that is?'

'No,' Leela said impatiently.

'Do you want me to explain it to you?' he asked.

There was no one else in sight, so Leela sheathed her knife. 'No. Which way do we go now?'

'Go?' The Doctor looked puzzled.

Leela's eyes narrowed slightly. 'The way out. Which way do we have go to get out of here?'

All doubt vanished and the Doctor said positively, 'We need the ship. I think I know where it is.'

It was Leela's turn to be puzzled. 'What ship?'

'Our ship. The ship we came in.'

Leela looked at the Doctor. It was definitely him. She moved closer and stared into his face. Yes it was him, of *course* it was him, but there was something changed about him. He looked much healthier than he did before. His skin was firmer, his eyes were clearer, his ridiculous mop of hair was curlier and shinier and... and he looked younger. Suddenly she thought of the louse and what the Doctor had said about it – '...and apart from what you've done to it there are no signs of damage of any kind. It's perfect' – and she had said that the reason was because it was young.

'What's the matter?' he asked now.

'You do not remember?'

He scowled. 'Of course I remember,' he snapped. 'Remember what?'

'We did not come in a ship. We came in the TARDIS hut.'

The Doctor stopped scowling immediately and beamed with delight. 'We came in the TARDIS hut. That's what I meant. I know where the TARDIS hut is.'

'The TARDIS,' Leela corrected herself yet again, only now she was not as embarrassed about it as she had been. 'I do not know why you have to keep saying it. Is it important? I know it is not a hut. I know it is just the TARDIS.'

'And just the TARDIS is?' the Doctor prompted.

'Time And Relative Dimension In Space,' Leela parroted.

'Time And Relative Dimension In Space,' the Doctor repeated slowly as though he had never heard of it before. 'Time And Relative Dimension In Space. What does that mean, exactly?'

Although she was less sensitive about her lack of knowledge now, the Doctor's teasing was beginning to make Leela angry. 'You do not know?' she said coldly.

He thought for a long moment. 'I don't seem to. No. It means nothing to me.' He smiled brightly. 'I take it you don't know what it means, either. Is that going to be a problem, do you suppose?'

'It has not been up to now,' Leela said. She knew the Doctor's humour escaped her sometimes and she hoped that this was such an occasion.

The passageway they were in was brightly lit from underneath, but Leela noticed that there were no shadows cast by the light, so that it was hard to judge distances properly. It needed extra concentration to get an exact feeling of where you were standing or how you were walking, and it affected the balance slightly if you were not paying attention. None of this seemed to bother the Doctor, who had set out boldly and then paused and waited, calm and smiling, to give her time to catch up. He showed none of his normal impatience and irritation. He was behaving very oddly, even for him, Leela decided, and it was not because he was lost in thought, the way he got sometimes. This was different. *He* was different.

The light that came from behind them and poured under and over and round them took Leela totally by surprise. In one smooth movement she pulled her knife, turned and dropped into a fighting crouch, but there was nothing there except a fat hungry glow blowing past her like a fire burning through grass. She was angry with herself that anything could creep up on her like that, and she was surprised that she felt no heat from the passing flare. There was no one in the passage behind them and nothing to show that the flame had gone through. She turned to watch it roaring silently on, leaving the light steady, unshadowed and unchanged. She found she wanted to follow it and see where it went.

In the distance, the ball of fire blazed and passed out of sight, leaving a strangely familiar figure coming towards them. Leela recognised the physical shape and the stride and the impractical outfit long before she could see the face. Beside her, the Doctor seemed blithely unaware that the Doctor was coming towards them.

'Leela?' the Doctor called as he approached. 'Is that you? More to the point: is that me?'

'Who is that?' the Doctor beside her asked. 'Do you know him?'

'You mean you do not recognise who he is?' she said.

'I don't think so.' He looked down at himself. 'Though he does seem to be wearing the same sort of clothes as I am.'

'He is wearing the same *face* as you are,' Leela said frowning. She could see that they were twins. Could he not see that? And if not, why not?

'He has the same face as I have. Really?' he said. 'That's going to be a problem. I think you'd better kill him. Or give me the knife and I'll do it.'

Leela sheathed the knife. The other Doctor stopped a few paces from them and stood watching them both. 'Uncanny,' he said finally. 'Does he think like me? I wonder. How much of what I know does he know? Not enough, obviously, otherwise why did he bother with me?'

'Are you a ghost?' Leela asked.

'You know better than that,' the other Doctor said. 'There are no ghosts, only the fear of ghosts.'

'What are you, then?'

'I'm the original of him. Are you the original Leela?'

'Give me the knife,' the Doctor beside her said.

'I'd rather you didn't,' the other Doctor said. 'He's probably stronger than I am. He certainly looks a lot healthier.'

'He's dangerous,' the Doctor beside her said. 'Kill him, or let *me* kill him, but don't listen to what he says.'

'But you do not kill, Doctor –' Leela began.

'Where are you going?' the other Doctor asked.

'Don't tell him!' the Doctor beside her hissed.

She still did not like to be told what to do. 'The TARDIS,' she said guardedly.

'The light takes you to it,' the other Doctor said. 'I expect you've felt the urge to follow as it passes.'

Leela was uncomfortable and a little afraid. She did not understand this and she did not know what she was supposed to do next. 'Where are you going?' she asked because she could think of nothing else to say.

The other Doctor smiled. 'I was coming to look for you and to try to find the control room for this complex.'

'You are not worried about the TARDIS?'

'Not as worried as he is.'

She looked at the Doctor beside her. 'The Doctor?'

He shook his head. 'The runner,' he said. 'And *he's* not the Doctor, I am. He's a clone. Well a sort of clone. Actually I think he's less than a clone but technologically he may be rather more impressive.'

Keeping her distance from the other Doctor, Leela stepped away from the Doctor she had been standing beside.

'What are you doing?' he asked. 'We're together. I released you. The electrostatic charge? Don't you remember?'

'She doesn't trust you now,' the other Doctor said.

'I can speak for myself,' Leela said. 'I do not trust you either.'

'That's good,' he said. 'Under the circumstances that's very good indeed, Leela.'

Leela bristled. 'I do not need your good opinion.'

'I don't understand,' the other Doctor went on, 'what the runner expected to get from you that he couldn't get from a copy of me. If he really thinks that I'm physically the key to the TARDIS.'

Behind him Leela saw a sudden burst of flame at the furthest point in the long passageway. The cold fire was returning from wherever it had been to. 'It is coming back,' she said.

The other Doctor glanced over his shoulder. 'That's odd,' he said. 'It's going the wrong way.'

As she watched the burning swell towards them, Leela was momentarily distracted. When she saw the movement at the edge of her vision, she was shocked and unprepared. Despite what she had said, she was not ready to mistrust the Doctor, either Doctor, because they were *both* the Doctor.

She felt the knife snatched out of its sheath and saw the Doctor, who could not be the Doctor after all, lunge at the Doctor who said he was the Doctor and whose not so healthy face showed surprise and dismay. And delay. And he could not dodge away from the knife in time to save himself.

Leela's counter-attack was unthinkingly fast and unblinkingly devastating. She stepped across the front of the lunge and caught the knife hand at the wrist. She pivoted so that he fell over her hip and she twisted the arm and, using the weight of his fall, broke it at the wrist and at the elbow. The knife fell from his nerveless fingers and she snatched it up. She stepped over him, pulled his head back by his hair and put the knife hard against his throat.

'Don't kill him, Leela,' the Doctor said.

'He was going to kill you,' she said coldly. 'Why do you want to protect him?' She was surprised at the icy fury she felt. Killing him was necessary. Killing him would be the completion of her moves. She took a deep shuddering breath and eased the pressure on the knife slightly.

'It's you I want to protect,' the Doctor said.

Leela said, 'I saved your life.'

'That's not why you were going to kill him.'

Leela stood up and sheathed her knife. The injured copy of the Doctor rolled on to his back and looked up at them. 'That hurt,' he said peevishly. 'I don't think you needed to be that violent. I rescued you, Leela. You wouldn't be running around now if it wasn't for me.' He sat up but made no attempt to get to his feet. 'What happens now? I'm in pain here.'

The fire, which had been rolling through the passageway more slowly than before, reached them now and Leela felt it pass this time. There was a flickering ache behind her eyes and a fluttering inside her ears like the wings of an insect beating very slowly. When it had gone she said to the copy of the Doctor, 'Why did you rescue me?'

The Doctor said, 'My guess is he wanted you moving and talking.'

'Is that why?' Leela asked.

'I made it easy for him,' the Doctor said. 'I talk too much. I expect you were sulking, weren't you?'

'No.'

'But you weren't talking?'

'Is that what it was?' Leela asked squatting down beside the copy of the Doctor. All her anger was gone now. The seated figure said nothing. He was sitting, cradling his damaged arm, with his head bent forward so that his chin was resting on his chest. 'Well, is it?' She poked him. Slowly he sagged over on to his side and lay unmoving.

The Doctor bent down and felt for a pulse. 'He's dead,' he said.

'Did I kill him?' Leela asked.

'No,' the Doctor said. 'It was that light, the radiation pulse.'

The Doctor shrugged. 'We're not the same. As I said, he's not a clone. He's a fabrication. A copy. He's more vulnerable to it.'

'I felt the light,' Leela said.

'So did I,' the Doctor said. 'He's a close copy, certainly.'

Leela stood up. 'Most of the time I thought he was you.'

The Doctor nodded thoughtfully. 'And if we talk and answer questions, the copies can be refined. They might even end up thinking like we do.'

The Doctor strode off down the passageway heading back in the direction Leela had come from. 'Come on, then!' he called without pausing or looking back. 'There's no time to waste.'

'Where are we going?' she demanded, loping after him.

'To find that control room,' he said impatiently. 'I've told you that already.'

Chapter Nine

The signal from the distress beacon was picked up by an unmanned ore freighter on its way in from the asteroid cloud and automatically boosted and relayed to the First Planet signal clearing centre. From there, it was routed to emergency assessment, where it was identified as an OIG-registered unit. The signal was then rebooted and relayed to the Second Planet clearing centre, which directed it to the OIG headquarters in Trikaybel City, where the Director himself was eventually informed.

Dikero Drew, known to his subordinates as Skinny-dick, was not pleased. For a slightly built man in early middle age he had a deep voice and a huge capacity for rage. 'Tell me this is not the disaster that I think it is,' he roared at the Deputy Director (Operations).

The DDO was used to being bellowed at; he didn't like it but he was used to it. In a way it was a compliment. There was none of that patronising firster–toody politeness between them. 'I don't know what it is,' he said calmly, 'not yet.' He looked at the magnificent views out across the city from the Director's rooftop office suite. 'I've activated search-and-retrieval. They're powering up a ship even as we speak.'

'I want two ships,' Drew snapped. 'And a backup standing off.'

'One up, two down? Are you serious? It's a minimum-strength patrol. There were only seven of them on the ground to begin with.'

'You heard me!'

Most of the building heard you, he wanted to say, but bit his tongue. 'This could just be a bag-and-tag lift. There could be more ships than there are survivors.'

'We owe our people the best!'

Since it was unlikely that Skinny-dick was developing a social conscience at this late stage, the DDO made a mental note to check out the personal links between the Director and the members of that patrol. Family, sex or money, one or all of them had to be involved there somewhere. He said, 'Have you found a new source of funding that I don't know about, Dikero, because Operations hasn't got the budget for that.'

'I'll cover it from the contingencies fund. Just do as you're told.'

'You are going to personally authorise this?'

'No, *you* are going to personally authorise this. You're the Operations Director after all. You don't want me undermining your position, do you?'

'But you are going to personally authorise the budget in advance of my rush of blood to the head. Right now would be a good time.'

Drew smiled. Not the open, handsome smile that looked so good on the interworld newslink screens, but the small amused smile of the schemer the DDO knew him to be. 'What makes you so suspicious, Feerlenator?' he asked.

'Working for you, Dikero,' the DDO said, smiling back.

The Doctor had reasoned that the complex was circular, so ultimately it would make no real difference which way they walked, but the guide pulses were obviously controlled and whoever was controlling them was putting increasing pressure on them to go the other way. As far as the Doctor was concerned, that meant they were moving in the right direction. He was slightly bothered that there might be a series of these circular complexes all over the planet and that they might be linked together. Without any clear points of navigational reference, he and Leela might wander off line and possibly lose themselves in a never-ending labyrinth of glowing passageways and galleries.

With her unnerving instinct for recognising the Doctor's unspoken doubts and voicing them as thoroughly irritating questions, Leela asked, 'Are you sure this is the right way? We have been walking a long time and nothing seems to have changed.'

'No, I'm not sure,' the Doctor said grimly. 'My feeling is that we have been walking round a circular perimeter.'

'Your feeling?' Leela asked incredulously.

'The centre of which,' he went on, indicating with his left hand the curvature of the circumference, 'is somewhere in there. If we can find a way in we should reach the control areas.'

'You *feel* as though we have been walking in a circle?' Leela said.

'Don't you?'

'It does not mean we have.'

'That's true,' the Doctor said.

'And what makes you think there is a way in?'

'Because there has to be a way out.'

Leela skipped ahead of him and turned and stood in his path. 'That is more like a hope than a reason. If there is no way in, there is no way out, so there has to be a way in.'

The Doctor had already noticed that Leela was showing signs of a more focused physical aggression and now he wondered if the sharpening of her fighting instincts was being matched by an increased intellectual aggression. Was it simply that he had never noticed how formidable she was? Or was it really possible that she was being refined and fashioned into a weapon. Training by any other name... Training taken to its logical conclusion.

'The runner,' he said, 'didn't make any of this. Nobody like him had any hand in this. It's a higher order of technology altogether. The people we've met come from a society that has interstellar space travel but hasn't got an efficient rechargeable power cell. Somebody found this place and it's as alien to them as it is to us.'

'So the runner is like us and he has to be able to come and go,' Leela said nodding. 'A way out, so there is a way in.'

'Exactly.'

The Doctor began walking again and Leela fell in beside him. They had gone only a short distance before Leela shook her head and said, 'No.'

'No?'

'He does not have to come and go through this passageway. If, as you say, everything is in there –' she pointed at what the Doctor hoped was the inner of the two walls – 'The way in and the way out be there as well.'

'Then what is this passageway for?' the Doctor asked, smiling reasonably.

'I was right,' Leela said triumphantly. 'It is more of a hope than a reason.'

They walked on in silence. Ahead of them, the inner wall had begun to change. The opaque, waxy yellow substance was becoming flecked with more and more of the tiny particles of sparkling crystal. Eventually they reached a point where the wall was made up entirely of tiny opalescent crystals and, as they walked on, these gradually coalesced into larger and larger forms until finally there was what appeared to be a single sheet of milky crystal. Then this too changed and became a grey membrane, which seemed to be pulsing and quivering rhythmically like a living thing.

The Doctor reached out to touch it and without the slightest sensation his hand went straight through it up to the wrist. He pulled it out again quickly and was relieved to find that he still had a hand, and that it was undamaged and unmarked in any way. The membrane was similarly unaffected.

Leela watched as the Doctor examined his hand and then looked closely at the quivering skin through which he had pushed it. It was typical of his carelessness, she thought, that he had no idea of the risk until after he had taken it. 'We were both right,' he said.

'Shall we go?'

'Go? Go where?'

He offered Leela his arm and, when she hesitated and frowned her puzzlement, he shrugged and smiled and stepped through the membrane and out of sight.

'Doctor?' Leela shouted at the gently throbbing grey skin. 'Doctor?' When there was no response, she drew her knife and ran the blade down the skin trying to see what was behind it. The greyness closed round the knife and the cut vanished as she made it, leaving no sign of itself and nothing on the blade. She tried again, cutting horizontally, cutting more quickly, cutting more deeply but there was no practical way to make a hole through which to see anything. Leela gave up and, keeping the knife ready, she took a step back and leapt through the membrane.

OIG search-and-retrieval asked for notarised confirmation of the unprecedented 'triple-A' Ops had given the rescue of the pursuit patrol led by Serian Kley. One wag suggested they should have it in triplicate but no one really had the nerve to go that far.

Nothing like it had been authorised since the third asteroid mining disaster had stranded a full shift of forty-three ore-seekers, with only emergency air and power and no way to get back to link up with their base supply ship. All the offworlds organisations – Csat, Dpex, Transorb, as well as OIG – had been drawn in on that one, and nobody paid any attention to the overspends. This was a stand-alone Group shout with no justification that anyone could see, and even with extra funds confirmed by the Deputy Director (Finance), the budget would be stretched to its limit. They were having to buy in the use of at least one orbit-to-ground jump ship, and if it had not been for the killer deal somebody cut on that particular subcontract, it would have been a no-go on the whole armada extravagance.

Of course the essence of search-and-retrieval is speed and by the time everyone had done their part and the ships were assembled, equipped, crewed and holding for the go code, the enterprise had taken on a justification of its own which was no longer questioned. Overreaction? What price do you put on a life, anyway? Wouldn't you want them to do the same for you, or your partner, or your son, or your daughter…?

News organisations that might otherwise have paid closer attention to what was happening in the Out-system Investigation Group were involved in the sudden excitement of an upcoming fight between two of the top contract duellists in either of the colonised worlds. With the toody Bardlenor due to face the firster Gex in an unlimited kill-zone combat to a finish, there was little interest in an attempt by a minor law-enforcement agency to hide its own incompetence behind flashy stunts.

All of this reaction and non-reaction was a reasonable response to Skinny-dick's insistence on sending three ships in response to the distress call. It was reasonable, but it was wrong. Dangerously wrong.

The control area was a high chamber, huge and circular and domed as the Doctor had expected. What he had not particularly expected was a brightly glowing, smaller, transparent dome in the centre of the larger one and within that a virtual-reality representation of himself and Leela in the gallery of the larger dome, looking at themselves in the smaller dome, which contained a virtual representation of himself and Leela in the gallery of the larger dome, looking at themselves in the smaller dome… On and on the images went, down and down. It was seductive to watch them. It was like standing at the edge of a precipice and feeling it tug at you, wanting you to jump, urging you to tip over and fall into it for ever… The Doctor closed his eyes and stepped away, turning his back on the glowing dome. When he opened his eyes again he could see that Leela was still staring deep into the vision created by the feedback loop. Conscious of the knife she was holding and her increasingly aggressive reflexes, he carefully pulled her away from the viewing side of the gallery and turned her towards the entrance side, the side through which they had stepped.

The inside of the grey membrane they had crossed was a soap-bubble kaleidoscope of colour and light and images. The patterns mixed and shifted in a band which stretched from the floor to just above the Doctor's head and ran round the whole of the giant chamber. There were so many images that it seemed as though they must be from all over the planet, but the Doctor quickly realised it could be that they were only from the immediate region. What he was looking at probably related solely to that small area above and below ground, around which they had been chased since they arrived. The images themselves were more than mere representations: they interwove and drifted, connecting to each other as they distorted and remixed bringing a strangely emotional dimension to the overall effect. Present real-time moments mixed with fading glimpses of what had happened already. It occurred to the Doctor that perhaps somewhere in among it there were projections of what would and could be about to happen.

'This must be a bit like how it feels to be inside a brain,' the Doctor said.

Leela woke from her trance and stared at the swimming band. She could see a passing shadow of herself coming into the chamber following the Doctor and, weirdly, she could somehow see what it felt like without needing to remember what it felt like – though she could remember what it felt like as well. And the two spoke to each other, seeing the feeling and remembering the feeling, and they were both stronger because they spoke to each other. The small fear she had felt then when the Doctor disappeared and the anger that had given her were getting narrower and tighter – and made her ready to kill again when it was time to kill again. To do better. To do it…

The Doctor heard Leela gasp, gulping and swallowing air as though sudden cold had taken her breath away. She said, 'It is telling me…'

'Yes?' the Doctor asked, eager for confirmation or contradiction of what he thought he was seeing.

'Killing is what I am. More killing gets better and more… balanced.'

'Fight it, Leela,' the Doctor said in a low voice. 'Don't look when it shows you yourself. There's some kind of a feedback system operating.'

'I think death is balance,' Leela said. 'Perfect balance.' She snorted, and sheathed her knife. 'No, I do not think that. It is not true, is it?'

'No,' the Doctor agreed, 'it's not true.' *Our essence is change. We are movement. Being out of balance is life. Perfect balance. Stasis. That is death. Life yearns for perfection. Death is perfection.* And he wondered which came first to this alien chamber: the runner or the madness. Did he learn that nonsense in here, or did he bring it with him like a virus? And where was he? The Doctor had expected to confront him here, finally, in the flesh.

'Can we get out the same way we got in?' Leela asked, putting her hand on the bright surface of the moving images. A whisper of electrical charges prickled against her skin and she found to her surprise that she could not penetrate the hardness. 'This is a trap,' she said. 'It let us in but it will not let us out again.'

'Don't panic,' the Doctor said reassuringly.

'I was not panicking.' Leela's voice was flat. 'I do not panic.' She was coldly angry. Was this thing still working on her reactions?

'We found the way in,' he said. 'We'll find the way out.'

Leela glared at him. 'If the prey cannot find a way in, it is not a trap.'

She was still pushing against the rigid crystalline structure which was the inside of the membrane. Where her hand touched, an image in the dreaming drift of colour and virtual feeling held its place and resisted the general flow. It eddied and gathered focus as if drawn to the hand. It was a vision of the pine forest where the Doctor had walked in the beginning. Gradually, the detail extended and intensified, and behind Leela in the brightly glowing inner dome the Doctor could see the reality take shape until it was complete and functioning independently of the physical cue.

'Take your hand away from it,' the Doctor said.

Frowning, Leela did as she was told.

'Look.' He nodded at the artificial forest behind her.

She turned and stared. 'It is magic,' she whispered. 'We are lost. We are the playthings of a mightier magician than you.'

'Don't go primitive on me,' the Doctor said, brusquely. 'Ignorance is no excuse for stupidity. There are no magicians. This is a machine. What you see is the work of technology.'

She looked at the forest and then back at the image now drifting away from them round the gallery wall, and then back at the forest again. 'That is out there on the surface, is it not?' she said.

The Doctor moved round the viewing edge staring out across the vista of pine trees. It was perfect in every detail and perfectly lifeless. 'The question is,' the Doctor said, 'did we just make that from scratch or did we call up some sort of surveillance of what was already there?'

'Who called us up?' Leela said.

The Doctor smiled. Now she was thinking again. He was about to congratulate her on it when he remembered how she felt about being patronised. 'I was thinking about that myself,' he said.

'It's possible that we stepped through our own images and that set it off. It's difficult to tell now, of course, because it doesn't all move at a uniform speed.'

'Where does all this come from to begin with?' Leela gestured at the wall. 'And where does it go to?'

The Doctor peered down the length of the gallery to where it curved away behind the central dome and merged into its glow. As far as he could see, when it emerged from the other side of the curve and ran back down an equally dizzying length of gallery to where they were standing, it was the same stream of sights and memories and feelings and combinations of all sorts of strangeness. 'It goes all the way round, I suppose. What goes around comes around. And once it's been started it keeps on going around, and coming around, losing things and gaining things as it does. I wonder if it learns as it goes.'

'How do you stop it?' Leela asked.

'Stop it?'

'If it is a machine you can stop it.'

'A better question is, how do you control it?'

'No, that is not a better question,' Leela said. 'You should stop it if you can. This is an evil thing.'

The Doctor was thinking aloud. 'The runner's been controlling it all very precisely.'

'How do you know?' Leela asked. 'How do you know he has been controlling it? Madmen do not control things.'

The Doctor wandered further down the gallery trying to see some order in the moving pattern. 'How does he pick out what he wants from this mess?'

'Maybe it tells him,' Leela said.

'What did you say?' The Doctor came back to where she was standing with one finger touching the wall.

'I said you should stop it if you can.' Below her finger a tiny swirl of blackness had formed in an otherwise plain white space.

The Doctor shook his head. 'You said maybe it tells him. And that's it.' His voice lowered to a stage whisper. 'Of course, that's it. You have to tell it what you want, and then it tells you how to achieve it. You have to commune with the system.'

'That is not what I meant,' Leela said, never taking her eyes off the swirl as up through its darkness a bipedal obscenity of flaky scales and fangs and patchy fur began to surface.

Leela rejected the biped by circling her finger the opposite way to the turn of the swirl. She said, 'One of the tribal shamans communed with things. Mostly trees and large rocks. He said there were spirits in them.' Another creature came up, eight legs this time and a smooth silvery carapace.

'Its mouth parts are underneath,' the Doctor said quietly, 'and very nasty too, as far as I remember.'

Leela consigned it back to the depths. 'How do I know how to do that, Doctor?'

The Doctor shrugged and shook his head. 'There must be other layers below the immediate surface. Perhaps nothing is ever lost. It just sinks down as it's overlaid by new data. This is infinitely more complex than I first imagined.'

Leela broke the contact with the surface and the swirl drifted away and faded and was gone. 'I did not ask for those monsters and I was not communing,' she said. 'This *machine* chose them.'

'Try thinking herbivores, something harmless and affectionate,' the Doctor suggested.

'You try,' Leela said angrily. 'I am not touching it again.'

The Doctor composed an image in his mind of a calmly grazing chumno, a charming animal he had once come across which was devoted to eating and grooming and loved to be hand-fed and stroked. He chose a blank spot on the wall and put a finger on the surface. Nothing appeared. The blank held its position as other images and textures and distorted visions flowed slowly past, but the blank remained stubbornly empty. He put his whole hand on it and concentrated fiercely. A herd of chumnos wandered over a lush plain in his thoughts but nothing happened to the blank on the wall. He gave up. 'Interesting,' he said. 'Cuddly is not an acceptable part of the repertoire it seems.'

'*It* tells *you*,' Leela said. 'It tells you what it wants you to want. Then it makes you want it.'

'That's what successful training does,' the Doctor said.

'My theory, for what it's worth,' the voice said behind them, 'is that it finds what it's looking for inside you and builds on that.'

The Doctor turned slowly. Leela did not turn but clapped both hands on the wall.

The runner was a handsome young man; younger, the Doctor thought, than his voice had suggested up to now. He had a confident, superior smile, and he was wearing what appeared to be the same uniform fatigues as the investigators who were chasing him. 'But as you say, Thedoctor,' he continued, 'that is what training does.'

In the inner dome something huge and multilegged reared up, roaring and lashing and smashing down trees. The noise was startling as it broke and, before the Doctor could move, Leela whirled round to face it. Pulling her knife as she went, she crossed the gallery and grabbed at the young man. As she reached for him he vanished and reappeared to one side of her. She dropped low and flashed a horizontal slash at the back of his leg with the blade, aiming to hamstring him. He was gone before the move was completed.

'It's no good, Leela!' the Doctor said loudly.

The young man reappeared on the other side of her. 'Magic,' he said chortling.

Leela stood up and sheathed the knife. In the inner dome the monster subsided and began to bury itself in the soil.

'Where are you?' the Doctor asked. 'Where are you projecting this hologram from?'

The man smiled smugly and ignored the question. He looked instead at Leela with open admiration. 'That was quick. It really does tune to you. It hasn't responded to anything that fast before. You're easily the best I've come up with. You have simplified my task enormously. I'm very pleased with you.'

Leela moved to stand beside the Doctor. She stared, eyes narrowed, at the image. The Doctor wondered if the young man realised how murderously angry the object of his admiration was. He didn't seem to, because he did not react to her expression. In fact, the Doctor realised the way he looked at her was arrogantly insulting. It was the open admiration a hunter might show for the perfect companion animal.

'Will you tell me at least what your name is?' the Doctor asked politely.

The man considered for a moment and then said, 'I don't suppose it will matter, Thedoctor. You're a clever toody, but not clever enough. My name is Monly. Assistant Chief Investigator Fosten Monly.'

The three ships got the priority go code for the inner-system jump as quickly as the normal single search-and-retrieval vessel would have done, even though three at once put a large and costly hole in the routine traffic patterns.

The navigation co-ordinator on Lead One was surprised to find that the go code for the inter-system jump was already contained and cleared within the first code for what amounted to a double jump. He recognised that somebody had to have pulled some serious strings and spread prime currency around to get that sort of clearance for this sort of mission. The navigation co-ordinator had been in OIG long enough to know that knowledge might not be strength but lack of it was definitely weakness, so he passed the information on to the captain of Lead One. It had to be useful to know that there were wheels within wheels on this job. He was disappointed by the captain's reaction, or rather his lack of it, but if he was honest it was no more than he expected from a toody. They did tend to be a bit slower to see the implications of things. Basically they lacked imagination.

Tragically, the navigation co-ordinator was killed soon afterwards in a freak accident. Apparently the pseudo-grav kicked in between jumps and he broke his neck. The captain was obliged to replace him by promoting a less experienced toody officer on a full mission contract credit.

'I thought you'd been eaten by lizards. In fact –' the Doctor pointed at the constantly moving images on the wall – 'it'll be in here somewhere, won't it? You being ripped to pieces.'

'That's what you were supposed to think,' Monly gloated.

The Doctor nodded. 'When did you substitute the copy of yourself? The copy that was set up to be lizard bait.'

'Does it matter? When a team is as poorly led and shambolic as that one and you've made yourself as unpopular with your leader as I had, there are plenty of opportunities to duck out of sight.'

'But you are the runner?'

'There never was a runner,' Monly said. 'Not as such.'

'No toody weapons technologist.'

Monly smirked. 'Oh yes. Of course there's a toody weapons technologist. That's me. I am a toody and I am a weapons technologist. I'm just not a runner, that's all.'

'What was the patrol for?'

'To catch me, obviously. Come on The, use your head. You're letting the side down.'

The Doctor took a step closer to the image. He peered theatrically at it and then shook his head dismissively. 'I don't know. Perhaps it's just a distortion of the projector,' he said to Leela. 'What do you think?'

'What are you asking her for?' Monly sniggered. 'I don't know where you found her, Thedoctor, but let's not pretend it was at an institute for higher learning.'

'I see,' the Doctor said. 'So you regard Leela as what?'

'A gifted fighter, but she's taken a few blows to the head along the way, yes? Or was she always one of the feeble-minded, ones?'

'Feeble-minded ones?' Leela murmured, smiling a small tight smile.

'I don't think your machine would be interested in the feeble-minded would it?' the Doctor asked.

'Why not?' Leela challenged. 'It is interested in him.'

Monly grinned. 'Not that I care, but what do you imagine is just a distortion of the projector?'

'As far as I can see you're not a toody,' the Doctor said, his voice ringing and full. 'You're a firster. You *are* a firster, aren't you? I mean, why bother with the pretence? What possible difference does it make to anything?'

Monly looked surprised and slightly shocked. 'You can ask me that?'

'I'm not trying to switch planets,' the Doctor said using the phrase he had heard Rinandor use. 'Are you saying I should be ashamed to be a toody?'

'No. Of course not.' He was outraged.

Looking. Always looking. Look for the opening. Look for your opponent's fear. If you cannot find fear look for desire. Both are weaknesses that can be used against them.

Leela saw the weakness the Doctor had been probing for. 'You are a firster,' she mocked and, remembering what Rinandor had said to her in the forest, she added for good measure, 'You have the name, you have the frame and you sound the same.'

'I'm a toody.' There was no smirking now. This was a challenge to his identity.

'I do not think so,' she sneered.

'You're not suggesting that you're doing all this for us toodies are you,' the Doctor said, frowning. 'You can't be that self-deluding. How many of us have you killed so far?'

'Who cares about that?' Leela was smirking now. 'He was not deluding himself. He was deluding stupid toodies. It is not difficult for a firster to do, Thedoctor.'

Monly's face twisted with anger. Abruptly the projection disappeared. The Doctor leaned close to Leela and muttered, 'I think you were right about the trap. He wouldn't have been so forthcoming if he thought we were able to get out of here.'

'What do you think he will do now?' Leela whispered.

'Make a mistake if he's angry enough. Be ready to move.'

Leela did not bother to acknowledge the pointless advice. Her silent glare spoke for her.

The Doctor smiled to himself. If they got out of this in one piece he must give her some advice about tact and diplomacy. It was something he knew he himself had always had a natural talent for. He stuck his hands in his pockets and made a show of wandering slowly away, stopping occasionally to look at the wall like some casual visitor to an art gallery. After a moment or two he forgot that it was a charade and lost himself in the wonder of what he was seeing. He was about to put his hand on an intriguing vision when Leela appeared beside him.

'It did not work,' she muttered.

'Patience,' the Doctor said. 'This machine is reactive. It takes time to react.'

'Doctor, what is Lentic?'

'Lentic? Where did you hear that name?'

'I think it was in the machine. What does it mean?'

Directly in front of them the wall blazed with sudden light. Involuntarily the Doctor took a step backwards and found Leela was already there, already in the half-crouch of her fighting stance. Out of the light four identical figures stepped forward and fanned out in front of them. They all had long dark hair and bright brown eyes. They were all dressed in short tunics of nondescript animal skins and crude calf-length moccasins, and they were all armed with razor-sharp hunting knives. They all dropped into identical half-crouched fighting stances.

All of them were Leela.

Feerlenator was tired. That was not a good sign, he knew. There was a time when he had enjoyed the politicking. There had been real satisfaction in the climb up the corporate ladder of the OIG; move and countermove had felt like a contest for grown-ups played for pride and other worthwhile prizes. Recently, though, the game had taken on a new edge. It was as if the rules had changed, the prizes had changed, and everything had got more dangerous suddenly and nobody had told him why. He gestured the willowy young man to the chair on the other side of the desk and said, 'You've double checked?' He was mostly tired of trying to keep ahead of the Director. On more than one occasion he had suspected that the man was clinically insane, and that to stay in the job of deputy director he had to be crazy too. 'Every possible connection from every possible angle?'

'Yes sir,' Frith said, sitting down. 'I've checked everything.'

'And Skinny-dick is not related to, bedding, or in business with any member of that team? We're quite sure?'

'There are no links of any kind between Director Drew and any member of the Serian Kley patrol.' His confidential assistant, Sol Frith, was a smart young firster of impeccable breeding. He was probably a bit too fastidious for crap-scuffling and snooping, Feerlenator knew, but he was the only person on his staff that Feerlenator trusted.

'He's up to something, Sol,' he said. 'And we're missing it. Let's hope it's not too important.'

'Too important?'

'Life-threatening?'

Frith looked dubious. 'Perhaps he means what he says about our people deserving our best endeavours.'

Feerlenator snorted. 'Dikero Drew has never meant anything he has ever said and that includes hello and goodbye.'

'Goes with the job, surely, doesn't it? The higher up the ladder you get the more hypocritical you have to become.' He grimaced, realising what he had just said to the second-ranking officer in the OIG. 'Did I say that?'

'Relax, Sol. We both know how the game is played. My point is that as far as he's concerned the definition of our people extends as far as Dikero Drew and no further.'

'You don't like him much, do you?'

'No,' Feerlenator said. Oddly, it had not occurred to him until he said it how much he actually hated the Director. 'I suppose I don't.' He smiled and rubbed his eyes. 'Maybe it's a toody reaction.'

'I doubt that.'

'I hope I'm not prejudiced.'

'For what it's worth I feel the same way about him,' Frith said. 'Do you want me to go on digging?'

For some obscure reason, Feerlenator felt that he had let Frith go too far. He was slightly offended by the young man's familiarity. No, it was by the young *firster's* familiarity. He would never be free of this feeling of resentment, he thought. It *was* prejudice. He hated Drew for being a firster as much as for being a selfish, arrogant, lying, craphead firster. 'No, leave it, Sol,' he said. 'Sooner or later he'll show his hand and we'll find out what's going on.'

Frith smiled. He was relieved. He had a genuine affection for his boss. One day he hoped to be able to take him into his confidence. In the meantime, he didn't want to arrest him unless he had absolutely no choice.

* * *

Leela had seen the copy of the Doctor and he had explained it to her, so why should she find these copies of herself so frightening? She kept her head high and her back straight as she walked. She was determined not to let them see how frightened she was, though since they were her perhaps they already knew. She was angry with herself that she had let one of them take her knife. She was angry with the Doctor for not letting her fight them. But most of all she was frightened. 'Do you know how the door worked?' she said to the Doctor's back.

'Not yet,' he said. He glanced over his shoulder at her. 'But that wasn't the control centre.'

'What was it, then?'

'Be quiet,' the Leela beside her said flatly. 'You are not allowed to talk.'

Leela thought it might be because there were four of them. She could see herself from different sides at the same time. Was that how she moved? It must be. Did she look like that? She must do. It was not working the way a reflection worked. It was working the way madness worked. They were not her. She was not them.

'It was a sort of processing centre. The way we were using it was crude. I think we might even have been interfering with the system. Like an infection. There has to be a more refined way.'

'Communing.'

'Exactly.'

'You were told to be quiet,' the Leela on the other side of her said.

'Talking is not allowed,' the Leela beside the Doctor said.

'Bossy lot, aren't you?' the Doctor said cheerfully.

'Is that how I sound?' Leela asked.

'Absolutely,' the Doctor said and flashed her a grin over his shoulder. 'I have tried to tell you but you simply didn't listen. Now you know what I have been putting up with.' He glanced back again and beamed. 'I'm sure you must be as impressed with my patience as I am.'

Leela knew he was trying to make her feel better, but she would have preferred it if he had been more serious. 'How do you know which one is me?' she asked.

'You're the one without the knife.'

'I am serious, Doctor.'

Abruptly the Leelas on either side of her took hold of Leela by the arms and, still hustling her along, each of them placed a knife against her neck with the points pressed under the angle of her jaw. The Leelas flanking the Doctor did the same to him. 'This really isn't necessary, you know,' the Doctor said. 'We're not going to run away.'

'You are not going to talk either,' one of the Leelas said flatly, pushing the knife point into his flesh so that it drew blood.

When the Doctor and Leela had walked in silence for a while the Leela copies relaxed their holds and their knives and the Doctor was able to extract a large white handkerchief from his coat pocket and dab at the cut on his neck. Ahead of them the lighting seemed to have failed so that it looked as though the passageway they were following ended in a dark blank. The Leela copies did not slow their pace so the Doctor and Leela had no choice but to hurry towards whatever the blankness was.

As they approached it Leela could still see nothing in the darkness. It was like the total dark of the cell she had been held in. Was that it? Were they to be put back in the cells? If they were then she would have to fight, whatever the Doctor said. In that cell she was dead. She was not going back there. She was a warrior. Warriors did not die in lightless cells.

The Doctor hoped that Leela would realise that what they were seeing was the same sort of coherent light effect that the runner, or Monly or whoever he was, had used on them before. Would she realise it was just another nervous-system illusion he was using the machine to generate? Always assuming he was using it and not the other way round. The more the Doctor saw of this machine, the more convinced he became that it was far beyond the technical competence of the people who were presently playing around with it. It was as if someone had stumbled over a stardrive and was using it to cut metal for a prototype internal-combustion engine. As they reached the edge of the blankness he said, 'It's just a trick door, Leela. Smoke and mirrors. Don't panic.' Then he stepped into it.

The two Leela copies who had been beside the Doctor stepped back and remained waiting on the threshold.

'I do not panic,' Leela said automatically and she was immediately propelled forward by the two Leela copies escorting her. She stumbled towards the dark but, as she came level with the Doctor's escorts, she suddenly regained her balance, grabbed one of them by the knife hand and swung her towards the other one. Once she got the Leela copy moving Leela pivoted hard and tripped her so that her knife arm was extended in a clumsy lunge. When she saw the knife thrust, the other Leela copy reacted instinctively, ducking to one side and aiming a murderous counterblow at the unprotected upper midriff of her attacker. The blow was an instant kill and, as the knife dropped from the lifeless hand, Leela caught it deftly and stepped into the darkness after the Doctor.

The dark had been momentary, like a brief loss of consciousness, except that there was no way to tell how brief it actually was. The Doctor stood in the bright centre of the perfectly circular domed chamber, which was perhaps a quarter of the size of the one he had just come from. It was huge even so, and he seemed to be standing at the lowest place in a shallow bowl-shaped pit. This time there was no central transparent dome, and instead of the band of moving images and sensations, a continuous series of semicircular alcoves stretched around the outer wall. In these alcoves, the Doctor could see what appeared to be separate subjects from the other chamber steadily unfolding, elaborating themselves and intensifying but with none of the dreamlike parallel drift and intermixing.

He turned slowly, straining to catch a glimpse of what individual alcoves were displaying. In some there were vistas of jungle and forest and desert, lifeless and unmoving as though frozen in time. In some there was nothing, and it was clear from their blankness that the alcoves themselves were shaped from the ubiquitous waxy material, flecked with its intricate patterns of minutely sparkling crystals. Isolated monstrous creatures, some in frozen motion and others twitching and flexing, apparently in the process of being created, featured in many of the dark booths. The Doctor was sure that, somewhere in this array of focus points, Leela was still being used as the basis of a development programme. It seemed likely, too, that among all these alcoves there were the control links that allowed for the manipulation of captives and which must drive the duplication processes. If he could find the right alcove or perhaps activate one of the blank ones he might be able to release what remained of the team of investigators. That was not why he had been brought here, of course. He was here because he and Leela had found a way to insult this maniac and force him into making a mistake. Was this a mistake? And where was Leela? Maybe she had resisted stepping into the void. He wouldn't have blamed her. She had shown remarkable resilience up to now but there must come a time when there would be too much pressure on her sense of reality for her to remain rational.

'Where is Leela?' he asked aloud. When there was no reply, he said, 'So you're still skulking in the shadows then. Typical firster behaviour in my experience.'

'Don't insult my intelligence, The,' Monly said from one of the alcoves the Doctor had not yet reached in his slow turn. 'I hate people to do that. It depresses me.'

'It wasn't deliberate, I assure you,' the Doctor said, peering at where he thought the voice was coming from.

'There you go again. Of course it was deliberate. You wanted me to react so you could see where I was.'

The Doctor finally located him. He was standing on the edge of an alcove that seemed to be active but was filled with thick darkness. 'There you are,' the Doctor said smiling.

'No,' said Monly, 'there *you were*, and there Leela still is.'

'May I come and see?' the Doctor asked politely.

'Why do you ask me?'

'Now you're insulting my intelligence.'

'Yes,' Monly said. 'You may come and see.'

The Doctor waited unmoving, partly because trusting Monly would be absurd and partly because flattering him might be a useful stratagem. 'Now?' he asked after a little while.

'What are you waiting for?'

'I'm a little unsure of myself,' the Doctor said, trying to sound suitably timid. 'You might have it in mind to punish me. To teach me a lesson...' He hesitated, wondering how far to take the grovelling but then added, 'For being disrespectful.'

Monly had come away from the alcove. He gestured at the Doctor to come to him. 'You needn't be afraid,' he said. 'You may come here and see.'

The young man's tone was magnanimous and his smile was a smug pantomime of reassuring warmth, and for the first time the Doctor understood completely Leela's aggressive reaction to feeling patronised. The brightness he had been standing in now dimmed slightly, confirming that his caution was probably justified. If he had tried to move immediately, there was a good chance he would have been given some sort of unpleasant shock to the nervous system. It could still happen, he realised, so he moved carefully out of the central pit and walked slowly up the slight slope to where Monly was standing.

'I told you you needn't be afraid,' Monly said impatiently. 'I'm a man of my word.'

The Doctor said, 'I find all this unnerving. It's hard to trust what you can't understand.'

'I understand it,' Monly said. 'You can trust me.'

The Doctor smiled and nodded. 'Where is Leela, did you say?'

Monly stepped aside to let the Doctor get a clear view of the alcove. The darkness was more than an absence of light: it looked like a physical presence, and the whole alcove was filled with it up to the open front, where it ended in a precisely defined and slightly flattened curve of black. The Doctor, making a show of nervous helplessness, said, 'I don't see anything.'

Monly smirked. 'That's where she is.'

The Doctor had a rough idea what you had to do to get these alcoves to work but until he knew what had happened to Leela it was important that this madman should not feel threatened in any way, so he shrugged uncertainly and took a tentative step closer to the dark. He hesitated and then, as if too frightened to go the whole way in, stopped and leaned forward, putting only his face through into the effect.

He found he was at once inside and outside so that what he saw was both real and an illusion. By stepping further in he reasoned he could become fully immersed but he was unsure whether this would mean losing direct contact with the way out of the darkness, and this did not seem like a sensible time to experiment. Directly in front of him, Leela was walking in the dark, unaware that she could see nothing and was going nowhere. In a bizarre reversal of physical reality, what he could see of himself was less substantial than she was. He reached out a transparent arm, took hold of her wrist and pulled her gently in the direction of the alcove edge where he was standing. It was clear that since he did not share her reality she could neither see him nor hear him. 'Listen to me,' he whispered, 'and remember this is your idea. When you find yourself in the light sit down. Do not move. Do not panic.' He pulled her across the threshold, and stepped back with empty hands held out in front of him, as though he was surprised to find them empty.

He had expected it, but he was still relieved that when he turned round Leela was standing in the bright centre of the chamber where he had first stood. She said, 'I do not panic,' and then she sat down cross-legged on the floor.

Monly was annoyed and suspicious. 'How did you do that?' he demanded.

The Doctor shook his head in mild amazement. 'I don't know,' he said. 'I saw her there and I tried to pull her out. Did I pull her out? Is that what I did?'

'What you did was ruin a perfectly good experiment.'

'An experiment?' the Doctor asked, interested and forgetting for the moment his timid disguise, which was beginning to bore him, anyway. 'What hypothesis were you testing?'

'That the blank zone I can create is infinite.'

'And you would test that how, exactly?'

'There are a number of ways. But I thought the most fun would be to see if she would walk herself to death in there.' He sniggered and walked closer to where Leela was sitting in the brightness and stared at her.

It was a timely reminder, the Doctor thought, of how easy it was to forget that this was not simply an irritating young man but a dangerously unpleasant psychopath. 'In that case,' he said, hoping it was not too late to get back into character, 'I'm glad I pulled her out. She's a valuable fighter. There are people who are interested in buying shares in her contract.'

'You mean Belay and his firster friends?' Monly said. 'Forget about it, The. Their time is over. He and all his kind are going to be… disadvantaged, shall we say?'

'What are his kind?' Leela asked loudly. She was standing now and glaring at Monly.

'Firsters,' he said coldly.

'And disadvantaged?' she demanded. 'Does that mean killed?'

'If necessary,' he said. 'We need to simplify things. What we need is a war. Wars simplify everything.'

'That's why you were sent here?' the Doctor said. 'To start a war?'

'To provide the weapons for a like-minded group of patriots.'

Leela toyed with her knife. She looked ready to leap at his throat. 'You mean there are others as mad as you are?'

'You'd be surprised how many.'

'Would I?' she said and threw the knife at him.

The move was so sudden and so blurringly quick that Monly had no time to react to it. Only the force field that surrounded Leela prevented the throw from killing him. When the knife struck it there was a vivid spark, which was immediately swallowed up in a black flash like a thunder storm recorded in negative. Static shimmered and sparkled over the knife as it lay at Leela's feet, and she made no attempt to pick it up again or to move from the spot where she was standing.

When Monly recovered from the shock he was furious at being made to feel vulnerable. 'Time for you to get back to my experiment, I think,' he raged.

The Doctor stood between him and the alcove. 'It was a fighter's natural response,' he said reasonably, holding up his hands in a placatory gesture. He did not want to take a chance on overpowering Monly without finding out what he had done to Kley and the others, and what little surprises he might have managed to embed in these systems. He could have rigged remote activation, fail-safes, booby traps, all kinds of nastiness. Monly was the type who would derive immense satisfaction from devising a hideous aftermath to his own defeat and capture. The Doctor had faced warped individuals like him so many times before, creatures lost in their fantasies of death and destruction.

'Get out of my way,' Monly said with enough casual confidence to convince the Doctor that he had indeed got unrevealed resources at his disposal.

The Doctor stood his ground. 'What satisfaction will you get?' he argued. If it came to it, in the end, he would have no choice but to risk stopping him physically. He could not let Leela be pushed back into the darkness.

'I shall expand the sum of all knowledge,' Monly said without a trace of irony.

It struck the Doctor that it was not just Leela's sense of reality that had been under severe pressure. How often had Monly visited this alien nightmare? If he was not mad to begin with but just slightly unbalanced, this installation would build a feedback loop in his brain chemistry to intensify whatever it could find that was destructive in him. 'Do you have time for that?' the Doctor asked.

'I will have when you give me the secret of the device that protects your blue box.' Monly stepped very close to him and stared into his face. 'A face-to-face deal, isn't that what you said?'

The Doctor returned his stare. 'Why is it so important to you?' he asked softly.

'Do you still deny it's your ship?'

There was an edge about the voice, a poorly disguised boredom. The Doctor realised Monly was asking a question to which he already knew the answer. Leela must have told the copy Doctor. 'I thought I'd already admitted it.'

'No.'

'Yes.'

'You didn't mean it.'

'Of course I meant it. The TARDIS is a vehicle.'

'TARDIS? Strange name. An acronym, perhaps, for –' he spoke the words with a flourish – '"Time And Relative –"'

'You knew,' the Doctor said.

'Of course I knew. I know everything about you. You have no secrets from me, Thedoctor. Which laboratory developed it, exactly?'

From the centre of the chamber Leela laughed mockingly. 'You are an ignorant fool. You know nothing about the Doctor and me.'

'Shut her up, Thedoctor. Or I will, and this negotiation will be at an end.'

'Be quiet Leela. Leave this to me.'

'We are not even from your planet, Monly!' Leela shouted angrily.

There was a silence. This was not exactly how the Doctor had planned to allay Monly's suspicions and find a way to get himself and Leela out of this mess in one piece.

'You think I don't know that?' Monly said contemptuously. 'I know you're not from my planet. I *know* that. But coming from First Planet is not going to be the advantage it once was. In fact it's going to be a distinct problem for some of you people.'

'That is not what I meant. Tell him who we are, Doctor.' Leela prowled round the inner edge of the brightly lit pit. She had worked out the significance of the light, and was making no attempt to cross the boundary at any point.

'You've said enough, Leela,' the Doctor warned.

'You are not afraid of him, are you?'

'Yes.'

'Well I am not! Get me out of here and I will deal with him for you.' For a moment it looked as though she was going to bang her fist against the force field.

'As you said,' the Doctor murmured to Monly, 'she has taken a few blows to the head. She's still a very effective fighter though. Very profitable.' The Doctor was aware that his grasp of how such things were organised back in the system where these people came from remained sketchy at best, but he knew he had to take the opportunity to elaborate on his story. 'I bought the TARDIS with the proceeds from a couple of her bouts.'

'Bouts?'

'Duels?' the Doctor suggested, remembering too late the advice of a successful politician he had once met: Keep the lies simple unless you've got a good memory and a high staff turnover. 'Fights,' he added.

Monly nodded. 'Private contracts, you mean.'

'That's right,' the Doctor agreed.

'Disgraceful,' Monly remarked disgustedly. 'Aren't you ashamed to be involved in such perversions?'

The Doctor was ready to laugh but he restrained himself. 'What is it you're doing here?' he asked. 'Remind me about that again?'

'It's not the same.'

'It never is.'

'What I'm doing is not for personal profit.'

'And that justifies hijacking my fighter, does it? Perversions indeed.' The Doctor was beginning to warm to his role as the outraged agent-manager of a promising contract duellist. He seemed to be making Monly slightly uncomfortable. 'You are planning to use her to kill people, aren't you? She is the basis of your new weapon, isn't she?'

Monly was definitely embarrassed now. 'I was hoping to make some useful developments in non-organic weapons,' he said.

'Weapons you're not allowed to develop back...' The Doctor was not sure whether 'home' was an appropriate word so he gestured vaguely over his shoulder.

'I had a cheap recharging handgun ready for testing,' Monly said. 'It was a beautiful device. Everybody could have had one.' He appeared to have forgotten everything else as he began to remember and rehearse his grievances. 'Imagine what that would have meant for the freedom of the individual.'

'Imagine that,' the Doctor said. 'What a sensible idea.'

Monly was already preoccupied enough for the Doctor to risk a look away in the direction of the darkness. The control mechanism that would free Leela from the force field had to be in there somewhere. Monly was standing there when he'd been released. Unless…

'You know what happened?' Monly demanded.

'They banned it?' Unless Monly had it on him.

'They banned *me*. I had the design for a bomb which was small and cheap and powerful.'

'And illegal,' the Doctor said. There was one other possibility…

'And illegal,' Monly agreed. 'I was working on a whole new approach to killing. A self-replicating protein fragment. Infectious but only under certain conditions. You can pick who dies and how long it takes them. They said the concept was immoral.'

'I have always been impressed by innovation,' the Doctor said peering round the gallery of alcoves again. Was that what he was looking for?

'You think that's impressive,' Monly was babbling, 'I have a device that uses radiation to addle brains. It can destroy minds.'

'And that was banned too, as far as you remember,' the Doctor said.

'What do you mean?'

The Doctor beamed at him. 'I mean it was probably a mistake to have tested it on yourself,' he said, and then, turning his attention to further along the gallery, he added loudly, 'You can come out now.'

An identical Monly stepped out of one of the alcoves. He was smiling broadly. 'If you want something done properly you really have to do it yourself, don't you?' he said. 'Very well.' He waved dismissively at the scowling Monly standing beside the Doctor. 'You can go.'

The Doctor shook his head. 'No. I hate people to do that. It depresses me.'

'Insult your intelligence?' Monly asked.

'Use the same trick twice.'

'There's another one, Doctor,' Leela said standing close to the edge of the bright force field and looking at yet another alcove.

'I thought there might be,' the Doctor said. His voice became low and grave. 'And it isn't Monly, is it?'

Chapter Ten

It had been a happy coincidence for the extravagant OIG search-and-retrieval operation that Bardlenor had chosen the unlimited-kill zone. Audiences on both planets were thrilled to see a death struggle, the stalking and countering of two fighters as they manoeuvred to kill each other, develop in the dull surroundings of normal everyday life. Duellists themselves disliked such contests because of the haphazard nature of stores and streets and offices, which took away whatever advantage their particular combat skills gave them. In addition to that, the instant death penalty for injuring a bystander was an unwelcome and dangerous distraction. Under the circumstances, no one was surprised that this type of fight was seen as rarely as a toody's ribcage. The convention was that, offered the choice, you opted for the ground that favoured you and paid a contract premium to your opponent to make up for the advantage. The system was obviously biased towards the rich and successful, since they could always bid the so-called death price high enough to ensure the fight was on their chosen ground.

In this case Bardlenor and Gex were equally rich and successful and as it happened they were both equally accomplished, multi-skilled, close-combat-and-pistol men, so an arena fight was the natural choice for them both. As it was a foregone conclusion, Gex indulged his reputation for firster charm and exquisite good manners and very sportingly and very publicly offered the formal choice of venue to his toody challenger. When Bardlenor specified the unlimited-kill zone everyone was shocked, especially Gex. The early press speculation was that Bardlenor did it 'to wipe the superior smirk off that skinny face'. Some reports had it that he said 'wipe the skinny smirk off that firster face', but people knew not to take the news reports at face value. When he went on to choose First Planet, however, and then to pick the city of Safedown there seemed little doubt that toody–firster resentments lay behind his decision.

What had been a contract challenge between two top professionals took on a new significance. As the camera teams set up well in advance so that they could practise for every conceivable fight variation, and the press besieged the duellists and their agents, there were ugly tensions underneath the general air of excitement. It was fortunate that the planets were run by the same authority and that there were no political or military structures separating them, because handled badly this combat could lead to serious unrest between First Planet and Second Planet – between firster and toody.

'I have no feeling either way, Director,' Frith said cautiously. 'I've never really been interested in contract duellists.' He had paused on his way out of the absurdly grandiose office and was standing at the door waiting to see what the obnoxious little man really had on his mind.

'Not a fight fan, then,' Drew boomed from behind his huge desk.

'No, sir.'

'Why doesn't that surprise me, Frith?'

Because you've read my file? Frith thought, but said, 'I don't know, sir.'

'A bit crude for your taste, I imagine.' Drew managed to make it sound as though Frith was lacking something important in his make-up.

Frith shrugged a small elegant shrug. 'Possibly.'

'I am a fan,' Drew said.

'Really, sir?' He smiled politely. Really, you little psycho, you don't imagine I don't know that and that I don't know about your links with Bardlenor.

'In fact I may decide to go to Safedown and see the fight first hand. If I do your boss will be standing in for me. He's not a fight fan either, it seems.'

Frith kept the smile in place. 'It's not something we've discussed.'

'You might find it difficult not to take sides,' Drew said. 'You and your boss.' And he dismissed him with a wave of his hand.

Frith left the office aware that Dikero Drew, the charismatic Director of the OIG, still didn't know whom he could trust. Did that make him leader or led in the conspiracy to overthrow the domination of the First Planet?

The two Monlys stood side by side and listened to the criticisms with swivel-eyed confusion and disbelief.

'I had to construct him out of what I could find in the main memory so I thought he did quite well. What do you think?'

The Doctor shrugged. 'I'm hardly an expert.'

Sozerdor strolled in a figure of eight round the two Monlys admiring them. 'He got a bit carried away with the mad routine. He wasn't entirely consistent. But then who is? And this place will drive you crazy if you're not paying attention. It could have been my fault though. Planting the idea that he was a toody weapons technologist was pushing him a bit far I think.' He poked each Monly in the chest with a chubby finger. 'You had no idea what you were talking about, did you?'

'*You* are the toody technologist, I take it,' the Doctor said. 'Or is there another one running about somewhere?'

'I am all the things he told you he was. Confusing, isn't it?'

'But he *was* your partner?' the Doctor suggested.

'Minder. He was supposed to be keeping an eye on me.'

'And he really was killed.'

'Right.'

'Whereas you really weren't.'

'Right again.' He put his arm round the Doctor's shoulders and squeezed. 'Tell me the truth now. I value your opinion more than you know. Were you impressed? Did you believe in him?' He leaned close to the Doctor's face. 'Were you fooled?' He was like a gleeful child. 'At least to begin with?'

'Why shouldn't I be? I didn't know him.'

'You saw his weak spot. You knew he wasn't a toody.'

'He knew he wasn't a toody. That's why it was a weak spot.'

Sozerdor said, looking the Doctor in the eye, 'I've watched you whenever I've had the opportunity and I have to tell you –'

'Doctor?' Leela interrupted from where she was standing in the middle of the central pit.

'Be quiet,' Sozerdor said firmly. 'We're talking. This is important. This is where I explain it all to him.'

Leela ignored him and said, 'The light cage is getting smaller.'

'Force field,' Sozerdor said. 'It's called a force field. She is a bit on the primitive side, isn't she? Where did you say you found her?'

The Doctor moved down to the edge of the shallow pit. The circular field no longer filled the area. The brightness remained at the same intensity, but it was shrinking quite perceptibly and continuously inward and downward. Already there was barely enough room for Leela to stand up.

'Another of your experiments?' he asked.

'That's uncalled for,' Sozerdor said sadly. 'That was Monly, not me.' His chubby middle-aged face broke into a sly, conspiratorial grin. 'I know what happens. Squelch. *Scream*, squelch, if you want to be entirely accurate. You remember your experience in the cell? This is a little more shocking but basically it's the same. From the spectator's point of view altogether more satisfying. Electrifying, you might say.'

'Controlled the same way?' the Doctor asked casually.

Sozerdor's face took on an expression of mock surprise. 'You wouldn't be trying to trick me into telling you how it works, would you?'

'I thought you said that's what you were going to do, before she interrupted. You said you were going to explain it all to me?'

'Not how it works,' Sozerdor explained with exaggerated playfulness. 'You know that's not what I meant.'

'Leela,' the Doctor said. 'Try not to touch it.'

'Good advice,' Sozerdor said. 'A little obvious perhaps but... good.'

Leela checked that she was in the exact centre of the pit and sat down cross-legged. The shrinking seemed to be speeding up. The force field reached the knife that she had not retrieved. With a vicious snap of static it flicked into movement and skittered across the floor. Leela stopped it with her foot.

'If you don't know how it's controlled do you at least know who's controlling it?' the Doctor asked matter-of-factly. 'Is it Monly?' He glared at the two Monlys, who were standing where they had been left and were looking lost and confused as though they had recently woken up in a place they didn't recognise. 'This toody says he created you. Do you think that's true?' Neither of them responded. 'If I were you,' he went on. 'I should want the toody punished for his presumption.'

'That's impressive. No, I really am impressed.' Sozerdor's grinning admiration might almost have been genuine. 'You never stop trying, do you? I'm controlling it of course.'

'I don't believe you,' the Doctor said.

'Yes you do.'

'Prove it to me.'

'By stopping it?'

'Yes.'

'Very well.' He held out an open palm towards the force field. With a theatrical flourish he closed the hand into a fist and clapped it to his chest. 'There. It's stopped.'

'It has not stopped, Doctor,' Leela called crouching lower, pulling her legs close to her chest and wrapping her arms round them.

'She's right, it hasn't stopped,' Sozerdor agreed. 'I lied.'

'You don't know how to stop it, do you?' the Doctor said with as convincing a sneer as he could manage. He strode away towards the two Monlys. 'Monly has got the controls, hasn't he?' He was quite sure that Sozerdor couldn't have resisted a small demonstration of his power if he had the control mechanism with him, so he reasoned that the alcove Sozerdor was hiding in had to be the key to it.

'This is disappointing,' Sozerdor declared, watching Leela with obvious enjoyment. 'You must know Monly couldn't control his *legs* without my say-so. I expected aliens like you and Leela here to be cleverer than this, Doctor.'

The Doctor reached the Monlys. 'That is a dangerous madman,' he muttered as he hurried on past them. 'He thinks that he made you and that I'm an alien.'

'Yes, Doctor,' Sozerdor was gloating loudly. 'I knew you were aliens from the start. But I know for certain now that you're not the aliens that made all this.'

'Stop him if you can,' the Doctor said.

'So I know for certain now that you're expendable.'

Leela could not get enough breath to shout as she cramped herself lower. 'Doctor?' she gasped. 'There is not much time left.'

'You're going to make a lot more noise than that,' Sozerdor taunted. 'Don't feel too badly – you'll live again in my little army of assassins.' Turning back to taunt the Doctor he said, 'Unlike you…' and realised as he spoke the words that the Monly outburst had been only a cover. 'Stop!' he bellowed.

The Doctor rushed on, hardly registering the weirdness in the active alcoves he was passing.

He had to pick the right one and he had to do it quickly. There was no time for mistakes. He hoped the Monlys might delay any attempt Sozerdor made to chase after him. The trouble was, there was nothing to distinguish one alcove from another except what they were monitoring or creating, downloading, uploading or controlling: the Doctor was uncomfortably aware suddenly of how little he really understood about this technology. There was no time for doubts, either. No time for mistakes and no time for doubts. Which one was it?

The shot took the Doctor by surprise. It missed him and chewed a chunk out of the forward edge of an alcove. He should have known Sozerdor would have kept a gun available. The power surge overloaded the alcove's output, which abruptly tumbled into a twisted chaos of fleeting impressions before everything faded to leave an inert, crystal-flecked hollow. The Doctor plunged on.

'I said stop!' The second shot flashed by the Doctor's face and deactivated another alcove.

Leela cried out as the force field touched her for one agonising fraction of a second before she struggled and managed to make herself smaller.

The Doctor reached what he thought was the right alcove. He paused.

Sozerdor took careful aim this time.

The Doctor hesitated. Was this the right one? Or was it the next one?

Sozerdor steadied his gun hand with his free hand and lined up the head shot.

Choose one. Choose one *now.*

Sozerdor squeezed the fire release smoothly and slowly.

With a shared yell of insane rage the two Monlys ran at Sozerdor, arms flailing, faces contorted. Sozerdor shot them both down.

Inside the alcove the Doctor found what looked like a small

holographic projection of the central pit and the bright, clearly deflating bubble of the force field. There was no sign of how it was controlled. He looked around urgently. There was nothing else to be seen. There were no doorways into a virtual guidance link. There was no directly slaved image of Leela. Control had to be exercised using the image itself. But how? If he got it wrong he could make things worse. Terminally worse. He thought of Sozerdor's theatrical display. Where had that come from?

Carefully he put his open hand on the top of the bubble and closed it and lifted his fist.

For a long moment nothing happened, and then the force field began to expand and inflate as it followed the movement of his hand.

'You should resist cheap jokes, Sozerdor,' he murmured, smiling with relief. 'They give things away.' With an upward gesture he opened his fist and watched carefully to see what effect that had. The image of the force field continued to expand. The Doctor wondered whether there was a direct correlation between the speed of the gesture and the rapidity with which the field changed. Perhaps it was possible with a series of identical gestures to pump up the acceleration? Would a reverse gesture slow it down or change the direction completely? He was about to test a couple of these possibilities when he realised what he was doing and remembered what Sozerdor said that he already knew: *And this place will drive you crazy if you're not paying attention.* He wasn't paying attention. He shouldn't be thinking about experimenting with the systems – he had to find out what was happening to Leela.

The Doctor turned back to the front and for the first time he registered that the alcove was closed around him in a complete circle. There was no front. There was no back. There was no feature by which to orientate himself. More disconcerting still, it appeared there were now no features at all, not even a recognisable wall he could feel his way round. If the Doctor had been given to panic, the dizzying absence of distance and perspective might well have made him lose his balance. As it was, he checked that the miniature force field was still expanding and then he set off to walk in what he hoped was a straight line.

He emerged from one of the hollowed-out places in the wall. It took a few seconds for his senses to rationalise that he was back in a more familiar landscape. He heard Leela calling out to him.

'Doctor? It is getting bigger. Does that mean I can get out now?'

Rubbing his eyes, he tried to focus on her. 'Soon.' His eyesight clear again he looked around, warily. 'Where's Sozerdor?'

'I do not know. He was gone before I could move enough to see.'

'A pressing engagement to which we're a possible threat or no threat at all,' the Doctor mused.

'When can I get out?' Leela demanded.

'If the light goes dim it's safe to step out,' the Doctor said.

'*If* the light goes dim?'

The Doctor walked down to look at the sprawled bodies of Monly. 'They must have heard what I said. I didn't think they were listening.'

'If the light goes dim?' Leela repeated.

'I think the field will weaken and dissipate eventually when it's expanded enough.' As he said it there was a dip in the brightness. 'You see.'

Leela gathered up her knife and stepped carefully out of the pit. Ignoring the Monlys, she said, 'Now what?'

The Doctor stared round the circle of bays. There were at least two hundred of them and most of those were active. 'Somewhere in one of these there's a mechanism which will release Kley and the others.'

'What mechanism?'

'Yes, exactly,' the Doctor said thoughtfully.

Leela frowned. 'Can we trust them? We could not trust Monly and Sozerdor. And they were both dead.'

'Sozerdor wasn't dead,' the Doctor said vaguely.

'He will be.' Leela's voice was flat with menace. 'It is a pity his Monly creatures are destroyed. They would have known how to find him.'

The Doctor beamed. 'Of course. Why didn't I think of that? Another good idea of yours, Leela.' He set off towards one of the inactive alcoves.

Leela followed him. 'What is?'

'We'll use a control bay to find the control bay,' the Doctor said. 'All we have to do is select here and specify that bay and when we have it identified either go directly to it or reselect it and operate it from where we are. It couldn't be simpler.'

He went straight into the alcove and rested his hands on the ghostly flickering of the crystal-flecked wall. A sparkling wave of energy washed through all the surfaces and returned to the Doctor's hands, where it faded and died away. Though his eyes were open and he could see the curved wall in front of him, the images of Kley, Rinandor, Pertanor, Fermindor and Belay stood out starkly behind the solid surface directly in front of him. Each one was life-size, each one was held in isolation, each one was simultaneously and separately in his eye line. He looked at his hands. 'Well perhaps it could be slightly simpler.' Focusing still seemed to be beyond him. Perhaps, he thought, his understanding of the system was fundamentally a misunderstanding.

Behind the Doctor, Leela searched the wall for a particular pattern among the crystal flecks. She no longer questioned how she knew what to look for. It felt natural, as though it was something she had always known. When she found the right points, she placed her fingertips against them, and the links came alive so that she was able to see and be seen. 'What do you want there to be?' she asked the Doctor.

It bothered the Doctor that Leela was now at home and comfortable with the technology. It seemed more than possible that it was working on her constantly, intensifying the feedback whenever she came into contact with any of the control interfaces. He would have to get her away from it soon or she might never be free of it.

'All the control bays in the chamber,' he said. The effects of the separate but at the same time superimposed images the machine had given him were still in his mind and he went on, 'All at once all alone.'

In the closed circle of the alcove, the two hundred or so other alcoves stretched away in a line that went nowhere, and had no length, and put no distance between first and last. In this array of single control bays, the one that held the key to Kley and the others was instantly obvious. 'That one,' the Doctor said, putting his hand on it.

Kley had tried opening her eyes, once, briefly. It was as she expected. She was dead. There was nothing. There was only the darkness. The whispering had stopped. The pain had stopped. The screaming had stopped. If she had been screaming. Had she been screaming? She couldn't remember. If this was death it wasn't so bad. It was the absence of everything, an infinity of absence, nothing for ever. It wasn't so bad... Oh, but it was. She couldn't bear the empty horror of it. She felt the scream gathering in the centre of her breathing. If she opened her eyes, she was lost. If she opened her mouth, she was lost.

'Kley?' the voice said. 'Open your eyes.'

It didn't sound like Monly.

'Come on, Kley,' the Doctor said. 'Open your eyes.'

Kley opened her eyes. She was standing against the wall in a small brightly lit room. The Doctor was standing in front of her smiling.

'Good,' the Doctor said. 'The way out is there.' He pointed at a hole in the floor. 'I'm not really here so you'll have to go it alone. Follow the light when you get into the tunnel. It should bring you to where the others are. Do you think you can manage that?'

'Yes,' Kley whispered. 'I can manage that.'

'Excellent,' the Doctor said. 'You've got blood on your chin by the way.' He smiled even more broadly and then he vanished, smile and all, leaving no sign that he was ever there. Without bothering to wipe her chin, Kley stumbled mechanically towards the hole in the floor. So this was death. It wasn't so bad...

Pertanor was suspicious and stubbornly silent. Leela had no idea how to persuade him that she was telling him the truth. It was more difficult because she did not entirely trust him anyway. She would not be surprised to find that the whole team were partly involved in whatever Sozerdor was planning.

'Listen,' she grated. 'Stay there if that is what you want to do. I do not care. I do not know why the Doctor is wasting our time with you people. I think you are stupid and treacherous and if the choice was mine I would leave you all to rot.'

'All?' he asked finally. 'What's happened to Rinandor?'

Leela said, 'The Doctor is releasing her.' Then she added, not without relish, Pertanor thought: 'You are weak-willed too. You cannot even remain silent.'

'Nice of you to wake me,' Rinandor yawned. 'At the risk of sounding obvious, where am I?' And where is everybody else?'

'Meaning Pertanor?'

She stretched and rubbed her eyes. 'If you like.'

'I think he's looking for you,' the Doctor said.

She yawned again. 'Let's go then,' she said. 'You lead the way.'

'I'm afraid I can't. I'm not here.'

'You can relax, The. Pe's not the jealous type. And you're not my type.'

'And I'm not here,' the Doctor said.

* * *

210

Leela found Belay talking in a conversational way about nothing very much to no one at all. His release, the light, her appearance, none of it made any difference; he just kept on talking. He babbled about his plans for the future, about his life in the OIG, about his friends. Leela could not shut him up and he did not seem to be listening to anything she told him. She tried standing very close to him. She tried shouting at him. She tried threatening him with her knife. Either something was wrong with the system and it was not showing her to him or something was wrong with him and he could not see her. After a while she gave up. The Doctor would have to deal with this one.

Fermindor listened to the Doctor's brief explanation and his instructions on where to find Belay. When the Doctor asked, 'Do you understand?' he simply nodded, and he was moving and on his way out of the cell almost before the Doctor vanished.

Sozerdor was nowhere to be found in any of the file of control bays and the Doctor had reasoned that he must be out on the surface somewhere. Although the Doctor's attempts to commune with the system all failed no matter what he tried, Leela was able to establish multi-layered links apparently at will. Sozerdor did not show up in any of them. They widened the search and, in the process, the Doctor confirmed that there were no other complexes linked to this one. They detected several heavily shielded power sources deep below them and what looked to the Doctor like a series of space-time anomaly loops which were being used to foreshorten physical perspectives.

'Shortcuts between places,' the Doctor explained in response to Leela's accusation of 'Shaman's gibberish.'

'The civilisation that put all this together,' he went on, 'had a rudimentary grasp of transdimensional engineering.'

'Does that mean your tribe are responsible for what has

happened here?' Leela demanded.

'My tribe?'

'You know what I mean. Your civilisation. You told me trans-that engineering was a discovery of your civilisation.'

'I did. It was. This is not the same.'

'Then why did you mention it?'

'I was just thinking that myself.' He looked around for the way out of the alcove, though he knew before he did it that there would be no way out other than the one he would choose. 'Shall we go?'

Leela gestured at the display. 'Do you want me to go on looking for it?'

The Doctor was becoming increasingly concerned about the time Leela had been in direct contact with the systems. He regretted calling it communing because that sounded innocuous and, far from feeling threatened, she was pleased that she could do it and he could not. In fact he was feeling guilty at using her that way despite his concerns. 'Leave it,' he said, and when she frowned at his tone, he smiled and added, 'We can come back and try again.'

The straight line, which he had found could subjectively be in any direction, took the Doctor out of the alcove, and Leela followed him. As with the rest of the procedures, Leela, however, was now quite unfazed by the bizarre discontinuities that bothered him and should have terrified her and filled her with superstitious awe.

Waiting in the pit, what remained of the OIG team was by contrast close to panic. At least the members who were still in touch with reality were. Pertanor looked shaken and the protective arm he had round a trembling Rinandor was clearly as much for his own comfort as for hers. Fermindor was grimly expressionless but the unconscious flexing and unflexing of his fists and the nervous shifting of his weight from one foot to the other suggested to the Doctor that he was struggling to stay in control. Kley was blank and unmoving. Belay was interested and relaxed as he stared around him, whispering to himself.

'You can come out of there,' the Doctor said.

Kley started to shuffle forward. Fermindor grabbed her arm and stopped her. She made no attempt to struggle but stood waiting for her next instruction. 'What's that about?' Fermindor said pointing at the two Monly corpses.

'Your friend Sozerdor has been experimenting,' the Doctor said. 'That's why you're all here of course. You were experimental subjects. You were chosen as cover and for him to use to test out the systems. You were sent here as laboratory rats.'

'Sozerdor's dead,' Pertanor said.

'I saw him die,' Rinandor said.

Fermindor said, 'We all saw him die.'

'I believe you saw Monly die, too, didn't you?' the Doctor pointed out.

'This is death,' Kley murmured. 'We are all dead.'

Fermindor turned her round to face him. 'Listen to me. You are not dead. Whatever this is, you are not dead.'

Her eyes were only half focused on his face, she could have been remembering rather than seeing. 'It's not so bad,' she said.

'*You* are not dead, Serian, and I am not dead. None of us is dead.' He took her face in his hands. 'Serian?' He had never noticed how soft her features were and how similar he was to her in height. 'Do you know who I am?' He was not that much stockier than she was, either, he realised.

Her eyes focused. It was as if she had woken up. 'Hello, Fe,' she said. 'You've never called me Serian before.'

'I've never been this scared before.'

'It's not so bad,' she said.

'Being dead?'

'Being called Serian by…'

He took his hands from her face. 'By a toody,' he offered.

She put a hand out and stroked his cheek. 'By you,' she said.

Kley turned and looked at the Doctor. 'Why are there two?' she asked.

The Doctor said, 'We haven't found out precisely where it's done yet, but somewhere in this complex you can put together copies of things.' He squatted down beside the bodies. They already had the beginnings of a slight sheen over them as though they had been sprayed with a fine mist of water. Things decomposed, or rather deconstructed, faster here than on the surface. Perhaps it was a design element which was intended to keep the creations separate from their creators. It could be that they were made to be more fragile down here. That would explain why the copy of him was vulnerable to the radiation pulse.

'Copies of anything?' Rinandor asked, moving to get a better look at the two dead versions of Monly.

'Anything alive,' Leela said. 'We think it has to be alive.'

'I thought Monly alone was one too many Monlys,' Rinandor said. 'So did someone else, obviously.'

'What about the clothes, then?' Fermindor asked. 'Where did they come from?'

'That is odd,' the Doctor agreed. 'Clothing and simple weaponry like knives and spears appear to be included in the process. Maybe the system interprets them as part of the organism. Theoretically, since it seems able to build from the atomic level, there should be no limit to what can be duplicated, but there obviously is. The machine must have been designed to work that way.'

'What machine? Where? What is it?' demanded Pertanor.

'It's not so much what it is,' the Doctor said, 'as what it was.'

'Very well, then,' Kley said. 'What was it?'

'It was the Lentic,' Leela said.

The Doctor nodded. 'Have you heard of the Empire of the

Lentic?'

'Should we have done?'

'I'm not sure when they are in relation to you,' the Doctor mused as he searched through the pockets and pouches of Monly's uniform fatigues.

'*When* they are?' Rinandor asked looking down at him.

'Interesting,' the Doctor said, examining coins and small personal items which were identical to both versions of Monly and in identical pockets. 'The machine's scanning must be automatic, immediate and thorough, but quite undiscriminating.'

'When?' Rinandor repeated.

The Doctor rubbed the surface of the coins. 'These deconstruct more slowly.' He looked up at Leela. 'What about the knife you took?'

Leela handed him the knife. 'It has not changed,' she said.

'Yes,' the Doctor murmured thoughtfully as he examined it. 'Of course it might just be your original blade.'

Leela's expression darkened. 'I should not have surrendered it.'

He handed it back, and began returning the items to the pockets and pouches where he had found them. 'Perhaps you didn't,' he said absently. 'In a way they were you. So in a way you were surrendering it to yourself.'

'You know that is not true,' Leela said. 'Making excuses will not help me or change what I did.'

'I'm patronising you again, aren't I? It's a difficult habit to break.'

'Did you say *when* they are, The?' Rinandor asked again.

The Doctor got to his feet and smiled. 'Ri Rinandor, my name is not The Thedoctor. I am simply known as the Doctor. Leela and I are not from your system. We are in fact –'

Belay lunged forward through the others. 'Aliens!' He had stopped whispering to himself and was looking at Leela in disappointed amazement. 'You're aliens. But that's not allowed. You can't take a contract duel if you're an alien. You originate out-system? Crumbling balls of crap, the Guild won't even allow *training* offworlds.'

There was a moment's silence and then Pertanor giggled. 'Does this mean we're not going to be rich after all?'

'If we back her we could lose everything,' Belay sniggered.

Before long they were all laughing hysterically.

'Belay's knack of seeing right to the heart of a problem is why he was chosen for the mission,' Kley choked.

'Do you think we should arrest them now, Investigator Belay?' Fermindor chortled. 'Or should we simply report them for contract violation and let them off with a standard warning?'

'I'm going to wake up soon and this is all going to have been a horrible dream,' Rinandor laughed.

'All of it?' Pertanor protested.

'The sex'll have to be pretty special to compensate for what's happened up to now,' she hooted.

'Living up to that will be a definite nightmare,' he howled.

Leela listened to the laughter and the jokes that were not funny and saw the fear that was in the faces and the movements. She hoped the Doctor understood that this was the way frightened people sometimes acted, and that he was not expecting these investigators to be of any help. Even warriors might break and run in a place like this, and they were no kind of warriors. She had seen warrior initiates, children, who were better prepared to face unknown dangers. She watched the Doctor smiling at them and nodding. He was not joining in the laughter but he was leading it, encouraging it. And he was wasting time.

'Doctor,' she said. 'What about Sozerdor?'

He leaned close and murmured, 'Smile, Leela.'

Leela frowned. 'I am not afraid.'

'They are,' he whispered. 'They're absolutely terrified. It'll help them if you look as relaxed and cheerful as they do.'

Leela smiled. For a shaman, she reminded herself, the Doctor could be a very wise and practical person.

Kley stopped laughing finally, and said, 'So you claim to be an alien, Doctor. We're hardly in a position to doubt you, are we? Unless we're all going to wake up with bad headaches.' She gestured round at the alcoves with their mysterious hints of depth and the occasional glimpses, showing at the surface of the access gaps, of the strange creations and locations within. 'I can't imagine what I could've taken to produce this effect anyway. So you're an alien. Are you one of these – what did you call them – Lentics?'

'No.'

'Is Leela?' Rinandor asked.

'No.'

'I can answer for myself,' Leela said.

'Are you?' Rinandor asked.

'No,' Leela said, feeling foolish.

'But you are different,' Rinandor suggested. 'From different planets, I mean?'

'You'd make a good policeman,' the Doctor said. 'You should consider taking it up professionally.'

'If that was meant to be an insult you'll have to try harder.'

The Doctor beamed. 'Or you won't notice you've been insulted? Actually it was meant to be a compliment.'

'You think this belongs to the Lentic then?' Fermindor asked. 'Is that what you're saying?'

'The Empire of the Lentic,' the Doctor began, walking slowly away from the pit towards the alcoves, 'was military. Quite striking in its way. Particularly striking if you got *in* its way. All military organisations are aggressive but the Lentic carried aggression to new extremes.' As he expected the others followed him in an attentive group. 'Eventually the Lentic became obsessed,' he went on, 'with the need to produce the perfect soldier. To that end they developed a semi-sentient, self-refining training facility. What the facility did was to analyse the strengths and weaknesses of the test subjects and then use the data to develop a training-and-selection process. To build the strengths up it exaggerated and fed back the weaknesses as physical threats. Think of it as a machine which created a working example of your own personal nightmare, and then made you fight it in some suitable location. The machine would observe how you reacted and, if it liked what it saw and you were still alive, it would try something more extreme. It was based on some halfwitted notion that whatever doesn't kill you will make you stronger. It was a cruel and ugly idea and, like all cruel and ugly ideas, it was ultimately self-defeating.'

'It kept on going until it killed you?' Pertanor asked.

'Apparently.'

'What was the point of that?'

The Doctor shrugged. 'Obsessions tend to lose sight of the point. The idea was that when the machine had defined and discovered the perfect soldier, it would copy it in sufficient numbers to maintain the empire for ever after.'

'So where is this empire?' Fermindor asked.

'Where indeed?' the Doctor agreed. 'It seems they tested the subjects in batches. It was a process of elimination which became known as Last Man Running. I think that's where we are now. I think we are in the barely functioning remains of the control centre of one of the Lentic's last-man-running facilities.'

Kley stepped in front of the Doctor and stared hard at him. 'You knew all this from when exactly?'

'Don't misunderstand me.' The Doctor put on his most serious expression and shook his head vigorously to emphasise the denial. 'I'm not even sure of it now.'

'Yes we are,' Leela said. 'It is remembered in the machine.'

'A suggestion,' the Doctor said, 'no more than that. It confirms some ideas. It fits the hypothesis.'

Fermindor said, 'You know a lot about it for someone who isn't sure.'

'I've only *heard* about the Lentic,' the Doctor said. 'I've never seen them in action. I've never seen them at all.'

'I think I have,' Leela said. 'Somewhere in all this.' She gestured round at the alcoves.

They had reached the entrance to an inactive control bay. Kley and Fermindor peered into it. 'What's happened to them then?' Kley asked. 'Where are they?'

The Doctor said, 'The empire collapsed the way empires do. Entropy, change, evolution. The Lentic were absorbed as everything and everyone is sooner or later.'

Pertanor and Rinandor were hanging back warily. They looked less than convinced. 'When did all this happen exactly?' Rinandor asked, not bothering to keep the scepticism out of her voice.

Pertanor said, 'As far as we know you could be making this up.'

'The Doctor does not make things up,' Leela said angrily. 'He is a powerful shaman who has saved your lives and you should show him proper respect.'

'So you are a contract duellist after all, then?' Rinandor said wryly.

'I agree with Leela,' Belay said. 'The Doctor may be crazy but that doesn't mean we can't trust him.' Belay was still fascinated by Leela and he had been rather clumsily trying to disguise it by glancing at her surreptitiously and then looking away quickly and feigning interest in the general surroundings.

'Do you trust me enough to go out on the surface and hunt for Sozerdor?'

'This would be the same Sozerdor we left in a seek-bag tagged for autolift? The dead one?' Rinandor asked.

'No. This is the live one,' the Doctor said. 'This is the runner

219

you've been chasing all along.' He stared at each of the OIG crew in turn. 'This is what you came for.'

Chapter Eleven

As soon as they reached the planet, they went into the preset search-and-retrieval routines. One of the ships made a series of powered sub-orbital sweeps at the edge of the atmosphere, beginning at the equator and working an overlapping search pattern towards the northern pole. A second ship did the same in the southern hemisphere. Co-ordination, analysis of ground-scan radar mapping and the identification of the distress beacon signals was carried out by Lead One from a stationary orbit. The absence of a fully experienced senior navigation co-ordinator seemed to make no difference to the efficiency of the operation, which went without a major hitch.

The beacon was still sending powerfully when they pinpointed it in an area of desert in the northern hemisphere. The urgency of the mission was obvious, a three-ship'er was a new experience for everyone involved, so no one had time to remark on the odd topography of that region of the planet. Since most of the ordinary crew members had no real idea what the special urgency was all about, and the captain of Lead One was generally accepted to be an uncommunicative type whose briefings were notably brief, there was already an unreality about the whole enterprise, which meant that anything strange would have fitted in with what was happening.

Voice communication from the group of survivors sheltering in a cave in the desert was faint and slightly garbled, but it seemed that the entire patrol lead by Chief Investigator Serian Kley had survived and were waiting to be picked up. The loss of their ship due to a failure of the main power plant had apparently left them without the bulk of their supplies, but they had managed to eke out what they had so that they were all in reasonable health, with the exception of the oldest member of the team, Senior Investigator Sozerdor, who was seriously injured and in need of urgent medical attention.

When the news was relayed from Lead One to the other two ships it was greeted with relief and excitement. It was not their job to worry about the runner or to look for the remains of the pursuit team's crashed ship. So none of them did.

The Doctor could see that they were not convinced. It was a pity. He had not wanted to risk their fragile mental equilibrium by showing them a control bay in action, especially not the one that presently contained an index of all the other control bays. It would be too disorientating for them; he wasn't that comfortable with it himself. He didn't know what the shock might do to them. The last thing he needed was for them to retreat into the defensive explanations they had made for themselves, which seemed to run the full spectrum from death to prisoner mind games. He had hoped they would take his word for things and allow themselves to be transported to the surface without any further questions. Close your eyes, walk forward, open your eyes. It would have been a simple and painless procedure, provided they did not think about it too closely. They weren't going to find Sozerdor out there, but there was a chance that Sozerdor might find them – which for his purposes would be the same thing.

'We need more to go on,' Kley said reasonably. 'We can't just take your word for things. It seems that's what got us into this mess in the first place.'

'You want us to chase someone we haven't seen, who is doing something we probably haven't understood,' Fermindor said. 'As far as I remember you didn't think that was such a good idea before.'

'You *have* seen him,' the Doctor urged.

'Tagged and bagged.'

'And I've told you what he's *doing*.'

'What you *think* he's doing.'

'And you think you're an alien,' Rinandor put in. 'So how reliable are you?'

'I mean Sozerdor's come here to start a war?' Pertanor said. 'Does that seem likely to you?'

'If it does you obviously are an alien,' Rinandor said.

'Very well.' The Doctor held up his hand in exasperation. 'If you insist on trying to understand then you're going to have to take the consequences.'

'Yes,' Kley said.

'And the problem with that is what exactly?' Rinandor asked.

Once again the Doctor had to wonder how the Lentic trainer might be affecting him. Trying to understand was one of the drives he had always recognised in himself. How could he be objecting to the same impulse in these people, just so it would be easier to use them as bait? 'I wanted to protect you,' he muttered. 'That was all.'

Leela led the way into the control bay. She was closely followed by Belay. Kley was more cautious but she led the others in and they followed her. Leela had already activated the mechanism by the time the Doctor joined the rather sheepish group, which stood waiting for something to happen.

What did happen could have been an accident. A coincidence of the sort that shamans and charlatans find convenient to build their reputations on. When the Doctor had a chance to think about it, however, it seemed more likely that the machine simply recognised the originals and their constructs and automatically offered a link for the purposes of comparison. Whatever the reason, the effect, first for Kley, and then for the others, was unnerving.

* * *

Kley walked out of the cave into the stark brightness. Light and heat were the same, a chest-burning breathlessness and the same dry smell of hot rock filled her nose and her eyes. She would have looked up to try to see the approaching rescue ship, but even peering out from the shade of both hands she could see nothing. She turned her face from the searing white sky, took the communicator from her hip pouch and pulled it out of its dark-wrap.

It took Kley a moment or two to recognise herself. 'Is that supposed to be me?' she asked watching the oddly short, slightly stocky figure standing in the unforgiving blaze waiting for the voice link aerial to deploy. 'That's not how I look, is it?'

'No,' Fermindor said.

'I thought I was taller.'

'You are.'

'I didn't think I was that plump.'

'You're not,' Fermindor said. 'It's a crap copy.'

'You're such a liar, Fe,' she murmured as Fermindor's exact copy emerged from the cave and was immediately joined by perfect copies of all the others except Sozerdor. 'I'll never be able to trust you again.'

Pertanor giggled nervously. 'How is it they got everybody else right and me wrong?'

'I knew it,' Rinandor said. 'This is a nightmare. How many copies of Monly are there?'

'What are they for?' Kley said. 'What are they doing?'

'My guess is they're decoying a rescue ship,' the Doctor said.

'Lead One, Lead One,' Kley said into her communicator, 'have you acquired visual lock? I repeat have you visual confirmation? Reset.'

'Serian Kley, this is Lead One. We have you on drone locator with visual lock. Orbit drop one is in ten. Reset.'

* * *

'But why? What's the point of it?' Pertanor said. 'I mean, have they decided they like being us so they're taking over our lives? What?'

The Doctor said, 'Not exactly. They probably won't know that they're decoys.'

'Search-and-retrieval would have dropped anyway,' Fermindor commented. 'All it takes is a distress beacon.'

'Would they have landed for a beacon?' the Doctor asked.

'Yes. They'd have to be sure.'

Leela asked, 'Would they have been armed and wary?'

As soon as she said it, they knew that was the reason but Kley said it just to be clear. 'They would be heavily armed and very wary.'

'If it wasn't us and it was remotely threatening,' Rinandor said, 'they'd blast the everlasting crap out of it. They don't call search-and-retrieval "the death detail" for nothing.'

Leela had put her fingers back on the control surface and the Doctor noticed that the bay seemed to be expanding slowly so that the figures and the landscape were getting larger. They were almost full size now and Kley and the others found themselves standing awkwardly close to the virtual representations of the copies of themselves. Strangely, there was no discernible change in their relative positions so that for a brief dizzying moment they were unsure whether the images were getting larger or they themselves were getting smaller. There was no change in the sounds, either, so that closeness was not closeness. But the awkwardness intensified as they strained to understand the detail of what the Kley copy was saying.

'Lead One, Lead One, this is Kley,' the figure said. 'Drop-zone co-ordinates are specified and acquired. It looks wide, Lead One. Is there a reason? I repeat drop zone has overextended error margin. Reset.'

In the unnatural stillness of the baking desertscape, the voice of the navigation co-ordinator on the orbit ship was just about audible over the communicator channel.

'Serian Kley, this is Lead One. Be advised we are briefed for a double-drop lift-out. Orbit drop two is in fifteen. Reset.'

Pertanor whispered, 'They sent two ships for us. Maybe three if Lead One's a stand-off.'

'Isn't it good to feel wanted?' Rinandor murmured with a wry smile.

'How did they justify that, do you suppose?'

'Not how,' Kley said quietly. 'Who.' She looked at the Doctor and nodded her acceptance of what he had told them.

Fermindor was nodding grimly. 'When we find out who it was who sent them,' he muttered, 'we'll know who we've got to deal with.'

'Why are you whispering?' Leela said. 'You are not with them. They cannot hear you.' She took her fingers from the pattern of crystals, which were by this time recognisable only to her.

The Doctor watched her staring intently at the virtual figures. She seemed completely absorbed by the vision of them standing in the thin dust outside the desert cave. She unsheathed her knife. Was she finally losing contact with her own reality? She examined the knife carefully and then she returned to gazing at what the control bay was showing. Was it the machine that was dictating her behaviour now? He tried to see precisely what she was looking at.

'Leela?' the Doctor said. She did not seem to have heard him. 'Leela,' he said more loudly.

She glanced at him. 'They are in the cave, Doctor,' she said, pointing into the starkly contrasted darkness. 'I cannot tell how many of them there are.'

They all peered at the cave. Fermindor tried to shift to a new position to get a better look, but found that nothing at all had changed. Pertanor shaded his eyes before realising how pointless the effort was.

'I can see them moving,' Belay said, suddenly excited. 'There must be dozens of them.'

'Dozens of what?' Kley demanded.

'Dozens of me,' Leela said flatly.

'Probably that's why Belay can see them,' Rinandor snorted, 'and we can't?'

'Probably,' the Doctor agreed, absently. 'Semi-sentient telepathic machines are strangely selective sometimes.' He had just noticed something that Leela had undoubtedly been aware of for some time. The Kley copy had a sidearm. 'The TARDIS can be quite arbitrary under certain circumstances.' He did a quick check. None of the people with them had guns.

'The TARDIS? That would be an alien artefact?' Rinandor asked.

The Doctor said, 'Where did Kley get the handgun?' He looked at Kley. 'You haven't got one so it wasn't duplicated as part of you.'

'Sozerdor had a gun,' Leela said.

'Yes but why would he give it to her?' the Doctor mused.

'Enough talking,' Fermindor said. 'What do we do to stop this happening?'

The Doctor struggled to establish the crossover point himself yet again, and yet again he had to leave the final details to Leela's unconscious interaction with the machine. The surface access shaft was formed within the link to the desert location that the system had already set up, but a collapsing temporal anomaly and a sealing shaft meant the only options for the new access seemed to be in the middle of the crowded cave, or well away on the reverse side of the giant column of rock. On balance, the reverse side of the column looked like the better choice.

As he had expected, the Doctor found the darkness of the crossover no less disconcerting because he knew what to expect.

Perhaps, he thought, it was the simple crudeness of the process that whispered to him of ancient dangers.

He stepped out of a fissure in the rock wall and found himself staring across the flat wilderness of stone and yellowy-grey dust.

Behind him, the others crowded out of the fissure: Kley first, then Fermindor, Rinandor, Pertanor and Belay. They all seemed to the Doctor to be quite comfortable with the experience, except for Belay, who looked mildly harassed. When Leela emerged with her knife drawn and an expression of irritated impatience on her face, it was apparent that he had probably attempted to be last in line and the chivalrous gesture had been abruptly rebuffed. The Doctor waited briefly while everyone got over the initial shock of the breathless heat before he set off to find a way round the huge pillar, the base of which – as well as being several thousand yards in circumference – was surrounded by mountainous heaps of large boulders and broken stone.

It didn't take any of them long to realise that there were disadvantages to the choice they had made. The scramble up and down through the rocks quite exhausted them – and they had covered less than half the distance to the end of the curve in the pillar that would allow them a first glimpse of what was happening on the other side. A short, bad-tempered discussion led them to climb down from the boulders and move out on to the flatter ground where they could walk more quickly. If Sozerdor had scouts posted or had surveillance monitoring looped up from the underground control centre, they risked being spotted more easily, but it was a chance they decided to take. On the featureless plain they were pitilessly exposed in the bright heat, but there was no other way they could get to the rescue site in time to prevent the retrieval of those first shock troops, the training-developed weapons for a war most people were not expecting back on First and Second.

They were tiring again, and slowing up, when they saw the

approach of the first search-and-retrieval ship. It came in under full power, low and slow, with the micro-touch reverse thrust and vertical braking switching through the drives in a flickering blur. By the time it had disappeared from view behind the column of rock, and whirling dust clouds were churning and boiling out on to the plain, they had forced themselves to speed up until they were almost running. The group began to string out as the stronger ones drew ahead and the less fit began to flag. Despite their efforts, the second ship came in long before anyone had managed to reach the front edge of the column.

The Doctor and Leela got to a vantage point ahead of anyone else, and peered through the gradually settling fog of gritty particles to see the copied OIG team, the survivors of which were even now struggling to catch up, greeting the pilot and medic from the first ship. Sozerdor was still nowhere in evidence.

'What are they waiting for?' whispered Leela.

'The pilot from the other ship?' the Doctor hazarded, catching his breath.

Behind them, Kley and the others staggered up gasping and exhausted. The Doctor ducked back to stop them going any further. 'Can any of you fly one of those?' he asked quietly.

'Yes,' Kley rasped.

'Which one of you?'

'All of us.'

'We're all flight-trained,' Fermindor wheezed. 'That's why they pay us the heavy currency.'

'Out-system Investigation Group,' Rinandor panted. 'You don't get to run to our assignments.'

'Not until now, anyway,' gasped Pertanor, leaning against the rock.

'How many crew do they carry?'

'Two for the drop usually. The rest transfer to the stand-off,' Kley said.

'In that case,' the Doctor said brightly, 'you can steal both of them.'

Kley was recovering. 'Is this another of your plans, Doctor?' she asked softly. 'Can I take a look first?' She moved past him to the curved edge of the eroded rock where the Doctor and Leela had been crouching.

That was when the Doctor realised that Leela had gone.

'Where's Belay?' Fermindor muttered. 'Anyone notice what happened to him?'

It was SOC – Standard Operational Caution, or Same Old Crap to the time-served sweats – that prevented the pilot of Drop Two from cracking the seals immediately and joining the Drop One jock and his bug-sniffer in the backslapping. Truth was, he couldn't see much point in both ships being down, but since those were the orders and since he had brought it in hot and hard and landed it close and cool, he sort of resented not being in on the first contact. Second didn't count for much, no matter how good you were. Ask any toody. It would be fairly stupid, though, to do the hard stuff right and crap up the details, so they waited on the flight deck – him and the field medic – for the initial analysis and safety clearance to come in from Lead One out there in orbit.

If he had been less impatient the pilot might have noticed that the clearance when it came was too fast for book-minimum SOC. Nothing could have been checked in that time, and he might have waited and queried the data. If he had been less eager to get his share of the glory he might still have been squinting out of the ground-exposed vision slots, or watching the dust-clogged visuals from the scancam, and he might have seen the danger while there was still time to do something about it.

He was a good pilot. He did the hard stuff right. Crapping up the details was what was about to get him killed.

Leela knew Belay was behind her and there was nothing she could do about it. As she crept along, keeping as close as she could to the cover of the wall of rock, she had slowed down slightly, reasoning that for him slower would be quieter, and she had signalled for him to keep his distance and to tread carefully. After that, she put him out of her mind and concentrated on the group ahead of her. The copies and the rescue team were talking excitedly, and there was a good chance that she could get within attacking distance before they saw her. She drew her knife.

She was almost in position when Monly and Belay brought Sozerdor out of the narrow mouth of the cave on a makeshift stretcher and put him down for one of the men from the ship to examine. It looked to Leela as though Sozerdor had been shot, and she remembered the Doctor's questions about the gun the Kley copy had. The Belay copy had been squatting by the stretcher helping to make the injured man comfortable. Now he stood up and Leela could see him more clearly. The closer you got to them the more real they were and that made the horror of them worse. At her back, the original Belay gasped. It was not a loud noise, but it was loud enough. The pilot standing by the stretcher glanced in their direction. Kley saw the look.

'Where did she come from?' the pilot said, smiling towards Leela. The smile disappeared as he got a good look at Belay. He looked from the Belay behind her to the Belay beside him. 'There's something wrong here, Boo,' he cried to the crouching medic and he tried to draw his gun. Kley shot him where he stood.

'Come on!' Leela shouted at Belay, and sprinted for the cover of the cave mouth. Belay stood shocked and unmoving.

Kley shot the medic as he tried to rise and as Sozerdor stirred she put a shot into him. Then she swung the gun at Leela as she ran. Kley poured a withering stream of shots in her direction and as Leela plunged towards the cave a chunk of rock blew out and caught her a glancing blow above the right eye. Leela fell. Kley took her time and aimed more carefully at her.

Belay came back to life with a rush. Silently, head down, he ran at Kley and before she could shoot he leapt at her, knocking her to the ground. They rolled and struggled for possession of the gun.

The pilot and medic from Drop Two had got the go and left the ship when the shooting broke out. They were halfway across the open ground when they saw the other team go down. That should have been it. They could still get back to the ship, back into orbit, get the crew back on board and burn out the place. But they hesitated when they saw one of the survivors tackling the one with the gun. Maybe it was all right. Maybe they could save the rest of them after all. Maybe they could be heroes.

They pulled their guns and ran on towards the struggling figures.

Leela recovered her knife and got back to her feet. She was dazed. Where was Belay? The copies seemed to be fighting among themselves. The two men from the ship looked dead. Two of the copies were crouching over them. What were they doing? What were they looking for? Guns! They were getting the guns. As it all came back into focus, Fermindor rose with one of the guns in his hand and immediately took a shot at her. She ducked back and into the cave.

As soon as the shooting started, the Doctor knew it was already too late for subtlety and persuasion. 'Get those ships out of there and do it now. Go on!' He did not wait for a response but pushed past Kley and set off after Leela. He should have paid closer attention to what she was doing, he thought angrily, aware as he had been all along of the way the machine was working on her instincts. He should have been ready for her impatience and aggression to touch off this fight. He should have stopped her.

Maybe he could still stop her.

He was running, half crouched, keeping close to the rocks. He had gone some distance before he realised he had no idea of what he was going to do. He ran on.

Belay was enraged at the Kley copy, and desperate, and so fiercely terrified that he lashed and wrenched and smashed and kicked and found himself suddenly in possession of the gun. He shot Kley at the closest of close ranges, pouring fire into her until the gun was empty and bits of burning flesh and chunks of bone were spattering over him. He screamed and scrambled away. Above him, the figure of Fermindor was firing at the cave. He turned and stared down at him and aimed the gun, and then something weird happened. Fermindor's head exploded in a cloud of white bone fragments and muddy goo, *there's something wrong here Boo*, and the headless body flopped and slopped towards him. He saw the gun in its hand and he grabbed at it. And now he was standing over himself with a gun shooting. He wrested the gun from Fermindor's hand and he fired at himself. And still there was running and shooting. He kept his finger on the trigger and he cut himself in half and he cut down the figures who were running at him and yelling or was it him yelling…?

Belay killed the pilot and the medic from Drop Two with more accurate shooting than he would have thought possible if he had been in a state to think. He felt better now that there was just him and not him and him again. Rinandor came across and took the gun from his dead hand. He had always liked Rinandor. She didn't seem to be confused that he was dead.

'I'm still alive, Ri,' he said. She pointed the gun at his face, and then he remembered that it wasn't really Rinandor.

Not far in from the entrance, the neck of the cave narrowed. Leela let her eyes adjust to the dimness before she moved any further.

This was the cave she had seen in the place of the communing. This was the cave she had seen them all in. The wider part must be further back than the machine had shown. She could not have seen them from outside the entrance any more than Belay could have seen them. And yet they both did. They must be much further back in the wider part. The machine must have used one of those short cuts the Doctor talked about to show them what it had shown them.

When she could see as much as she could see, she ghosted over the smooth rock floor and into the narrow opening. It was only a few paces long and then it turned to the right and opened out suddenly into a much bigger cave which glowed very faintly with strange light, the same strange light – only much weaker – as there was in the underground passageways and caverns. There in the cave, in the half-darkness, just as the communing had shown, Leela found them. They were all her. There were at least fifty of her, maybe more. Everywhere she looked she stood with her knife drawn, waiting to fight, waiting to kill. Even though she had been ready for something like this, the number of them and the reality of them was too wrong. She could not keep ahead of this madness, she could not keep fighting it. She heard a low moan of horrified fear and she realised it was coming from her. She felt the muscles of her legs and arms starting to tighten and twitch. Part of her knew she was about to lose control of everything.

'My word,' the voice whispered behind her. 'He has been busy, hasn't he?' She turned to find the Doctor peering past her at the crowded cave. 'It's entirely possible,' he went on softly, 'that producing all those meant there wasn't enough capacity left to keep track of us and counter what we were doing. There must be a limit to what the machine can cope with at any one time.'

Leela felt the panic drain out of her, and her muscles stopped twitching.

* * *

Rinandor's damaged leg hadn't been giving her trouble and she had more or less forgotten about it until she tried to sprint across the open ground to the closer of the two ships. Then, suddenly, it hurt like hell, and she grunted with the pain as she hopped and staggered on. A shot burned past her face and another kicked a chunk of dusty rock out under her heel. The compression wave jagged at her foot almost tripping her over. For the moment she forgot about the pain and sprinted on.

Who'd have thought that terror's an analgesic? she found herself thinking, and saw with bizarre clarity that it was she herself who was firing at her. Self-destruction made easy, she thought, and shouted, 'You're me, you crap-head! Stop shooting at us!' But it made no difference. The firing went on. If anything it got worse, and she ran on desperately.

It would have been a sort of relief if they had attacked. They looked to Leela like standing corpses. It was only the small movements, the tiny shufflings, the odd twitch of a head that told her that they were not dead. Or at least that they were not dead and gone.

There are no ghosts, she thought, and looked at the Doctor. 'What are they waiting for now?' she whispered, 'Why are they not out there with the others?'

'I don't know. Maybe he's saving them for a rainy day.'

Leela frowned. What did that mean? More silliness. This was a desert cave. 'I do not understand,' she said quietly. 'It will not rain here.'

That was better, the Doctor decided. He could see that she was getting back in control of herself. He could understand her panic – he wasn't at all sure how he might have reacted if suddenly confronted with massed ranks of himself standing to attention in some gloomy tomb waiting for a signal to go into action. The immediate question was: what was that signal going to be?

'Never mind,' he said. 'Bad joke. Is that light getting brighter?' Of course it was getting brighter. That would be the activation signal. A radiation pulse was coming.

Leela stared round. 'Yes. It is getting brighter.'

The Doctor tugged at her arm. 'They're not going to be waiting for much longer,' he said, and they retreated back through the narrow opening.

The firing stopped abruptly as she approached the ship, and with a yell of relief Rinandor dived into cover behind one of the stabilisers. Why did she stop firing so soon? Had she emptied the gun? Rinandor took a quick look. No, she was firing again towards the rocks.

'They're frightened of damaging the ships!' she yelled to no one in particular.

Pertanor came slogging across the open ground and plunged into cover beside her. 'What did you think you were doing?' he demanded, gulping for breath. 'If you ever take a risk like that again I'll kill you myself.'

She smirked at him. 'Can't have you taking me for granted,' she said.

The Doctor examined the rock round the narrow opening.

'What are you looking for?' Leela asked.

He pulled at some loose material. 'A way to delay the copies long enough to get those ships off the ground without them.' It didn't look like a promising stratagem.

'That will not work,' Leela said flatly.

'No, it won't,' he agreed, giving up on the idea.

'I will stop them,' she said, moving to stand in front of the opening.

'There are fifty or more,' the Doctor said. 'But they can only come through that gap one at a time or they'll get in each other's way.'

Leela said, 'I will get tired eventually.' She was holding her knife and waiting to fight, standing uncannily like the copies had stood, waiting to fight.

'The guns are key,' Fermindor said to Kley, squinting into the brightness out beyond the shelter of Drop One's main drive housing. 'If they get to them first, we're dead.' The bodies of the pilot and medic from Drop Two lay in the open between the two ships. The guns they had been using had fallen near them, spilled from their hands as they were cut down by Belay's deranged firing.

'I don't understand why they've left them lying there,' she said, 'when it's get 'em and game over.'

'They may look like us, but that doesn't mean they're bright.'

'You mean *we* are?'

The copies of Rinandor, Monly and Pertanor were standing in the mess of bodies and bits of bodies left by the fire fight that Belay had triggered. Rinandor was the one with the gun and she was watching intently for movement in and around the ship. The other two were simply standing and waiting.

'It could be a trap,' Fermindor conceded. 'Or it could be that Belay confused them. Maybe they're not sure whether we're armed.'

'They can't be that stupid. I think they're following orders.'

'Which would be?'

'Get the ships down. Protect them at all costs.'

He smiled at her in admiration. 'Yes,' he said. 'You're right. They couldn't have been expecting us so killing us isn't a priority. And if we're not armed we don't feature. They don't give a damn about us as long as we can't threaten the ships.'

She peered round. 'Where are Ri and Pe now?'

Behind them Rinandor and Pertanor were carefully crawling out into the dazzling light heading for Drop Two. They were keeping

Drop One between them and the watching Rinandor, but they would be fully visible sooner or later. It looked like sooner to Kley.

They were obviously not expecting resistance, because the first two of them came through the narrow gap together, one slightly behind the other. Leela stepped across the opening so that the lead one turned to thrust at her and impeded the attack of the second. Leela killed them both as they were struggling to get at her. The second pair were stumbling over the bodies before they realised the full danger and Leela dispatched them with equal skill. After that there was a lull.

'They will come one at a time now,' Leela said with grim satisfaction. 'They do not learn quickly, but they learn.' She glanced at the Doctor. 'Is that how I am?'

'No,' the Doctor said. 'You're a quick study.' The narrow gap was already partially blocked with dead versions of Leela. For a moment he wondered what these constructs would have felt before they died. How fully formed and individual were they? He put the thought out of his mind. Now was not the time for philosophising. 'I'll see if I can do anything to speed things up,' the Doctor said, hurrying to the cave entrance and out into the harsh light.

'I'll take the pilot, you take the medic, yes?' Kley was crouched and ready.

Beside her, Fermindor was poised to make the dash to the guns as soon as Pertanor and Rinandor reached the limit of their crawl and made a run for the other ship. 'Look, Chief,' he said. 'We only need one gun. Let me do this?'

'Chief?' She looked hurt.

'I don't want anything to happen to you, Serian.'

'We do it together,' she said.

'I'll go for the gun, you go for the ship,' he suggested.

'I'll take the pilot, you take the medic,' she repeated. 'Are you ready?'

As they watched, the Rinandor copy tilted her head slightly and took a couple of steps to one side.

'She's seen them,' Fermindor said, glancing back to where Pertanor had paused with Rinandor close behind him.

'Get ready,' Kley said.

'Excuse me!' the Doctor shouted from outside the cave.

The Rinandor copy turned and swung the gun towards the cave.

'I hate to interrupt,' the Doctor went on, holding his hat up to shield his eyes from the glare, 'but what exactly do you imagine is being achieved by all this?'

'Do it!' shouted Kley. Fermindor was already up and running by the time she kicked off her sprint.

Pertanor and Rinandor got to their feet and ran for Drop Two. Rinandor was limping badly now, and Pertanor threw an arm round her waist and hauled her against him. They shambled on together.

The Rinandor copy hesitated and then, loosing off a quick shot at the Doctor, she turned back to the ships, which were her first priority. With one pair heading away from the first ship, a second pair running towards the second ship, and Rinandor shooting at an unexpected intruder, the Monly and Pertanor copies followed their orders and set off to protect the ships by intercepting the pair who most immediately threatened one. They ran at Pertanor and Rinandor as they struggled to reach Drop Two.

By the time the fake Rinandor had turned back to the flurry of activity among the ships she was already too late. Fermindor had reached the medic's gun. It was of better quality than the stuff they had brought with them on the patrol. He shot the Rinandor copy and then he swung round and took down the copies of Monly and Pertanor. 'You see,' he said breathing hard. 'I told you we only needed one.'

'My hero,' Kley rasped as she looked around for someone to shoot at.

'I was the best shot in the team. As far as I remember that's what the computer stats said.'

'I'm the best pilot.'

'And you're team leader and you're a firster.'

'Why do you keep reminding me of that?'

He sighed. 'Because it's true.'

'Yeah, well, you're a fool but I don't keep reminding you of that.'

Pertanor and Rinandor had reached the second ship. They paused by the hatch. Kley signalled them to board and they climbed on and closed up.

Kley and Fermindor were holstering the guns and moving back to the other ship as the Doctor hurried towards them. 'Get off as quickly as you can,' he said. 'Leela's holding the pass but I'm not sure how much longer she can do it.'

'Aren't you coming with us?' Kley asked.

'No. We have unfinished business here.'

'Listen,' Fermindor said. 'Once we're off they'll blast every colour of crap out of this place.'

'You listen,' the Doctor said. 'This was a high-level conspiracy. Don't count on everyone out there being on your side.'

Kley snorted. 'Don't worry. We know who to trust.'

'We do?' Fermindor said.

'Each other,' she said, smiling into his eyes. 'The rest of them have things to prove.'

'And the same goes for when you get back to your home system,' the Doctor said. 'Whoever's behind this is not going to be pleased to see you.'

Fermindor smiled grimly. 'Oh, I can guarantee that,' he said.

'My hero again,' Kley mocked, cheerfully.

'I hope it's some skinny-brained firster,' Fermindor said. 'They're always overconfident so they're easy to best.'

'You're still only second in command, toody.'

'Clerical error,' he said. 'Just a question of time before it's sorted it out.'

'Be nice to me,' she said waggling her wrist log under his nose. 'If I lose this you won't even be second-in-command.'

As they reached the ship the Doctor called to them, a fist raised in triumph or congratulation. 'Kley? Fermindor? Make sure it *is* every colour? Insist on it, yes?'

The Doctor reached the cave with the first of the dust devils whirling into life and battering the sand and grit against his back. As he went in, the sound of knife blades clashing and soft grunts of effort was drowned by the sudden rush of wind and power outside. The distraction affected neither of the combatants. The knives parted. Leela stepped back slightly, allowing her opponent to overreach herself, and then dispatched her by pulling her on to an upward blow under the left fifth rib.

Behind the Doctor a voice said above the noise, 'Stand perfectly still, please, Doctor, or I will place a large hole in your back.'

The Doctor did as he was told, and stood quite still. 'I thought you must have made a copy of yourself, Sozerdor,' he said loudly. 'A camouflage decoy and an extra gun. Why only one?'

'I only needed one,' Sozerdor said.

'It seems to me an egomaniacal psychopath like you would want lots of copies of himself.'

'I prefer to be unique. That's the way of us egomaniacal psychopaths.'

'My mistake.'

Leela pushed the dead copy away from her and back into the narrow gap.

'They don't fight as well as I'd hoped they would,' Sozerdor commented. 'They need work. The next generation will be stronger and more aggressive.'

Leela turned and stared at him coldly. 'Do you think we are going to let you make more of these?'

'I think it's out of your hands.' He gestured with the gun. 'Come now, we're wasting time. Over here, please.' Leela did not move. 'I will kill the Doctor unless you do as I say.'

In the narrow gap a new Leela showed herself. Sozerdor fired and the shot smashed her back and brought down a fall of rocks and debris. 'I will kill the Doctor,' he repeated, 'unless you do as I say.'

Outside the cave the noise was diminishing. 'You've lost, Sozerdor,' the Doctor said calmly. 'The ships are gone.'

'Lost?' Sozerdor sneered. 'You don't imagine that a few suicide troops, fairly primitive ones at that, were anything more than a trial run, do you?'

'Yes, I do.'

Sozerdor chortled. 'You've been spending too much time with that simple-minded savage over there. You should get out more.'

The Doctor grinned at Leela. 'I remember thinking something of the kind myself. I was wrong.'

'Those things,' Sozerdor said, 'would just have been a destabilising diversion in the overall plan. We can do without them. I've barely scratched the surface of this place yet.'

The Doctor said, 'I think the survivors of your investigation team are about to do that.'

'The vengeance of search-and-retrieval?' Sozerdor sounded positively gleeful. 'They couldn't put a dent in this installation no matter how much fire they bring down on it.'

'They could put a dent in us, though,' the Doctor suggested.

'Out-system ship-mounted gunnery is crude but it's powerful,' Sozerdor agreed. 'Shall we go?'

'Go where?' Leela asked, still not moving.

'Wherever I tell you to,' Sozerdor snapped. Angrily he gestured with the gun for her to leave the cave.

'He hasn't given up on the TARDIS, Leela,' the Doctor said.

'You're such a clever alien, aren't you?' Sozerdor sneered.

'We can bargain with him later,' the Doctor said, looking hard at Leela, 'but right now it's essential that we're back in that control centre if the ships attack.'

Leela could see that the Doctor wanted her to do as this flabby-faced bully with the gun ordered but the thought of it made her angry. She was also reluctant to go back down into that underworld of magic and demons, even though she knew it was not magic and there were no demons because that was what the Doctor had told her and she knew he was right and she trusted the Doctor... So why was she hesitating? She walked to the cave entrance. The expression on the Doctor's face said she was doing the right thing. Inside her head something was screaming.

The new access and crossover were quite close on the other side of the cave entrance. Sozerdor had no difficulty in herding the Doctor and Leela into it, and as they stepped out into the pit of the control suite – what Leela thought of as the place of communing – he was chortling again.

'Keep it simple, that's the secret. All this alien technology,' he said. 'I think magic is the word for it. Isn't that right?' He poked Leela in the back with the gun. 'All this magical technology and finally what it comes down to is a man with a gun. That's what it always comes down to.'

'Not always,' the Doctor said stepping out of the pit and striding towards the control bays.

'Wait!' Sozerdor called. 'Stay right there.'

Leela hesitated at the edge of the pit. As she had hoped, Sozerdor tried to hurry her along by prodding her in the back with the gun. As soon as she knew precisely where it was she dropped below the gun, at the same time twisting and lunging upward. She grabbed Sozerdor's wrist with her left hand and drove her right shoulder up into his armpit, levering the arm stiff against the elbow. As she straightened up she butted him on the bridge of the nose with the back of her head. The gun fell from his hand. Leela caught it and turned with it pointing at his head.

'Sometimes,' the Doctor remarked, 'what it comes down to is a *girl* with a gun.'

Sozerdor moaned in anger, never taking his eyes off Leela and the gun.

'Don't kill him,' the Doctor said, and then corrected himself quickly. 'What I mean is I don't think you should kill him.'

'Why not?'

Sozerdor was beginning to cower.

'Because you don't have to,' the Doctor said.

Leela did not lower the gun. 'We cannot leave him with all this.'

'I agree.'

'Do you mean to take him with us, then?'

'No.' The Doctor laughed. 'Certainly not. Do you want him as a travelling companion?'

Leela did not laugh, nor did she lower the gun. 'What then?'

'I think we should destroy all this.'

'Good plan,' Sozerdor sniggered. 'That one's got my vote.'

'He does not think we can do it,' Leela said, coldly. 'Neither do I.' She stepped backwards out of the pit, never taking her eyes off Sozerdor and never lowering her aim. 'I think I *must* kill him.'

The Doctor could see that she meant it. Leela's training as a warrior made killing and being killed a logical part of life, and the machine had been working on that among other things.

'Wait,' he said. He hurried into one of the inactive alcoves. He could recognise patterns in the crystals now. Setting up a force field was one of the simpler procedures, so he picked a simple pattern, little more than a slight curve, and put his fingers against it. He had come to the conclusion, finally, that the machine was either set up to tap directly into the subconscious, or else it was designed to resist conscious interference and amendment of its basic control systems. Either way, what it could not accommodate was online analysis. Thinking about it, he had realised that thinking about it was not the way to work the machine. He did not mentally specify the details and the function of the force field but merely allowed the fact of it to be in his mind. The control booth flowed smoothly into action. The Doctor imprisoned Sozerdor in the force field and tried not to be pleased with himself. Function without thought? What could be admired in that?

When he emerged, Leela had lowered the gun and was smiling at Sozerdor. 'How does it feel to be on the inside?' she asked. 'Try not to touch it. You were right. It hurts very much.'

'I think that solves the problem, don't you?' the Doctor said.

Leela looked at the Doctor and said, unsmiling, 'I think it would have been kinder to shoot him. I prefer it this way.'

'You're not going to leave me in here?' Sozerdor demanded of the Doctor. 'I'll starve to death.'

'No,' Leela said flatly. 'You will die of thirst long before that.'

'Actually,' the Doctor said, 'you'll be able to escape when the systems overload. With luck, you'll find a way up to the surface.'

'In that case kill me now. It's never going to happen.'

The Doctor smiled. 'Leela and I are going to set off every major function that we can find. As you discovered, there is a limit to what the system can cope with at any one time.'

'That's your plan? You really are an alien halfwit, aren't you?' Sozerdor raged. 'It won't *let* you overload it.'

'Why would the machine destroy itself, Doctor?' Leela asked thoughtfully. 'You showed me that it had great power stored –' she gestured at the floor – 'down there.'

'That's true,' the Doctor said. 'We can't overload the power source, but we can overload the systems that use the power.'

'No you can't!' Sozerdor shouted furiously. 'It has self-control built in.'

'Unlike you.' The Doctor smiled bleakly and, turning back to Leela, went on, 'We *can* overload them, because when the control systems are already fully extended, there's a good chance they won't be able to defend the machine from a major bombardment – say from three search-and-retrieval ships.' His smile became broader. 'That's an unusually large number, it seems.'

'Will they attack?'

'I think so,' the Doctor said. 'They have things to prove. Those of Sozerdor's co-conspirators that are out there will think the way *he* does, that it's not going to have any effect.'

Leela nodded. 'I am ready.'

The Doctor wandered down to the edge of the force field. 'We won't be seeing each other again, Sozerdor, so I'll say goodbye.' He smiled. 'Pay attention, and the chances are that with one mighty bound you'll be free.'

'What does that mean?' Sozerdor demanded.

'It is another bad joke,' Leela guessed. 'Is that not it, Doctor?'

Kley and her second in command had formally requested a full bombardment of the whole area they had gone down in, as was their right by custom and practice. They'd lost three men: ACI Monly, SI Sozerdor, and Investigator Belay. The two drop ships had both lost two crew members and the rest of their complements were angry enough to risk straight suborbital attacks. But still nothing was happening. Pertanor and Rinandor, both armed now, waited outside the control deck while Kley and Fermindor pressed their claim in person.

The captain of Lead One was not a happy toody. 'It's a pointless waste of armaments,' he said, his face an expressionless mask. 'There's nothing down there.'

'How would you know that?' Kley demanded.

'There has been a full instrument search,' the navigation co-ordinator, also a toody, said.

'I'll bet there has,' Kley snapped.

'With respect, Captain,' Fermindor said, 'but aren't you required to decommission all ships' weaponry before the return jump anyway? So what's the difference?'

'Word is,' the captain said, watching Fermindor for a reaction, 'there's unrest back home. We may stay primed.'

Several members of the Lead One crew looked up from their consoles. This was clearly news to them.

'That's against every regulation in the code,' Kley protested 'Even to think that is treasonable. You cannot enter the system armed.'

'Don't presume to give me orders, madam. Or to tell me my duty. You have no firster rank here.'

'She has an OIG rank,' Fermindor said. 'It's Chief Investigator. I suggest you use it. She outranks you, Captain.'

'Not on my ship she doesn't,' the captain said tersely. He was getting angry.

'She outranks you and so do I.' Fermindor was very calm. 'You have the request. You have the ordnance. You have no shortage of volunteers to do the job. What's it to be, Captain?'

Outside the entrance to the deck, as they waited to see which of the crew were in this thing with the captain, Pertanor said, 'Do we stay together now, Ri?'

'The four of us?' Rinandor said.

'The two of us,' he said.

'You're easy to tease,' she said, and then nodded. 'I will if you will.'

'You have to promise me something first,' Pertanor said.

'Already there are conditions?'

'If we find out it *is* Skinny-dick, I get to arrest him.'

'Before or after I kill him?'

He shrugged and grinned. 'Whichever.'

The Doctor began modestly. He set a small range of mountains rising, put tropical savannah to replacing the pine forest and resited the jungle where the pillar stood in its desert rockscape. Satisfied that he could build up and tear down the environments at will, he then tested the speed at which it could be done and found that spare capacity in the system was used up by pushing the time limits for completion. Finally, when everything was in motion, he experimented with pick-and-mix, covering mountains with tropical swamp, growing deciduous woods in the middle of deserts, and discovered that this seemed to put a disproportionate additional strain on the processes.

Beside him in the gallery, Leela conjured nightmares from the depths of the machine's memory and freed them to fight and rage in the Doctor's weird and unquiet worlds.

'How long must we do this?' she asked.

'Until the attack,' he said, glancing back at the latest grotesque fantasy lurching into life in the glowing inner dome.

'What if they do not attack?'

'Plan B,' the Doctor said.

'What is the B for?'

'Boredom.' He beamed at her. 'We get bored with this and we do something else.'

She looked unconvinced. Something bright flared and bloomed in the inner dome.

'Did you do that?' Leela asked.

The Doctor shook his head. 'I think we can forget about Plan B.' He turned back to the wall. 'More monsters. More mountains,' he urged.

The reports, particularly from the first low-level runs, made unlikely claims for raging monsters and major changes of landscape and topography showing up between attacks. The captain of Lead One tried to abort the bombardment, citing regulations on 'unknown and unnecessary hazards', but it was little more than a token effort.

The wild rumours that four officers, among them the captain and the navigation co-ordinator, might be involved in some sort of anti-government conspiracy meant that no one was in a hurry for confrontation. And as long as there was ammunition left, the survivors – investigators and flight crews alike – wanted the whole place levelled to the ground.

The Doctor and Leela left the gallery when he judged the systems were teetering on the brink of collapse. They stepped through the link he had left open to the edge of the recycling floor where the TARDIS was still nudging gently in the unending eddy, still battered by ball lightning. There they stood on the narrow ledge, bathed in the cold brightness of the searing power, and waited for the final crash.

'When it goes dark,' the Doctor said, repeating himself. 'Do not assume –'

'That everything is cool and safe, I know,' Leela said. 'You told me. You keep telling me.'

Behind them a voice said, 'Good advice. A little obvious perhaps but… good.' They turned to find Sozerdor smiling a fat smile and brandishing the gun Leela had discarded. 'You were right about the systems, Doctor,' he said. 'The force field went down all of a sudden. I didn't even need a mighty bound.'

Leela pulled her knife and tried to get past the Doctor. He put a hand on her arm. 'Stay here. Please,' he said softly. 'I'll need you to know exactly where the TARDIS is when it goes dark.'

Leela stopped reluctantly. 'What are you going to do?'

'I'm going to reason with him,' the Doctor said, loudly.

'Excellent,' Sozerdor sniggered. 'I'm a reasonable man.'

'We are not taking you with us,' the Doctor said, taking a step towards him.

Sozerdor took a step back and aimed the gun. 'Oh yes you are,' he smirked.

'You're beginning to irritate me,' the Doctor said, and took another step towards him.

'Stop doing that,' Sozerdor ordered, taking another step back. 'You are in range and I am out of reach.' He gestured with the gun.

The Doctor took another step towards him, and then another.

Sozerdor stepped backwards again. 'What are you doing? It isn't going to work. I'll kill you. I *will* kill you.'

'No you won't,' the Doctor said, taking another step towards him. Sozerdor took one step back and then he stood his ground.

'Enough of this crap,' he shouted. 'Stay where you are!'

That was when the systems crashed and everything went black.

'Wait, don't move!' Sozerdor bellowed, lost in the darkness.

His fingers brushing the wall, the Doctor ran back to where Leela waited. 'It is five paces forward and one out,' she said.

Sozerdor was still groping his way forward when the light from inside the TARDIS shone briefly on the Doctor and Leela, and then the door disappeared, leaving him in total darkness again. 'No!' he screamed. 'That isn't fair!' He fired the pistol at where the TARDIS had been.

He was still firing and screaming when the huge dome collapsed and buried him.

As the TARDIS carried them away, Leela still had questions she wanted answered and arguments she wanted to make, but she knew more about herself now. Some of it, she understood, might make the Doctor uncomfortable. Some of it made *her* uncomfortable.

The Doctor was smiling to himself. The TARDIS's sampling image locator was not at fault after all. 'That planet simply shouldn't have been there,' he said.

'Then how *did* it get there?' Leela asked.

'I have no idea,' the Doctor said cheerfully.

'You must have a theory, though, Doctor,' Leela prompted. 'You always have some theory.'

'No,' he said. 'I haven't. And you can stop patronising me. And I will do my best to stop patronising you.' He beamed a smile at her. 'Young lady.'

Leela was about to protest – but then she seemed to recognise the joke.

And smiled back.

Watch out for DOCTOR WHO: EARTH AND BEYOND *on audio:*
Three exciting short stories read by Paul McGann –
the Eighth Doctor!